THE FORGETTING ROOM

K.G. LEWIS

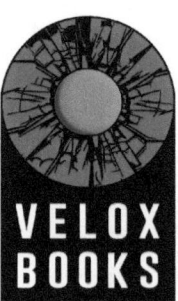

Published by arrangement with the author.

Copyright © 2026 by K.G. Lewis.

All rights reserved.

No part of this publication may be reproduced, distributed, or transmitted in any form or by any means, including photocopying, recording, or other electronic or mechanical methods, without the prior written permission of the publisher, except as permitted by U.S. copyright law.

The story, all names, characters, and incidents portrayed in this production are fictitious. No identification with actual persons (living or deceased), places, buildings, and products is intended or should be inferred.

YOU'RE READING ANOTHER TERRIFYING COLLECTION FROM

FOLLOW VELOX TO KEEP THE NIGHTMARES COMING:

CONTENTS

Mickey D's	1
The Body	13
Pistachio Place	19
Forest for the Trees	28
Going Down	37
Kiss and Tell	47
Damned	60
The Forgetting Room	70
Subdivision	81
Family Matters	99
Final Report Card	114
Double Vision	124
Typewriter	131
Mom	142
Mud Mouth	149
Good Timing	157

The Hollow Ween	162
Winny	171
Grief Support	179
Photograph	193
Itzpapalotl	205
Hostage Situation	216
Holy Shit	224

MICKEY D'S

"I'm hungry," my girlfriend, Samantha, said.

She was sitting in the passenger seat, staring at me with an apologetic look in her eyes.

"I knew this was going to happen," I said. "That's why I told you to eat something before we left."

I'd warned her that the route we were taking to my parents' house was through a lot of small rural towns and nothing was likely to be open because of how late we were driving. I would've preferred to have left earlier, but I couldn't get anyone to take my shift at the grocery store the day we left.

"I know," she admitted. "But I wasn't hungry then."

"There are some chips and granola bars in that plastic bag in the back seat." I hooked my thumb over my shoulder.

I always packed a bag of snacks whenever I went on a road trip. I'd picked up the habit from my mom, who didn't like stopping to eat when we were traveling.

"I don't want junk food," Samantha said. "I want real food, like a cheeseburger."

"I don't think cheeseburgers qualify as real food," I teased.

"They do to me," she said.

"It's only two more hours until we get to my parents' house," I gestured at the road ahead of us. "If you can wait until then, there's a Denny's right up the road from their place. We can eat there."

"I don't think I can wait," she said, placing her hand on her stomach.

"You might not have a choice."

"What's the next town we're going to pass through?" she asked, pulling out her phone.

"Salt Mill," I replied. "Why?"

She held up her phone. "I'm going to see if I can find something to eat there."

Salt Mill was a small farming town. I doubted she was going to find anything open this late, but I didn't tell her that. She would soon find out for herself.

"That's annoying," she sighed in frustration a few moments later.

"Couldn't find anything?" I asked.

"No," she replied. "I can't even search. I don't have any service out here."

That was another problem with driving through the country. Cell service was spotty.

"It's only about 20 miles to Salt Mill," I said. "We'll be there soon. Hopefully, we can find something for you."

Samantha's stomach growled in response.

"Hopefully," she repeated.

"That's Salt Mill," I pointed at the lights in the distance. "Keep your eyes open and let me know if you see anything."

I didn't expect Samantha to find anything. I was just trying to be nice, hoping she would figure it out on her own and just eat some of the snacks until we got to my parents' house.

"That's it?" she scoffed. "It looks so tiny."

"It just looks small because everything is closed for the night," I explained. "If we'd gotten here a few hours earlier, there'd be a lot more lights on. It's actually a decent-sized town."

"It's only 11:00," Samantha said. "Why does everything close so early out here?"

"Most of the people who live here are farmers," I explained. "They tend to start their days a lot earlier than the rest of us. I assume that means they also go to bed earlier. There's no sense in businesses staying open late if all their customers are asleep."

"I'd hate to live in a town like this," she grumbled.

Having lived in small towns most of my life, I didn't share her sentiment, but I wasn't going to argue the point with her.

Samantha didn't say anything else until we reached the center of town.

"What's that?" she pointed down one of the side streets.

"What's what?" I looked in the indicated direction but couldn't tell what Samantha was pointing at.

"That sign," she clarified. "It looks like McDonald's. See the two arches over that building?"

"Are you sure?" I asked after seeing the top of the sign. "I thought the McDonald's arches were supposed to be yellow." The two arches visible above the building were red.

"Let's go find out," Samantha said.

When the restaurant came into view, it was clear that it was not a McDonald's but had obviously been one at some point before the new owners redecorated.

"Mickey D's," Samantha read the name on the sign beneath the red arches.

"Looks like a knockoff," I said.

With that name, they weren't even trying to hide it.

"I don't care," Samantha replied. "That's the only thing that I care about." She pointed at the neon open sign hanging in the window.

"It doesn't look open." The restaurant looked empty. I could see the dining area and front counter through the window, but I didn't see anyone inside. "Maybe they forgot to turn off the sign before they left for the night."

"Maybe," Samantha agreed. "But I doubt they'd forget to take their cars with them." She looked over at the four cars parked on the opposite side of the parking lot from the restaurant. "Let's go inside and find out."

"Go inside? Why do you want to go inside when we can just go through the drive-thru?" I pointed at the drive-thru lane that ran behind the building.

We were already going to be getting to my parents' house later than I wanted to, and I didn't want us to be any later than necessary.

"Because I have to pee," Samantha said.

After I pulled into the nearest parking spot, I turned to Samantha and said, "I'm not really hungry, so I'm just going to stay here and wait for you."

"You're seriously going to make me go inside by myself?" she sounded disappointed.

When I looked over at her, she was pouting.

"I guess not." I turned off the car.

We got out and approached the door. When I reached for the handle, a part of me hoped the door would be locked so we could get back in the car and leave. But it wasn't.

"Looks like they're open," Samantha smiled when she saw that the door wasn't locked.

She rushed inside and hurried across the dining room to the women's restroom to go pee.

As I stepped into the restaurant, a teenage boy came running out of the men's room.

"Don't shut the door!" he yelled, holding out his arm as if he could prevent it from happening.

By the time I turned around, it was too late. The door was already shut.

The teenager, whose name tag identified him as Brent, ran up and started pushing on the door.

Frustrated that he couldn't get it open, he turned around and threw his arms into the air. "Great," he snapped. "Now we're all stuck here."

"What?" I was confused. "It shouldn't be locked."

I brushed past Brent and pushed against the door, trying to open it, but it wouldn't budge.

Brent opened his mouth to say something but stopped when he heard a clatter from the kitchen.

He suddenly looked frightened.

"Hide," he hissed, running back to the men's room as Samantha was coming out of the women's room. Once he was inside, he locked the door, changing the colored indicator on the outside of the lock from available to occupied.

"What the heck is his problem?" Samantha asked, looking back at the restrooms.

I shrugged. "I have no idea, but it seems to have something to do with the doors being locked," I said, gesturing at them.

"What do you mean they're locked? We wouldn't have been able to come inside if they were locked." She walked over and tested the doors herself. "That's weird," she said when she found they were really locked.

"Welcome to Mickey D's," a gravelly voice announced from behind us. "How can I help you?"

I turned to address the man who had spoken. "Well—for starters, you can unlock—" but it wasn't a man. It was a creature of some sort. Seeing it standing there behind the counter made me forget the rest of what I was going to say.

The creature stood seven feet tall and was wearing a blood-stained fast-food uniform. The name tag pinned to its shirt said its name was Mickey. Its hairless skin was dark brown and wrinkled like overcooked meat. On top of its bald head were two curved horns.

"What the hell is that?" Samantha whispered, clutching my arm and moving to stand behind me.

"I'm afraid I can't unlock the doors," Mickey smiled, showing his pointy yellow teeth. "Not until the end of my shift."

"Wh-Wh-When's that?" I had to force the question out.

Mickey turned to look at the clock on the wall beside him. "Forty-five minutes," he replied.

In 45 minutes, it would be midnight.

"So," Samantha said from behind me, "if we just wait until then, you'll unlock the doors and we can go?"

Mickey held up one long finger tipped with a black nail. "One of you can go," he said. "The other has to come with me."

I got a sinking feeling in the pit of my stomach.

"Why do either of us have to go with you?" Samantha was feeling a lot bolder than I was. "We're not a part of whatever is going on here." She made a circular motion with her hand. "We're just passing through."

"You became a part of it the moment you walked through that door," Mickey replied.

"A-A part of what?" I asked.

If there was any hope of us escaping the restaurant with our lives, we needed to know exactly what was going on.

"The sacrificial circle," Mickey said. "The geniuses who work here thought it would be fun to summon a demon using frozen beef patties and chicken tenders. You should have seen the look on their faces when it worked."

"But we had nothing to do with that," Samantha said, stepping out from behind me. "Why should we be punished for their stupidity?"

"I don't make the rules." Mickey spread his hands in a mock apology.

"What are the rules?" I asked.

If there were rules, there could be loopholes we could exploit.

"You'll have to read them for yourself." Mickey suddenly turned and started walking to the back of the restaurant.

"Where's he going?" Samantha whispered in my ear.

"How should I know?" I whispered back.

"Do you think those are locked?" She pointed at the doors on the other side of the restaurant, opposite the ones we entered through.

"I doubt it," I replied. "But we should check just to be sure."

Samantha and I rushed over to the doors. When we were about halfway there, we heard Mickey call out behind us.

"They're locked," he said, "and will remain that way until I am paid what is owed."

We stopped and turned to face him. He was standing behind the counter, holding a large leather-bound book in his left hand.

"Go ahead and try." He gestured at the doors.

Samantha walked up and pushed on both doors. They rattled in their frame but didn't open.

"You wanted to know what the rules are," Mickey said to me. "Here they are."

He set the book down on the counter, opened it, and flipped through the pages. When he found the one that he wanted, he turned the book around so I could read it.

Cautiously, I approached the counter. The closer I got to Mickey, the more I could smell him. He reeked of rancid meat and sulfur. By the time I reached the counter, my eyes were watering from the overpowering stench wafting from him.

"Something wrong?" Mickey asked after seeing my discomfort.

"Uh, no," I stammered.

I wasn't about to tell him that he stank so bad it was making it hard for me to focus on the book.

"Can I take this over there?" I asked, gesturing at the dining area of the restaurant.

"Knock yourself out," Mickey replied. "I have some things to take care of in the back. When I return, we can discuss which one of you is going with me."

I picked up the book and carried it over to the nearest table, ignoring his last comment.

Samantha came over to the table and sat across from me.

"Why does it have to be one of us?" she kept her voice low. "Why can't he take the kid in the restroom?"

I'd completely forgotten about Brent, the employee we'd encountered when we first walked into the restaurant.

"That's a good question," I said. "It's like Mickey doesn't even know he's here."

"I'm going to go talk to him," Samantha suddenly declared, pushing herself up from the table.

"What if he doesn't want to talk to you?"

"Then I'm going to drag his ass out of that bathroom," she snapped, "and if he's responsible for what happened here," she jabbed her finger toward the floor, "then it should be his ass on the line, not ours."

She was right, but I didn't think we were going to get out of there that easily.

I watched Samantha storm off toward the restrooms before turning my attention to the book on the table in front of me.

"Maybe something in here will help us," I said to myself, focusing on the open pages.

As I sat there reading the book, Samantha was pounding on the men's room door, threatening Brent in every way imaginable, trying to get him to talk to her. After she realized there was no way she was going to be able to force her way into the restroom, she gave up and returned to the table.

"Any luck?" she asked, plopping herself down into the seat across from me.

"Maybe," I said. "But I don't think you're going to like it."

I'd read the pages indicated by Mickey and learned that the restaurant employees had performed something called the Ritual of Request. The ritual required five people to perform, four of whom were to be unwitting sacrifices, and the fifth, the ritual leader, was the person whose request would be granted by the demon summoned.

"If I'm reading this correctly," I pointed at the book, "I think Brent is the one who summoned the demon, offering up his coworkers as sacrifices. That's why Mickey isn't messing with him; he's the ritual leader."

"If he's the ritual leader, why'd he try to leave when we got here?" Samantha asked.

"Because Brent didn't have enough sacrifices to pay Mickey," I said. "He was one short, and I think that meant Mickey was going to take him as the fourth sacrifice. At least he was until we showed up."

"So, one of us becomes the fourth sacrifice," she gestured back and forth between the two of us, "and that little shit hiding in the men's room gets some sort of special favor from Mickey?"

"Essentially," I replied.

"I don't see how that's going to help us." She frowned.

"You didn't let me finish," I said.

"Then hurry up and finish." She looked over at the clock on the wall. "We've only got about twenty minutes left before Mickey comes to collect."

"There's a way for one of us to become the ritual leader," I explained. "But I'm not sure you're going to like the cost."

"Spit it out," she snapped.

"You have to give up your soul—" I started to say.

"That's it?" Samantha interrupted. "That's a small price to pay to walk out of here alive."

"...and you have to kill the current ritual leader," I finished.

"Anything else?"

"There's an incantation you have to say to become the ritual leader, but that's essentially it."

Samantha pushed herself up from the table.

"Where are you going?" I asked.

"To become the ritual leader," she replied. "Unless you want to do it." She gestured at me.

When I didn't respond, she turned and started to walk away.

"That's what I thought," she muttered.

I sat at the table and watched her walk behind the counter and into the kitchen area of the restaurant. She was back there for two seconds before she came rushing back out with her hand over her mouth.

"Are you okay?" I got up and met her in front of the counter.

She shook her head. "The sacrifices..." She suddenly started retching, making it impossible for her to continue.

I stepped back to give her some space in case she was going to puke. Thankfully, she didn't.

"Go look," she panted, gesturing to the kitchen entrance. "See what's going to happen to us if we don't find a way out of here."

After seeing her reaction, I didn't want to go back there.

"Go," she insisted.

Hesitantly, I walked over to the entrance and peered around the corner. Like Samantha, the scene before me made me instantly nauseous.

The kitchen looked like a slaughterhouse.

Mickey had placed all three bodies of the sacrificed restaurant employees across one of the prep tables so that their heads hung over the edge. He then slit open their throats, letting their blood drain onto the floor. When I peeked my head through the entrance, he was in the process of disemboweling one of them.

"Did you need something?" Mickey asked. In his hands was a thick rope of glistening intestine.

I shook my head and quickly turned away.

"That's going to be one of us if we don't get that guy out of the restroom," Samantha jabbed her finger toward the kitchen.

Before I could respond, Mickey returned. In his left hand was a knife.

"Did you finish reading the rules?" he asked, gesturing at the book lying open on the dining room table.

"Yeah," I replied. "I did."

"Then you know why I have to do this," he said. "It's nothing personal, just business. I would let you go if I could." He placed his right hand over his chest to emphasize his sincerity. "Seriously."

"Well," I looked over at the clock, "we still have 10 minutes."

"That you do," Mickey replied. "You should probably use that time to decide which one of you is going to be the sacrifice." He gestured from me to Samantha.

"Can I ask a favor?" An idea started to form in my mind.

"Depends on what the favor is," he replied. "Most people who ask something of me have to pay a steep price." He gestured toward the kitchen and the bodies within.

"It's nothing like that," I said. "I just wanted to know if I could borrow your knife." I pointed.

Mickey eyed me for a moment. "You're not thinking of trying to be a hero, are you? Because it would take a lot more than this"—he wiggled the long knife, which looked small in his large hands—"to harm me."

"What are you doing?" Samantha whispered.

"If you want to get that guy out of the men's room, we need something to pry the door open," I whispered back. "That knife is our best shot." To Mickey, I said, "I'm not stupid. The knife isn't for you."

"Okay," Mickey said, flipping the knife around in his hand and offering it to me by the handle.

I didn't know if he agreed so readily because he heard what I said to Samantha or because he knew I wasn't a threat to him. It didn't matter. The important thing was that I got the knife.

"Thanks," I said, taking the knife from him.

The handle was slick with blood, but I did my best to ignore it. I didn't have time to be picky.

"Come on," I motioned for Samantha to follow me to the restrooms.

"Tick-tock," Mickey said as we walked away.

"Do you really think you can get the door open with that?" Samantha gestured at the knife.

"I don't know," I shrugged. "But I'm going to try."

The men's room door was locked with a deadbolt that had an occupancy indicator on the outside, which was currently red and displayed the word "occupied" in white letters. Below the indicator was a small slot that, with the appropriate tool, could be used to unlock the door.

Since I didn't have the appropriate tool, I was hoping the knife would be a good substitute. Turns out it wasn't. The blade was too wide and didn't go in far enough to reach the mechanisms inside.

As I kept working at it, trying to force the knife in deeper, Samantha leaned in close to get a better look at my progress. "I don't think that's going to work," she said after watching for a moment. "Here, let me try." She reached up and tried to take the knife out of my hand, but I moved it before she could grab hold of it.

When I saw the frantic look in her eyes, I realized that our time was almost up. There was no way we were going to get Brent out in time. That meant that one of us was going to be the last sacrifice.

"Give it here," Samantha snapped, grabbing for the knife again.

The wild way she came at me made me realize she had no intention of using the knife on the door. She'd decided that I should be the last sacrifice.

"Stay away from me," I held the knife out, threatening her.

"You should be the last sacrifice," Samantha said to me.

"Why me?" I said. "Why shouldn't it be you?"

"Because I'm pregnant," she blurted out.

"No, you're not." I didn't think she really was pregnant. "You're just saying that to save yourself."

"It's true," she insisted. "Why do you think I'm hungry all the time, or why I seem to have to pee every hour?"

I lowered the knife, wondering if she really could be pregnant. The more I thought about it, the more I realized that it could be true. We had engaged in some risky behavior on more than one drunken occasion.

"Why didn't you say something sooner?"

"I was waiting for the right time," she replied.

The knife was now at my side, pointing at the floor.

Seeing that I had let my guard down, Samantha seized the opportunity and lunged for the knife.

What happened next was a blur, but I swear it was an accident.

"You stabbed me," she grunted, looking down at my hand on the handle of the knife sticking out of her abdomen.

"I'm sorry." I let go of the handle and stepped back. "I didn't mean to. It was an accident."

"Well, well, well, what do we have here?" Mickey had come out from behind the counter to see what all the commotion was about.

"She was going to kill me," I said to him. "I was just trying to protect myself."

Behind us, the doors clicked unlocked.

Mickey heard it too and said, "Looks like you're free to go."

Without hesitation, I started walking toward the doors.

"Aren't you forgetting something?" Mickey called out.

I turned around to see him gesturing at Samantha.

"You're not just going to leave her here, are you?" he asked.

"I thought she was the last sacrifice."

"She wasn't," Mickey revealed. "He was." He pointed at the knife sticking out of the lower part of her abdomen.

THE BODY

"I came as soon as I got your call," Sheriff Morgan said after I greeted him in the hall of the morgue. "What did you want to show me?"

"Come with me." I motioned for him to follow me into the autopsy suite.

Once we were inside, I led him over to a lighted panel on the wall where I'd hung several X-ray films earlier.

"These are from the John Doe you brought in this evening," I said, gesturing at the films. "Notice anything odd about them?"

"Can't say that I do," Sheriff Morgan admitted after studying them for a moment.

On a nearby table was a stack of X-rays from a different corpse. I grabbed the top one and hung it next to the X-rays of John Doe.

"What about now?" I asked, gesturing at the new X-ray. "Notice anything different?"

Once he looked at the new X-ray, it didn't take him long to spot the difference.

"I can see bones in this one," Sheriff Morgan said, tapping his finger against the new X-ray. "I don't see any bones in any of the others." He gestured at the X-rays of John Doe.

"I took over a dozen X-rays, and not a single bone or organ appears in any of them," I said. "All that shows is his skin." I traced my finger along the white outline on one of the X-rays.

"How is that possible?" The sheriff looked to me for an answer.

"It's not," I explained. "It's like he's completely hollow inside." I walked over to the sheet-covered body and lifted John Doe's arm free.

"But he doesn't feel hollow," I said. "I can clearly feel his elbow." I gently placed the arm back on the table.

"Why call me about this?" the sheriff asked.

"Because I need you to tell me I'm not going crazy," I said.

"You seem perfectly sane to me."

"Maybe, maybe not," I said. "There's one more thing I need to show you." I reached up and pulled the sheet off the body, exposing the open abdominal cavity.

"Jesus fucking Christ," Sheriff Morgan cursed. "What the hell am I looking at?"

"I have no idea," I replied. "I called you as soon as I opened him up. All I can say for sure is that it's not natural."

We were standing on opposite sides of the autopsy table, staring into the void inside John Doe's body. There were no bones, no muscles, no organs, and no blood. There was just a vast empty space contained within the body's skin.

Sheriff Morgan looked under the table and then back into the hole. "If you're going crazy, then so am I," he said.

"What do you think we should do?" I asked.

The sheriff unhooked the flashlight from his belt and shined it into the hole. "Any idea how deep it is?"

I shook my head.

Sheriff Morgan reached into his pocket, withdrew a penny, and dropped it into the hole. The coin fell for a second before it clattered to a stop.

"That's odd." The sheriff was looking into the hole with his flashlight, but the beam couldn't penetrate the darkness within. "It's not that deep; we should be able to see the bottom."

He put his flashlight away and started looking around the room. When he couldn't find what he was looking for, he turned to me and asked, "Do you have a broom or mop or anything else with a long handle?"

"Yeah," I replied. "In the maintenance closet across the hall."

"Perfect, go grab me one."

"A mop or a broom?" I asked. He wasn't clear on which he preferred.

"It doesn't matter," he said. "Whichever has the longest handle."

I left the autopsy suite and returned a minute later with a broom.

"Here," I held it out to him.

"Thanks." The sheriff took the broom and began lowering it into the hole. He kept lowering it until his arms were in the body cavity up to his elbows. "That's as far as it goes," he declared. "Rough estimate, I'd say it's about seven feet deep." He pulled the broom out and handed it back to me.

I didn't see the point in holding onto it, so I leaned it against the wall, intending to put it away later.

"It must be some sort of pocket dimension," I declared when I returned to the table. "That's the only thing that makes sense."

I was familiar with the idea, having seen it used as a plot device in a few different science-fiction shows. After thinking about it, that was the best explanation I could come up with for the existence of the hole.

"Pocket dimension?" Clearly, Sheriff Morgan hadn't heard of the concept, which didn't surprise me, given his rural upbringing.

"It's a big space contained within a smaller space," I pantomimed, making a big circle and then a smaller one with my hands as I spoke.

When I saw that he still didn't understand, I walked over to a nearby desk and grabbed a piece of scratch paper and a pen. I folded the paper in half and then drew a small circle on one side and a big circle on the other.

"This side represents our dimension," I said, showing him the side with the small circle on it before flipping it over and adding, "and this side represents a different dimension."

While he stood there watching, I took the pen and jabbed a hole through the paper, extending from the center of the small circle to the center of the large one.

"Because of this hole I made between dimensions," I said, pointing, "I can now go from the smaller circle to the larger circle." To drive home my point, I returned to the body of John Doe. "This body is the small circle," I said, gesturing at the parts we could see. "While whatever is inside is the large circle." I gestured into the hole.

"So," I could tell from the look on his face that he was processing my explanation, "you're saying this body is some kind of a doorway to someplace else."

"Yeah," I nodded. "That's one way of putting it."

"Has anything like this happened before?" he asked.

"If it has, I've never heard about it," I replied.

"We should tell someone, but I just don't know who," Sheriff Morgan said, taking off his hat so he could scratch his head. "I'm not sure whose jurisdiction this falls under."

"I have a friend at the university I can call," I offered.

"I don't think that's a good idea," the sheriff said. "We don't want something like this getting out to the public just yet." He paused to think for a moment. "I could call the FBI and see if they can send one of their boys out here to take a look at it. See what they think we should do." He looked to me for affirmation.

"Whatever you think is best," I said.

He went to reach for his phone but stopped when he realized it wasn't in his pocket. "I didn't think I was going to be in here long, so I left it in the truck," he sighed.

"You can use mine," I offered.

"Thanks, but I need mine," he said. "I don't have the number memorized." He started walking toward the exit. "I'll just be a minute."

While Sheriff Morgan stepped outside to retrieve his phone, I returned to the body to examine it further. I knew I wasn't going to get another chance once the FBI arrived, and I wanted to make the most of the time I had left.

The first thing I did was reach into the body cavity and feel along its edge. We had a good idea about the depth of the dimensional space, but we didn't know how wide it was. All I could tell was that it was wider than the body.

When I stepped back, I looked up at the film hanging on the lighted panel. Pictured on the X-ray was the outline of John Doe's chest, shoulders, and upper arms. It was the arms that I was focused on.

I wonder...

I grabbed a scalpel from the tray of tools at the head of the table and used it to make an incision on John Doe's forearm. When I peeled back the skin, I was not surprised to see the same emptiness inside the arm. I expected that. What I was trying to do was find the edge of the space so I could better gauge its dimensions.

When I reached into the hole, I could feel resistance along the outside of the space. It didn't feel as hard as I expected. It felt like firm gel. It was really unnerving to touch, prompting me to withdraw my hand.

The space is the same shape as the body. I had assumed that would be the case, but I didn't know what would happen if I moved the arm.

Wanting to test the idea, I lifted the arm and inserted my hand into the incision. It felt the same inside, regardless of the position I held the arm.

I wonder what would happen if I put the arm inside the hole in the abdomen.

I probably shouldn't. I talked myself out of it. I wasn't a physicist and had no clue as to what laws of physics governed the hole. *Best to quit while I'm ahead.*

"What the hell are you doing?" Sheriff Morgan snapped.

He returned to the autopsy suite to find me standing over the body, holding the arm in the air. The sudden sound of his voice startled me, causing me to drop the arm, which fell into the exposed abdomen. I tried to catch it before it fell, but I wasn't fast enough. I only succeeded in pushing it into the hole faster.

As soon as the hole I'd made in the forearm entered the larger hole in the body, the room started to shake violently, sending loose items to the floor and making it hard for us to keep our footing.

"What have you done?" The sheriff looked alarmed as he reached out to steady himself on an empty table.

Behind me, a hollow ripping sound came from the body. The room stopped shaking after that.

"Do you feel that?" I felt a faint draft brush across my face.

The ripping sound came again.

The draft grew stronger. I could feel the air being pulled past me into the body, and that scared me.

"We need to leave—right now!"

I rushed past the sheriff on the way to the exit.

"What's going on?" the sheriff yelled.

I didn't have time to answer before the ripping sound came again. The pull of the air into the body suddenly became too great to resist. As soon as I felt myself being drawn toward it, I threw myself to the ground and started crawling toward the door.

The sheriff wasn't so lucky. As close as he was to the body, he didn't have a chance. It pulled him in before I could shout a warning. I'll never forget the look of surprise on his face as he was sucked into the hole.

Not wanting to follow him, I used every ounce of strength I could muster to pull myself out into the hall.

"Once I was able to, I stood up and ran out of the building, and I didn't stop running until you showed up," I said to Agent Michaels, the FBI agent who was sitting across the table from me.

"The breach has stabilized," another FBI agent said, entering the room.

"That's good, right?" I looked at Agent Michaels.

"No, it's not," he replied. "It means things are about to get a whole lot worse."

"What do you mean?"

"This isn't the first time we've encountered one of these dimensional bubbles," Agent Michaels explained, using their official term for the anomaly. "They've been appearing for a couple of decades now."

"What's causing them?" I was surprised to hear they already knew about them.

Agent Michaels shrugged. "We don't know. All we know is that something on the other side is trying to use people to break through into our dimension. Whenever it does, it leaves behind one of the bubbles like the one you found."

As soon as he said that, it dawned on me why he said things were about to get a whole lot worse.

"And I popped the bubble," I said.

"That you did." Agent Michaels got to his feet. "Now whatever is on the other side can just walk right on through."

PISTACHIO PLACE

"Hey, Hazel! I finally found out what dad was hiding in the attic," my brother, Thomas, announced as he descended the stairs.

"Good for you," I said. "Now that you've gotten that out of the way, maybe you could help me organize all these bills." I gestured at the stack of envelopes sitting on the table in front of me.

"Not until you come see this." He hooked his thumb over his shoulder.

"Unless it's a million dollars," I quipped, "I don't care what you found up there. You heard what the lawyer said; we're not supposed to touch anything in here until we settle these accounts." I waved the envelopes I was holding.

Our estranged father passed away a week earlier, and since he died without a will, we were tasked with going through his belongings and settling his affairs. Based on all the bills he had amassed, it was clear that he was in massive debt and doing nothing to rectify the situation. It was starting to look like we were going to have to sell the house to pay his creditors.

"Aren't you just the slightest bit curious about what he kept locked up there?"

For as long as I could remember, our father kept a padlock on the attic door and would threaten us with corporal punishment if we went anywhere near it. I remember the day Thomas tried to sneak a peek after our father left his keys on the counter. He had trouble sitting for a week.

I think that incident might have been the final straw for our mother because she packed us up and left a couple of months later. That was over thirty years ago.

When I didn't make a move to get up, Thomas tried a different tactic. "What's up there might be worth more than the house and everything else in it," he said.

"Seriously?" I set the bills down and stood up. "How much more?"

Thomas smiled. "A lot more. Come on, I'll show you."

I followed him up to the second floor, where he stopped in front of the attic stairs. "Go check it out." He nodded.

I hurried up the stairs, pushed the already ajar door the rest of the way open, and stepped into the attic.

"Oh my God! Is that what I think it is?" I gasped upon seeing the monster puppet sitting in a display case on the far side of the attic. Its body was covered with a lime green fuzz, and its face, topped with two large white eyes and a bulbous yellow nose, was instantly recognizable.

"I told you it was valuable." Thomas had followed me up the stairs and was watching from the doorway so he could see my reaction.

"But what's it doing here?" My surprise at seeing the puppet quickly turned to confusion. "Dad said they were all destroyed in the fire."

When we were kids, our dad worked as a prop maker on a local children's television show called *Pistachio Place*. It was like *Sesame Street*, except that it didn't feature any live actors. The entire cast consisted of puppets, all of which were designed by my father.

The show was a huge hit locally, and after airing for only a year, discussions had begun about turning it into a nationally syndicated show, but that never materialized. A fire swept through the studio, destroying the *Pistachio Place* set and all the puppets along with it—or so we thought.

After the fire, the station began discussing rebuilding the show, bigger and better than before, but our father had no part in it. That's when the rumors that he started the fire began. The rumors eventually led to an arson investigation, but it was dropped due to a lack of evidence.

The studio fired him long before the investigation was over, essentially ending his career in television. He never managed to hold down a steady job after that.

That was also around the time he started locking up the attic.

"He obviously lied." Thomas stepped into the room and stood next to me in front of the display case.

"I wonder why he kept it." I took a step forward and placed my hands on the glass.

As soon as my fingers touched the case, the puppet shifted, rolling its head from left to right, startling me.

I jumped back with a gasp.

Thomas laughed.

"The same thing happened to me," he said. "It's the floorboards." To emphasize his point, he stepped up to the case and started bouncing on the balls of his feet. The floor creaked, and the case started to rock back and forth.

"You'd better stop before you knock it over," I warned, reaching out to steady the case.

Once the case stopped moving, the puppet fell forward, causing its large plastic eyes to click against the glass.

"Which one is that again?" Thomas pointed at the puppet. "I could never get their names straight."

"Seriously?" I scoffed. "How could you not know which one that is?"

"I think you've forgotten that I never watched the show," he replied. "You were the one who was obsessed with it, like all the other preschoolers in the state."

I had forgotten that.

But it made sense. When *Pistachio Place* first started airing, I was five and Thomas was eight. He'd already outgrown shows like that. What little he knew about it, he likely learned in passing from all the times I sat in front of the television watching it.

"That's Pistachio," I said. "The main character of the show."

"If he's the main character, that makes him the most valuable one, right?" Thomas replied.

"I guess," I said. "Assuming anyone even remembers it."

"Do you think the other puppets might be up here somewhere?" Thomas looked around at the stacks of boxes that filled half the attic.

"It's possible," I said. "But doubtful."

"Why do you say that?"

"That's why." I gestured at the case holding Pistachio. "Why keep him locked up and not the others?"

"I'm still going to look," he said, walking over to the nearest box.

"Okay," I said. "I guess I'm going to go back downstairs and finish figuring out just how much Dad owes."

I turned and left the attic.

"$62,000," I said, reading the number from the calculator.

I'd finished organizing the bills, and that was the amount my father owed to all his creditors, assuming I didn't find any other outstanding bills lying around. It wasn't as bad as I thought, but it was still a lot.

We could easily sell the house and pay everyone off, with a decent amount left over to split between Thomas and me, but I wasn't sure I wanted to do that. Part of me wanted to keep the house and turn it into a rental property. The only way I could do that was to find an alternative way to come up with $62,000.

As cool as finding the puppet was, I didn't think it was as valuable as Thomas believed. I figured we'd be lucky to get a few hundred dollars out of it.

I got up and started walking around the house, looking at all the stuff my father left behind, assigning values to everything I could potentially sell if I were to have an estate sale.

It didn't look good. Most of the furniture was old and well-worn, and all the appliances were outdated by several decades.

He must have some money hidden away somewhere.

I'd seen his bank statements. He kept just enough money in his account to keep it open but hadn't made any deposits or withdrawals in over two years. There was no way he'd be able to take care of himself for that long without an income of some sort. That meant he had another bank account we didn't know about, or he started using cash. I was hoping it was the latter and he had a stash of it hidden somewhere in the house.

Where would I hide my money if I were you?

I scanned the kitchen, dining room, and living room, noticing how sparsely furnished they were.

When we lived in the house with him, there were all sorts of furnishings spread throughout the house: pictures on the walls, shelves full of books and knick-knacks. All that stuff was gone.

I don't think I'm going to find anything down here, I decided.

After climbing the stairs to the second floor, I made my way to the end of the hall where my father's bedroom was. Once inside, I started going through the drawers of his dresser. When I didn't find anything there, I checked under his bed but found nothing but dust. From there, I moved into the closet.

"Nothing," I sighed upon seeing a well-worn collection of clothing that wasn't fit to donate to Goodwill.

I was about to turn and leave the room, but something out of the corner of my eye caught my attention.

There was a dark spot on the ceiling of the closet.

Upon examining it, I realized that there was a gap. Someone had created a small access panel in the closet ceiling and forgotten to reseat it properly, which is why I noticed the gap. If it had been seated properly, I probably never would have noticed it.

That looks like the perfect hiding place.

Since the panel was in the ceiling, I was unable to reach it on my own and had to go downstairs and grab a chair to boost me up. Once I had the chair in position, I reached up and carefully moved the panel out of the way.

I hope there aren't any spiders up there, I thought as I reached my hand through the opening and started feeling around the edge of it.

"Gotcha!" I yelled triumphantly when my fingers brushed against the edge of a small wooden box.

When I tried to pull the box free, I was surprised by how heavy it was. I had to use both hands to drag it to the edge of the opening so I could pull it down.

Unable to keep my curiosity in check, I remained standing on the chair, undid the little metal latch on the front of the box, and then swung the lid open.

I should've waited.

The act of opening the lid unbalanced the box and sent it tumbling out of my hands, spilling its contents all over the closet floor.

"Well, shit," I muttered, stepping off the chair to pick everything up.

I was disappointed to see that there wasn't any money in the box. There was just a stack of old Polaroids and a couple of small books.

I tossed everything back into the box and carried it over to the bed so I could sit down and look at it.

The first thing I pulled out was the stack of Polaroid pictures. They were originally held together by a rubber band, but that snapped when the stack hit the floor.

All the pictures were of Pistachio. In most of them, the puppet showed signs of having been in a fire. In a few of them, he was barely recognizable due to how charred his body was. As I was looking at the photos, I noticed that handwritten dates were on the back of them. I quickly put the photos in order from oldest to newest and then reviewed them.

The dates listed were a week apart and seemed to show the restoration of Pistachio from an unrecognizable lump of charred fur back to the puppet that was sitting in the case in the attic. The last photo was dated a few months before our mother took us out of the house for good.

Why did you hold on to these?

What was the point in keeping the photos? Especially in a box hidden in his closet.

I set the photos aside and picked up the smaller of the two books, trying to identify it, but I couldn't find the title or author anywhere on its cover. Its pages were yellowed with age, and its leather binding was well-worn. It was clearly very old.

Carefully, I cracked open the cover. On the first page was a list of names. There were a dozen of them, all handwritten. My father's name was the last one on the list.

After flipping through a few of the pages, I quickly realized I wasn't going to be able to identify the book. It was written in a language I wasn't familiar with.

Might be worth something.

I set the book aside and grabbed the other one. That one I recognized. It was my father's old journal. It was where he wrote out all his design ideas for the props he made for the television studio. He carried it with him everywhere he went and was always writing inside it. He was writing in it so much that my mother had to ban him from bringing it to the dinner table.

I opened the journal and started flipping through the pages. It was interesting to see the diagrams he'd drawn of his props, along with the notes about functionality and the materials to use when building them. It wasn't until I was halfway through the journal that I got to the section where he'd started designing the puppets and sets for *Pistachio Place*.

This is so cool, I thought, marveling at how much effort my father put into creating the props and set pieces for the show. Every little detail was accounted for.

I continued flipping through the journal until I got to the last few pages. Those pages were different from the rest of the journal. Instead of being filled with diagrams and design notes, they were filled with my father's crazy thoughts about the puppet Pistachio being alive.

I never should have used that book. If I had known what I'd be creating, I never would've done it. That was the first thing he wrote about it.

I looked over at the old book, wondering if that was the one he was referring to.

There was another accident on set today, the next entry in the journal said, *but I know it wasn't an accident. It was Pistachio.*

The next few entries discussed the specifics of the accidents that had occurred on set, along with my father's belief that the puppet of Pistachio was responsible. They sounded like the ravings of a madman.

He finally killed someone today. That was written on the top of the next page. *And it's all my fault. What was I thinking! Success is not worth the lives of my coworkers. I have to do something.*

The entry that followed stated: *The producers refused to shut the show down. They brushed the stagehand's death aside, calling it an unfortunate accident, and then wanted to start talking about filming two episodes a day, airing one in the morning and one in the afternoon. If that were to happen, Pistachio would be unstoppable. I can't let that happen.*

The more I read, the more unhinged I thought my father was.

The next entry confirmed just how crazy he'd become.

I was told that Pistachio Place *had been picked up for syndication. The thought of Pistachio appearing on millions of TV screens across the nation is* terrifying. With that kind of adoration, I can only imagine how powerful he'd become.

Beneath that entry, he had drawn a huge bonfire and wrote: *This is my show; I get to decide its future.*

That was confirmation to me that my father really had burned the studio down like everyone had suspected.

"What the hell, Dad?" I said, turning the page so I could continue reading.

I thought I'd put an end to Pistachio's reign of terror, he wrote, *but I was wrong. He's coming back. All the reruns they've been running must be helping him. At the rate he's regenerating, he'll be good as new within a month, maybe two. I can't keep him locked in my attic any longer. It's not safe.*

I looked over at the stack of photos of Pistachio—the ones I thought showed my father's restoration efforts repairing the burned puppet.

This just keeps getting weirder and weirder, I thought, but I kept reading.

They wanted to redo the show, bigger and better than before, but I refused. Because of that, someone started a rumor that I was the cause of the fire. There's no way they could actually know that, and there's no way the police can pin it on me. I made sure of that.

That entry was followed by: *They fired me today.*

I was beginning to understand why our mother left him. There was a lot more going on at the time than we thought. It was starting to look like he had become delusional. I wondered how much my mother knew about his obsession with the Pistachio puppet.

I caught Thomas going into the attic today and overreacted. He had no idea of the danger he'd put himself in. I need to find a way to get rid of that infernal puppet once and for all so it can't hurt anyone else.

The following entry was just two words. *Mary left.* Mary was my mother's name.

Thank God they finally stopped airing those reruns. He's finally quieted down. Now's my chance to get rid of him.

Knives, fire, acid—nothing works. He's still too powerful to destroy, so I had to change tactics. I used the book to build a containment chamber and was able to lock him inside. As long as he doesn't get any stronger, that should hold him until I can find a way to get rid of him for good.

The next entry was written with a different colored pen, and the handwriting appeared to be a bit shakier, making me think it was written a long time after the previous ones.

Someone has started sharing episodes of Pistachio Place *online. I've done my best to get them taken down, but there are just too many places where they are being shared. That containment chamber won't hold him for long.*

The final entry sent chills up my spine.

If this is the last thing I write, it means that all my efforts to stop him have failed.

"I have to show this to Thomas," I muttered, closing the journal before standing up and carrying it out of the room.

"Hey, Thomas," I called out as I approached the attic door. "You're not going to believe what I found."

He didn't respond.

"Thomas?" I repeated, pushing the door open and stepping inside. "What..."

I forgot the rest of what I was going to say when I saw Thomas's lifeless body lying on the floor in front of Pistachio's case. The door to the case was open, and Pistachio was nowhere in sight.

FOREST FOR THE TREES

"Hey, Hank!" I called out to the site foreman. "Where do you want us today?"

Hank walked over to where I was standing next to my truck with Thomas, Bode, and Travis, my crew of loggers.

"I need you and your boys to start working the southwest quadrant," he said, pointing behind us.

"I thought that quadrant was off-limits," I replied.

A local conservation group had filed an injunction against us several months ago to prevent us from logging that specific area on the grounds that it was the natural habitat for an *at-risk* species of salamander.

"The injunction was lifted this morning," Hank said. "But I'm not sure if it'll stay that way, which is why I need you to get in there ASAP and do a select cut. Get the best timber you can, as quickly as you can."

"You got it." I turned to the trio of men to address them. "All right, you heard Hank, we're working the southwest quadrant today! Get your gear in the truck and let's get to it!"

As Bode and Travis were unloading the gear from the truck, I pulled Thomas aside.

"Go do your thing," I said, handing him the can of orange spray paint we used to mark the trees we were going to cut down. "Select cut only today," I added to remind him that we were only after the best trees in the quadrant.

"You got it, boss." Thomas put on his hard hat and started making his way into the forest.

While he went off to mark the target trees for the day, I inspected the crew's equipment like I did every morning. I expected them to maintain everything to the highest possible standards to avoid unnecessary accidents. Anyone who had a problem with that was not welcome on my crew.

Just before I finished, Thomas returned.

"The first sector is done," he said, setting the can of paint back in the truck. "There's a lot of good timber in there. It would've been easier for me to mark the ones we shouldn't take."

I liked the sound of that; it meant we were going to have a productive day.

"All right, let's get cutting," I said.

Fifteen minutes later, the crew felled their first tree of the day, and then our day went to shit.

"Hey, boss," Bode called over the walkie. "I think you need to come take a look at this."

I looked over to where the three men were gathered around the stump of the tree they'd just felled, staring at something.

"On my way," I replied.

When I approached the stump, Bode stepped aside so I could get a closer look.

"What do you make of that?" he asked, gesturing at a hollowed-out cavity in the center of the stump, which contained the mummified remains of a large, hairy humanoid. I could only see its head and the top of its shoulders.

It wasn't uncommon for us to find dead animals in the hollows of trees, but it was usually things like birds, squirrels, and other small animals. This was the first time we'd ever found anything like this.

"I think it's Bigfoot," Travis blurted out. "Doesn't it look like Bigfoot?" he directed the question at me.

I could see why he'd say that. The head was very simian-looking and covered with remnants of dark brown hair, which brought to mind all the supposed images of Bigfoot I'd seen.

"I don't know what it looks like," I said, not wanting to jump to any conclusions and have the guys start spreading rumors among the other cutting crews.

"What should we do about it?" Bode asked.

"We need to shut down and cordon off the area," I replied. "Thomas, can you go grab the tape?" I gestured over my shoulder toward the truck.

"Seriously?" Bode scoffed. "Can't we report it after we're done for the day? It's not like we're going to disturb it by felling a few more trees."

"You know we can't," I replied.

If we went ahead and kept felling trees and the area was later deemed to be of historical significance, we could be fined or, worse, lose our logging rights.

"Let's pack it up," I said. "I'll radio Hank and see what he wants us to do."

While Bode and Travis packed up the equipment and Thomas cordoned off the area around the mummified remains, I sat in the cab and radioed Hank, explaining to him what we found.

Ten minutes later, Hank pulled his truck up alongside mine and got out.

"Show me," he said.

I led him to the tree stump and pointed into the hollow.

"There it is," I said.

Hank leaned over the stump to get a closer look at the remains.

"Any idea what it is?" he asked.

"I have no clue," I replied.

"What do the boys think?" Hank nodded toward the trio of men who were loading the last of the equipment into the back of my truck.

I hesitated before recounting it, knowing I was going to sound crazy if I told him what Travis had said.

Hank noticed my reluctance to answer and said, "Say it."

"Travis thinks it might be Bigfoot," I said.

"Jesus Christ, I hope not," he grumbled, rubbing his head. "That's the last thing we need up here. Can you imagine the shitstorm that would follow if people thought we found Bigfoot?"

He looked back at the men for a moment before continuing.

"Make sure they keep their mouths shut about this," he said, jabbing his finger at my chest. "At least until we know what we're dealing with, got it?"

I nodded. "Got it."

Hank looked back at the body in the tree. "Goddammit!" he cursed.

"Do you want me to contact the preservation office, or do you want to do it?" I asked.

We were supposed to contact the state historical preservation office if we ever found anything of historical significance. They would then send someone out to assess the site and let us know how to proceed.

"We should hold off on that," he said, holding up a hand. "I think we need to figure out exactly what that thing is before we contact them. We've spent too much money procuring this site to lose it over something like that," he nodded toward the stump.

"What do you want us to do?" He was asking me to step outside the bounds of standard protocol, which was something I was uncomfortable with, but he was the boss, and I wasn't going to go against his wishes. At least not until he gave me a good reason to.

"Your daughter is a vet, isn't she?" Hank asked. "I seem to recall you saying something about that a few months back."

Hank had overheard me talking to one of the other crew chiefs about his sick dog. I recommended that he take the dog to my daughter's veterinary practice in town, and that was the end of the conversation. I was surprised Hank remembered it.

"Yeah," I confirmed. "She is."

"Do you think you could convince her to come out and take a look at this thing?" he asked, pointing at the body. "Maybe tell us what it is."

"I can ask," I offered, "but I'm not sure she's really qualified for this sort of thing."

My daughter's expertise was with cats and dogs, not whatever the hell the thing in the tree was.

"Call her," Hank said.

"I doubt she'd be able to get here until this evening," I pointed out as I pulled out my phone and started to make the call.

"That's better than being shut down for a week waiting on the preservation office to send someone," he countered.

Having to wait a week was an exaggeration on his part. The preservation office had never made us wait that long before, but they had been known to make us wait a day or two before sending someone out.

My daughter, Ashley, answered on the second ring.

"Hey, Dad," she said. "What's up?" She sounded a little worried, which I assumed was because I rarely called her while she was at work. When I did, it was usually bad news.

"Is Mom okay?" she asked, assuming the worst.

The last time I called her, I had to tell her I put her mother in a special care facility at the recommendation of her neurologist. She'd been diagnosed with early-onset Alzheimer's and had deteriorated to the point of needing round-the-clock specialized care that I couldn't provide on my own.

"Your mother is fine," I replied, putting her fears to rest. "I'm calling because we need your help with something we found today."

"Why me?"

"Do you think you can come out to the site today?" I asked. "You'll understand why once you see it for yourself."

There was a brief pause before Ashley answered. In the background, I could hear her typing on a keyboard.

"Yeah," she eventually answered. "I can meet you out there later this afternoon."

Ashley pulled up in front of the foreman's trailer eight hours later.

"I appreciate you coming out," I said as she climbed out of her jeep.

"What's with all the secrecy?" she asked.

"Come on," I said, motioning for her to follow me over to my truck. "I'll show you."

Ten minutes later, we were standing next to the tree stump, staring down at the strange body entombed within.

"Any idea what it is?" I asked.

Ashley had been staring at the body for quite some time without saying a word before I broke the silence with my question.

"I honestly have no idea," she said, shaking her head. "And I don't want to make any guesses based on appearance alone."

"Do you think you could figure it out?"

She sighed. "I can try, but this isn't really my area of expertise. You'd have better luck calling in a cryptozoologist."

"A crypto what?" I'd never heard the word before.

"A cryptozoologist," she repeated. "It's someone who specializes in the study of unverified creatures. They'd be better qualified to tell if that is what you think it is." She gestured at the body.

"We can't afford to have this area shut down for an investigation like that," I replied. "Is there anything you can do to help us stop that from happening?"

"Nothing ethical."

"What did you have in mind?"

I could tell she'd already thought about it.

"The way I see it," she explained, "you have two options. You can bury it and pretend that you never found it, or you can move it some place out of the way and let someone else find it."

I'd already thought about burying the body and trying to forget about it, but I hadn't considered moving it.

"That said," Ashley continued, "given the potential importance of a discovery like this, and assuming I can't convince you to leave it where it is and call the proper authorities, I'd suggest moving it."

"It's not my call. I'll have to check with Hank," I said, which was only half true.

I could go over Hank's head and report the body, but doing so would piss him off, and that's not something I wanted to do. I'd seen what happens when someone gets on his bad side. He wouldn't fire me, but he'd make my life miserable to the point I'd want to quit. The best thing I could do was convince him to let us move the body.

I pulled out my phone and called Hank. After speaking with him for a few minutes, I was able to convince him that moving the body was the best course of action. He reluctantly agreed, with the caveat that it be moved far enough away that its discovery wouldn't impact the logging site in any way.

That was a reasonable request. If the body were discovered too close to the logging site, the authorities might shut us down and want to reinspect the area.

"I'll take care of it," I promised him.

"So, we're moving it?" Ashley had eavesdropped on my conversation.

I nodded. "You don't have to help if you don't want to."

"I'm already here," she said. "And if you help me get the body into my truck, I know the perfect place to move it to."

"Where?" I hadn't thought that far ahead yet.

"Remember when we took Mom to the lake last summer?" she asked.

"Yeah," I replied.

The lake was my wife's favorite place to go before Alzheimer's took away her independence. We brought her out there to see if it might help bring her thoughts back to the present day, if only for a little while.

"While we were out there, I found a small cave," she revealed. "I think we should put the body there. Lots of people frequent the area. Someone is bound to find the cave sooner or later. Plus, all that land is already owned by the state, so it won't inconvenience anyone once it's found."

"Okay," I agreed. It sounded like a good idea to me.

"Do you have a tarp or something we can wrap the body in once we remove it from the stump?" Ashley asked.

"I think I have one in my truck," I said. "I'll go check."

I started walking back to where my truck was parked. I was about halfway there when Ashley called out to me.

"Um... Dad!?" she yelled. "You might want to come look at this."

I stopped and turned around, thinking, *Now what?*

Ashley was standing next to the stump with her hands on her hips, staring down at the body.

"What about the tarp?" I called back, gesturing toward my truck.

"We might not need it," she replied.

I made my way back up to the stump and stood next to Ashley.

"What did you find?" I asked.

"How closely did you examine that thing when you found it?" she asked, pointing at the body.

"Not very," I admitted. "Why?"

"Because I don't think it's real," she said.

"Why do you think that?" It looked real to me, but I was no expert.

"When you went to get the tarp," she explained, "I wanted to see how easy it would be to free it from the stump, so I started fiddling with it, and that's when I found this." She held up a tuft of fur.

Again, I was no expert, so I had no idea what the significance was.

"This is synthetic fur," she said.

"How can you tell?"

"For starters, it's too perfect." She held the tuft up before her eyes. "Every hair is exactly the same length and color. If this were real fur, there'd be a lot more variation to it. Secondly, real fur wouldn't come free from the skin this easily, and if it did, there'd be follicles attached to the end of each hair, but that's not the case with any of these." She held the tuft out for me to examine.

"I believe you," I said, taking her word for it.

"We need to pull it out of there and take a closer look at it," she said.

I agreed, so the two of us set about pulling the body free from the stump, which was surprisingly easy to do. Once we got it out, we laid it on the ground.

"This is definitely fake," she declared. "It would be a lot heavier if it were real."

"Why would someone hide a fake Bigfoot body in the middle of a tree?" It didn't make sense to me. We were in the middle of nowhere, miles from the nearest civilization.

"Let's see if we can find out." Ashley leaned down, grabbed a saggy patch of fur, and pulled it, ripping it apart.

Doing so exposed the inner framework of the body, which didn't look anything like bones.

"That looks like plastic," I said.

Ashley tapped one of the exposed pieces with her fingernail. "I think it is plastic," she agreed.

"I should call Hank and tell him about this," I said, pulling out my phone.

As I did that, Ashley ripped an even bigger hole in the fur, exposing more of its interior.

"Oh my God," she gasped upon seeing the little skeleton nestled in a harness in the center of the fake Bigfoot body.

"Is that a child?" I also gasped upon seeing the skeleton.

Ashley shook her head. "Whatever that is," she pointed at the oddly shaped skull with the oversized eye sockets, "it isn't human. I think it's an…"

"Don't say it," I cut her off.

Believing we'd found Bigfoot was one thing; finding an alien was a whole different problem.

"What should we do with it?" she asked.

I thought about it for a moment, and then ultimately decided that I was too old for this shit.

"I think we should get rid of the skeleton and take the fake body to Hank and tell him it was all a hoax of some kind."

"Why would you want to do that?" she scoffed. "We have evidence that aliens came here dressed in Bigfoot costumes. We have to tell someone."

"Listen to what you just said," I appealed to her common sense.

"That does sound kind of crazy," she admitted.

"Exactly," I replied. "Which is why we need to cover this up as neatly as possible and pretend it never happened."

"Okay," she said. "I'll take care of it. Go ahead and call Hank."

That's what I did.

Once Hank heard that the body wasn't real, he was relieved and wanted me to bring it down to his trailer, which I agreed to do.

By the time I got off the phone, Ashley had extricated the small skeleton, wrapped the bones up in her jacket, and carried them back to the truck, where she stowed them under the seat.

As we were driving back to the trailer, Travis called me over the radio.

"Hey, Boss," he sounded excited. "We just found another Bigfoot body."

I looked over at my daughter and said, "I think it might be time to retire."

GOING DOWN

"Where do you want to eat?" I asked my girlfriend, Verity, as I reached out to push the button to call the elevator.

"Why do you always make me pick?" she teased.

"Because you're the picky one," I said, smiling at my lame play on words. "Every time I pick something, you find something wrong with it."

Verity had a habit of adopting whatever diet plan was popular at the time, so I never knew what she would or wouldn't eat. That's why I started making her pick where we ate whenever we went out.

The elevator dinged, signaling its arrival.

"That's a lot of pressure," Verity whined as she stepped onto the elevator.

"I can pick if you want," I said, following her inside and pressing the button for the first floor. "But if I do, you can't complain about it."

"No, I'll pick," she said. "I just need to think about it for a minute."

"Well," I pushed the button for the first floor, "you have until we get to the lobby to figure it out."

My condo was on the twenty-eighth floor of the building, which meant she had about two to three minutes to make her decision, assuming the elevator didn't stop on any other floors.

Apparently, Verity realized that as well, because she quickly stepped forward and mashed her hands against the panel, pushing as many buttons as she could to stall for time.

She had a smug look on her face as she folded her arms across her chest and said, "That should give me enough time to think of something."

The elevator doors closed.

"Why aren't we moving?" Verity asked a few moments later.

I didn't have the answer to that question. We should have already started to descend.

I looked over at the panel and noticed that all the buttons were flashing, but they weren't flashing in sync. Different ones would flash at different times, and some would flash two or three times before going dark for a few seconds.

"I think you might've broken it." I pointed at the erratic light show on the panel.

"All I did was push the buttons," she huffed. "How could that break the elevator? You're supposed to push them."

"True," I agreed. "But I don't think you're supposed to push them all at the same time."

A loud grinding sound echoed through the elevator shaft. Whatever was causing it was also making the elevator floor vibrate.

"That doesn't sound good," Verity said, stepping closer to me and grabbing my arm.

The lights on the panel suddenly stopped flashing. A moment later, the grinding sound stopped, and the elevator started to sway.

"That doesn't feel right," I said, planting my feet farther apart to maintain my balance.

Verity tightened her grip on my arm.

"Maybe you should push the alarm," she said, pointing at the darkened panel.

That sounded like a good idea, but before I could do that, the elevator started descending.

I relaxed my posture. "It seems to be working now."

We stood in silence for a minute before Verity spoke again.

"Are you sure it's working?" she asked, releasing her hold on my arm. "None of the floors are lit up." She pointed at the panel. "How will it know where to stop?"

She had a point.

"Maybe you should push the button again," she suggested. "Just to make sure."

I had the same idea and was already leaning forward to press the button for the lobby again.

"It doesn't seem to be working." I pressed the button several times, but it never lit up.

That was when I looked at the digital floor indicator above the panel. It should display the current floor we were on, along with an up or down arrow indicating the direction we were traveling. Nothing was displayed on it.

"I think you might've fried it," I said. It was the only explanation for why the panel was dead, even though the elevator itself seemed to be moving.

"Try pushing the alarm button," she suggested.

Even though I had a pretty good idea that the button wasn't going to work, I pushed it anyway to show Verity.

"None of them are working," I replied while repeatedly jabbing the button with my index finger.

"What if it doesn't stop?" Verity sounded worried.

Her comment made me realize something.

It should've already stopped.

The elevator had started descending at least two minutes ago. If I recall correctly, it took about four or five seconds to travel between floors. If that were the case, we should've already reached the lobby.

Even stranger was the fact that we hadn't stopped at any other floors as we descended. I'd never used the elevator without it stopping at least once to pick up other passengers.

"It'll stop," I said. "It has to." I based that assumption on the fact that the elevator seemed to be descending without issue. It had to reach the bottom at some point, and when it did, the doors would open. I was sure of it.

But after waiting for several minutes, it was clear that wasn't going to happen.

"This is ridiculous," I griped, reaching behind me to pull my phone out of my pants pocket.

"What're you doing?" Verity asked.

"Calling 911," I replied.

"That's a good idea," she agreed.

I unlocked my phone and dialed the number, but there was only silence. I tried a few more times, but I couldn't get the call to connect. That's when I noticed the "no service" icon at the top of the screen.

"Well, that's just great," I sighed.

"What's wrong?" Verity asked.

"I don't have any service in here." I showed her the phone screen.

She pulled her phone out of her purse and checked it. "I don't either."

Frustrated, I walked back over to the elevator panel and repeatedly pushed the alarm button. I must've pushed it a hundred times. Still, nothing happened. Momentarily enraged, I stepped back and kicked the panel with the bottom of my shoe.

Verity walked over and pulled me away before I could kick it again.

"I don't think that's going to make it work," she said.

"I know," I huffed and shrugged away from her. "I know." I took a deep breath and tried to relax.

Even though whatever was going on with the elevator was more than likely Verity's fault, I didn't want to take my frustration out on her.

"I just don't understand why we haven't stopped," I said. "Hundreds of people use this elevator every day. Someone should've realized it isn't working right by now."

"Maybe they have," Verity said, trying to sound optimistic. "Maybe it's just taking them longer than normal to fix whatever is wrong."

"Yeah, you're probably right," I agreed reluctantly. "It hasn't really been that long."

I pressed my back against the elevator wall and slid down until I was sitting on the floor with my knees up. Verity sat down beside me.

"I guess we wait," I said.

We sat there for fifteen minutes before my butt couldn't handle sitting on the hard floor any longer.

Groaning, I got to my feet. As soon as I was standing, the elevator stopped.

The sudden lack of motion made me feel dizzy for a moment.

"Did we stop?" Verity asked, grabbing hold of my arm to pull herself up.

"I think so," I replied.

The elevator made a dinging sound, and the doors slid open.

"Finally," I sighed. "Let's get out of here." I motioned for us to leave.

Verity walked out before me, stopping just outside the doors.

"Where is everyone?" she whispered.

I stepped out beside her and scanned the lobby of the building. It was completely empty. For a Friday night, that was really weird. Normally, there'd be dozens of people coming and going or just milling about at one of the tables in the lounge.

"I have no idea," I replied, walking away from the elevator so I could get a better look around.

"It's kind of creepy, don't you think?" Verity asked, following close behind me.

"A little," I agreed.

"What do you think is going on?" she asked.

I shrugged. "It's probably nothing."

It wasn't the first time I'd been in the lobby without anyone around. If I ever came home late or left early, I'd often find it empty.

"Come on," I nodded. "Let's go get something to eat. I'm starving."

"Wait," Verity stopped and tilted her head. "Listen… do you hear that?"

"Hear what?" I asked, stopping to listen. "I don't hear anything."

"Exactly," she said. "This is New York. It's never this quiet."

She was right. Being close to the street, we should be hearing horns honking, sirens blaring, and angry drivers yelling. But there was nothing. It unnerved me a little but also piqued my curiosity.

I turned the corner and started heading toward the exit doors.

"Where are you going?" Verity asked, lagging a few steps behind me.

"To find out what's going on," I replied, striding up to the exit doors.

"I think I'm just going to wait here." She stopped and retreated a few steps.

Without breaking my stride, I reached my hands out to push on the inner set of doors. Instead of swinging open as I expected, they stayed firmly shut, causing me to collide with the glass.

Annoyed, I stepped back, grabbed the bar, and tried to force the doors open, but they wouldn't budge.

"Are they locked?" Verity called out behind me.

"They shouldn't be," I grunted, putting all my weight against the doors as I tried repeatedly to open them.

When that didn't work, I started banging on them, hoping I might be able to get someone's attention, although I knew that wasn't likely. I could see the street out in front of the building; it looked deserted.

"I still don't have any service," Verity announced.

I turned and saw her standing with her phone in her hands. I pulled mine out and saw that I still didn't have any service either. That's when I remembered the emergency phone that was hanging on the wall near the elevators. It was a landline. It should work.

I walked back across the lobby to where the elevators were. Verity fell into step beside me as I passed her.

"What are you doing now?" she asked.

I pointed at the red phone hanging on the wall. "I'm going to call for help."

I picked up the receiver, held it to my ear, and waited for it to connect.

"That won't work," a man declared behind us.

Verity yelped at the unexpected intrusion. "Oh my God, you scared the crap out of me," she hissed, placing a hand on her chest as she turned to look at the oddly dressed young man who had just entered the lobby.

His dark brown hair was well-styled but overgrown, and he was wearing a mustard-colored, double-breasted suit with a lime-green tie. A matching handkerchief was hanging out of the breast pocket of his jacket. He looked ridiculous.

"Why doesn't it work?" I asked, keeping the phone to my ear in case he was wrong.

The stranger shrugged. "If I knew that, I might be able to find a way out of this place," he replied, making a sweeping gesture with his hand.

I hung up the phone and took a few steps closer to him. "What do you mean by that?"

"Isn't it obvious?" he scoffed. "Haven't you tried to leave?" He gestured at the exit doors.

"Yeah, I tried," I admitted. "But the doors were locked."

The man shook his head. "They're not locked, man," he gave me a humorless smile. "They just don't work. Just like the phones don't work, or the elevators, or anything else in this endless maze of lobbies."

"If the doors don't work, how did you get in here?" Verity asked.

"From the adjoining lobby," he pointed toward a hallway to the side of the elevators. A hallway that I knew led to the restrooms. When he saw the skeptical look on my face, he said, "Come on, I'll show you."

He started walking toward the hallway. When he noticed that neither of us was following him, he stopped and turned back. "If you want to survive in this place, you're going to have to trust me, man," he said.

"I don't think we have a choice," Verity whispered to me. "He seems to know a lot more about what's going on than we do."

Reluctantly, I agreed, and the two of us followed the man into the hallway, which I was surprised to see did not lead to the restrooms as I had thought. It really did lead to another lobby.

"Where the hell are we?" I asked, looking around the garishly decorated lobby. It looked like the décor hadn't been updated in decades.

"I've heard a lot of theories about that," the man explained, "but the truth is nobody really knows where we are. The only thing I can say for sure is that when you got off that elevator, you stepped right into *The Twilight Zone*."

Verity started walking around the lobby, examining our surroundings.

"It looks like there's another lobby through there," she pointed at an archway.

"And you'll find another through there," the stranger pointed to another archway opposite the one Verity was pointing at.

"How is this possible?" I stood in the center of the lobby, looking at the other lobbies. One of them occupied a space that seemed to be right in the middle of the street in front of the building.

"Your guess is as good as mine," the man replied. "But I'd wager it has something to do with the elevator ride that brought us all here—the flashing lights, the long descent. That's the one thing we all have in common."

I looked over at Verity, knowing she was the reason we were there. If it weren't for her little stunt with the buttons, we'd be sitting down to eat somewhere.

Verity saw the look on my face and quickly turned away.

"What's your name?" she asked the stranger, trying to deflect attention from herself. "I'm Verity," she placed her hand on her chest, "and that's Connor." She pointed at me without bothering to look at me.

"Ian," the stranger replied.

"How long have you been here?" she asked.

"I have no way to tell time, but if I had to guess, I'd say about a week," Ian answered.

"Can I ask you a personal question?"

"Sure."

"Why are you dressed like that?" Verity pointed at the suit Ian was wearing.

"Like what?" Ian looked down at his clothes.

"Like you're going to a costume party," she said.

"Why would I wear this to a costume party?" Ian sounded confused. "These are my work clothes."

"What year is it?" I interrupted, directing the question at Ian.

Looking at the different lobbies surrounding us and listening to the exchange between Ian and Verity made me curious about something.

"What?" He was confused by the question.

"What year is it?" I repeated.

"1968," Ian replied. "Why?"

Verity and I shared a look.

"To us, it's 2024," I said.

"That's impossible." Ian didn't want to believe me. "But it makes sense."

"How so?" I asked, because it didn't make sense to me.

"Look at this lobby," he spread his arms. "To me, this looks like something from the future. But that one over there," he pointed through the archway where you could see several gas lamps, "that one looks about fifty years out of date."

"They both look out of date to me," I said.

Before we could ponder the implications of our discovery any further, a noise drew our attention to the hallway that led back to my building. It sounded like something rhythmically slapping against the floor and walls, and it was quickly getting closer.

"What's that?" Verity asked.

Ian looked frightened.

"Run!" he yelled before taking off toward the nearest lobby.

As soon as he said that, an enormous spherical conglomeration of intertwined bodies came rolling out of the hallway. Dozens of arms and legs slapped against the floor as it rolled toward us.

Verity ran toward the lobby on the left while I ran toward the one where Ian had fled.

The rolling ball of bodies split into two smaller balls. One followed Verity, and the other followed me and Ian.

I ran as fast as I could for as long as I could, crossing dozens of lobbies that spanned an untold number of decades. Eventually, I was able to lose the ball by hiding and doubling back the way I had come.

I kept running, putting as much distance between me and the ball of bodies as I could before I couldn't run any longer.

Exhausted, I hid behind a reception counter where I eventually fell asleep.

When I woke, I tried to make my way back to the lobby of my own building, thinking that's what Verity would do, but I couldn't find it. I was hopelessly lost.

I wandered for what felt like days, avoiding more of those rolling death balls as I continued to search for Verity and Ian, but I never saw any sign of them. I tried leaving them messages in the lobbies I'd passed through, but I quickly discovered that was a fruitless endeavor. Whenever I'd leave a lobby and return to it at a later time, I'd find that everything in it had reset to how it was when I'd originally entered it.

The only good thing about the lobbies resetting is that the ones with food in them would restock, keeping me from going hungry.

I tried making a map of the lobbies, but that too was a waste of time. I quickly discovered that the lobbies never stayed connected in the same way for longer than a day or two.

Frustrated and losing hope of ever returning home, I chose a lobby that seemed secure and decided to camp there for a while. Running around aimlessly wasn't helping, so I was going to try waiting to see if my lobby would appear whenever the adjacent lobbies rearranged themselves.

I don't know how long I was in that lobby before I heard the chime of an elevator. I followed the sound into a new lobby where I watched a family of four step out of an elevator, looking around with confused looks on their faces.

Before they could stop me, I ran past them and into the elevator they had just exited just before the doors closed.

As I did, I heard the mom say, "That was rude."

I didn't care, though. My only thoughts were of finally getting out of that hell of lobbies.

After the doors closed, I walked over to the panel and reached out to press the button for the tenth floor. It was the highest floor of whatever building the elevator had come from.

To my surprise, the button lit up and the elevator started to ascend.

KISS AND TELL

It was well after midnight when I pulled into the parking lot of my apartment complex.

I would've been home hours earlier if my boss hadn't asked me to stay and help close the store after one of the other employees had to leave early. If I didn't need the extra money, I would've said no.

"Well, shit," I cursed when I saw that all the parking spaces near my building were taken. That meant I had to turn around and drive back to the front of the complex and park in the overflow lot near the pool.

They really need to start assigning parking spaces, I silently griped as I got out of my car and started the long walk back to my apartment. There were too many residents with more than one car, and that wasn't fair to the rest of us.

The rustling of a hedge that flanked the walkway between two of the buildings startled me out of my thoughts. When I looked around and saw how poorly lit the area was, it made me feel isolated, even though I knew there were dozens of people in the apartments around me.

Normally, I would've taken that walkway to get to my building, but the noise had prompted me to move on to the next one.

I hurried my pace, thinking I was being overly cautious and that it was just an animal I'd heard, but the sound of footsteps rushing up behind me proved me wrong.

As I started to run, I cast a quick glance behind me. Seeing the man's gruesome visage heightened my fear, making me wish I hadn't turned around.

What the fuck is wrong with his face!

That thought echoed through my mind as I raced toward the next walkway, hoping I could stay ahead of him long enough to reach the safety of my apartment.

In the meantime, I did the only thing I could.

"HELP!" I screamed.

I'd hoped that would be enough to scare the deformed-looking man off, but unfortunately, it wasn't.

Come on, come on, I silently begged for someone to hear me as I repeatedly yelled for help.

I was running as fast as I could, but it wasn't going to be enough. The man pursuing me was much faster and would catch me well before I made it to the next walkway.

That was when I decided I was going to have to stand my ground and fight.

I stopped and whirled around, clutching my keys in my fist, holding one of them between my knuckles like a knife.

"STAY AWAY FROM…" I wasn't able to finish my warning.

The man, who was about ten feet from me, ran and then launched himself into the air before tackling me to the ground.

My keys flew from my hand when the two of us tumbled to the ground.

He recovered much quicker than I did, climbing on top of me and pinning me down.

Now that the man's face was only a foot away from mine, I could clearly see his deformed lips. They looked like two overinflated pink balloons protruding from his jaw.

I struggled to free myself, but the man's grip was too strong.

At any moment, I expected him to start ripping my clothes off, but that's not what he did. He just sat there huffing his fetid breath into my face.

When I turned my head away from him, he grabbed hold of my chin with one of his hands and turned it back so I was facing him.

"What the fuck is wrong with you?" I snapped, struggling to escape his grip the entire time.

His response was to let a rope of thick saliva descend from his mouth onto my cheek.

I closed my eyes and gagged, fighting against the urge to throw up.

When I looked back up at the man, I realized I could no longer see his eyes. His lips had continued to swell to the point that they were now the only thing I could see.

And they were continuing to swell.

Oh my god! I think they're going to...

His lips exploded before I could finish the thought, showering my face with bits of broken flesh, blood, and mucus. The fluids flowed into my eyes, nose, and mouth.

"HEY!" a man shouted. I could hear his feet slapping against the pavement as he ran over to where I was.

Someone had heard me.

The man's body slumped over, releasing me enough to roll out from under him. Once I was free, I frantically started wiping the gore off my face.

"Are you okay?" the man asked.

In response, I got to my hands and knees and puked all over the sidewalk.

"No, I'm not," I groaned before another wave of vomiting hit me.

"What the hell happened?" My would-be savior was standing over the body of the freak who'd attacked me. "Is he dead?"

"I don't know," I panted, wiping away the vomit that clung to my cheek. "And I don't care."

Getting to my feet was a struggle, but I managed to do it on my own. Once I was able to walk, I retrieved my keys and started walking away.

"Where're you going?" he called out to me.

"Home," I replied, pausing a moment to spit the sour taste out of my mouth. "To take a shower."

"What about him?"

"Call the police," I said. "When they get here, you can tell them they can find me in apartment 23-B."

There was no way I was going to stand there covered in gore and wait for the police to arrive.

"I don't..." he started to protest, but I tuned him out and just kept walking.

I knew he'd do the right thing and call the police.

Twenty minutes later, there was a knock on my door.

Freshly showered, but still not feeling entirely clean, I let the two officers standing on my doorstep into my apartment.

"Sorry to bother you at this late hour, miss. I'm Officer Barnes," the taller of the two said, gesturing to himself with the small notebook he was holding. "And this is Officer Porter." He indicated his partner. "We were told you had some information about the unconscious man that was found outside."

"He's still alive?" I was surprised to hear that.

"For now," Officer Barnes replied. "What can you tell us about him?"

I told them everything that had happened to me, starting with getting off late from work and ending with the freak's lips exploding in my face.

"That's... quite a story," Officer Barnes said, exchanging a look with his partner.

"I know it sounds crazy," I said, "but that's exactly what happened. You've seen him, right?"

"We have," Officer Barnes replied. "Which brings me to my next question." He paused for a moment, making sure he had my attention. "Did you recognize the man who attacked you? Maybe seen him around the apartment complex or where you work?"

I scoffed at the question. "If I knew who he was, I would've told you. You don't forget someone who looks like him." The image of his deformed lips filled my mind.

"I'd like to show you a picture if I may." Officer Barnes pulled out his phone and held it out to me.

I took the phone and looked down at the screen. The image was of the man who'd attacked me. Only the top half of his face was visible because someone had wrapped a bandage around the lower half.

He looked mostly normal now.

"Are you sure you don't recognize him?" Officer Barnes asked.

I stared at the photo for a moment. "Sorry, I don't," I shook my head as I handed the phone back to him. "Should I know him?"

Officer Barnes shrugged. "He didn't have any identification on him. That's why we were hoping you might be able to tell us who he is."

"Sorry," I apologized again.

"No worries," Officer Barnes replied. "We'll figure it out." When he was done talking, he reached into his pocket, pulled out a card, and offered it to me. "We'll be in touch if we have any more questions for you," he said. "In the meantime, if you think of anything else that might help us, call the number on this card."

"I will," I promised, taking the card.

After the officers left, I tried to get some sleep, but all I could do was lie there, staring at the ceiling, replaying the attack in my mind.

The sound of my alarm going off jolted me awake.

I was surprised that I'd been able to fall asleep. The last thing I remembered was lying in bed, worrying that I might have caught something from all the blood and mucus that'd been splattered all over my face.

Thinking about that made me want to take another shower. Which I was definitely going to do, but first I wanted to call the clinic and make an appointment to get checked out.

When the receptionist came on the line, I didn't give her the specifics about what happened. I just told her I'd been involved in an accident where I'd been exposed to another person's blood and was worried about potential infections.

"The first available appointment I have is in two days," she said.

"You don't have anything sooner?" I'm sure I sounded whiny.

"Sorry," she apologized. "That's all I have."

"That won't work," I sighed. "I need something today."

"You can call around to some of the other clinics," she suggested, "but I doubt you're going to find an earlier appointment. If you really want to be seen today, your best bet is to go to the ER."

"I was hoping to avoid that," I said. I couldn't really afford it.

After I got off the phone with her, I did try to call the other clinics in the area, but, as the receptionist had warned, none of them had any availability.

Maybe I should just go to the ER, I thought.

It sounded like that was going to be my only option, but I wasn't going to make up my mind until after I'd taken a shower.

Feeling clean and refreshed, I stepped out of the shower, wrapped a towel around myself, and walked over to the mirror to start drying my hair. When I saw my reflection, I stopped and stared at it.

Do my lips look bigger?

I held up my hand and ran my fingertips gently across both lips, seeing if they felt swollen or tender.

I can't tell.

That started to worry me.

Still dripping water, I went into the bedroom, retrieved my phone, and then returned to the bathroom, where I scrolled through my photos looking at the most recent selfies that I'd taken. I was trying to compare the size of my lips in the photos to what they looked like in the mirror.

I still can't tell.

I dropped my phone on the counter and sighed in frustration.

Paranoid, I decided that the only way I was going to be able to ease my troubled mind was by going to the emergency room. So, after I got dressed, that's what I did.

"How can I help you?" the nurse at the desk asked as I approached.

"Um..." I didn't know how to explain what had happened to me without sounding crazy, so I decided to be vague and hope that was enough. "I was attacked last night and wanted to make sure I didn't catch anything."

A concerned look crossed her features. "Have you notified the police?" she asked.

I nodded.

"How long has it been since the attack?" was her next question.

I looked at the clock on the wall. "About nine hours ago."

"Are you on any kind of birth control?"

I was initially confused by the question, but then it dawned on me why she was asking. When I told her I'd been attacked, she thought I meant I was sexually assaulted.

"Yes, I am," I said, "but it wasn't that kind of attack."

"What kind of attack was it?" Now she was confused.

"This is going to sound crazy," I said, "but I swear to you it's the truth."

She listened quietly as I told her the same story I'd told the police.

"I'm not sure you're in the right place," the nurse started to say, but she was cut off when a doctor who was standing nearby interrupted her.

"It's okay, Marie," he said to her as he approached the desk. "I'll handle this."

"Hi," he said to me. "I'm Dr. Ferguson. I overheard what you said to Marie." He gestured at the nurse. "And I don't think you're crazy."

"You don't?"

I wasn't sure if he was telling the truth or not. The nurse didn't seem to take me seriously. Why would a doctor?

"Let's talk over here," Dr. Ferguson said as he placed his hand on my back and led me a few steps away from the nurse's desk so Marie couldn't overhear us.

"I shouldn't be telling you this," his voice was barely above a whisper, "but I think the man who attacked you was admitted into our ICU last night."

That made sense; Eastside Hospital was the closest hospital to my apartment complex.

This is good, I decided.

If the guy had anything, the hospital would know and could treat me.

"Do you know if he's contagious?" I decided to be direct and get right to the point.

Dr. Ferguson shook his head. "Even if I did know, I couldn't tell you because of patient confidentiality."

"He attacked me," I snapped, "and bled all over my face. Don't I have a right to know?"

"You're worried he might've infected you with something," Dr. Ferguson stated the obvious. "That's why you came here."

"Yeah," I sounded snippy. "Wouldn't you be worried?"

He ignored my attitude and retreated into his thoughts, deciding if he should help me.

"Come on," Dr. Ferguson said a moment later, motioning for me to follow him.

He led me further into the ER and into one of the exam rooms.

"Have a seat," he gestured at the bed. "I'm going to see what I can find out." He walked over to a rolling cart that had a laptop on top of it.

As I sat down on the edge of the bed, I got a sharp pain in my bottom lip, which caused me to cry out.

"Are you okay?" Dr. Ferguson asked, turning his head to look at me.

"There's something up with my lip," I replied, gently touching it with the tips of my fingers.

"Let me take a look at it," he said, walking over and standing before me. "Tilt your head back," he instructed.

He examined my lip, gently moving my head up and down and side to side with his fingers on my chin.

"Does it hurt when I do this?" he gently palpated the lip with his index finger.

"A little," I admitted.

"Stick your lip out like this." Dr. Ferguson made a pouty face, which would have been comical under different circumstances.

I did as he instructed and let him continue his exam. When he was done, he stepped back with a concerned look on his face.

"It looks like it might be a little swollen to me," he said.

"Seriously?" That was not what I wanted to hear. "Does that mean I have what the guy who attacked me has?"

Images of my lips swelling to the point of exploding filled my mind.

"Let me see what I can find out," Dr. Ferguson said, walking back over to the computer cart and starting to type on the laptop. As he typed, he said, "This is highly unethical, so I would appreciate your discretion if anyone asks."

"You don't have to worry about me saying anything," I assured him. "The fewer people who know what happened to me, the better." Plus, I wasn't going to rat out someone who was going out of their way to help me.

There were several minutes of silence as Dr. Ferguson focused his attention on the computer screen.

"According to what I'm seeing here, all of his blood work came back normal," he eventually said. "And his condition has been upgraded to stable," he added.

"Did they ever identify him?" I asked.

"His name is listed as David Duncan," he replied, "so I'm assuming that means yes."

I stood up, walked over to the computer cart, and started reading the screen over Dr. Ferguson's shoulder.

"It says he's awake and responsive," I pointed at the screen.

Seeing that gave me a crazy idea.

"Do you think we could maybe talk to him?" I asked.

"You want to talk to him after what he did to you?" Dr. Ferguson turned and gave me a look of incredulity.

"His lips were as big as water balloons before they exploded in my face, and none of your tests can tell you why," I explained. "But I know there was something wrong with him. I think he might be able to tell us what happened."

When I finished speaking, I got a sharp pain in my upper lip.

"Ow," I winced, instinctively reaching up and touching it, thinking that might stop it from hurting.

"Your lip again?" Dr. Ferguson asked.

"Yeah," I nodded, "but it's my upper lip this time."

"Let me see." He gently placed his hands on the side of my head and tilted it back. "It looks a little swollen now too," he said after examining my lip.

"And that's why I must talk to that guy as soon as possible!" I snapped. "I can't just sit around and wait for my lips to explode. I have to do something!"

"We don't know for certain that's what's going to happen to you," Dr. Ferguson countered.

"But it could," I said. "Right?"

"I suppose it could," he conceded, "assuming you weren't in shock and misremembered what actually happened."

"I wasn't in shock! I saw what I saw. Why won't anyone believe me?" I was starting to get annoyed with him.

"I believe you," Dr. Ferguson insisted. "I just think your anxiety is getting the better of you."

His comment pissed me off.

"You think this is all in my head?" I scoffed, gesturing at my lips, which still hurt a little and which also felt a little bigger to me.

"It's possible," he admitted. "Anxiety can manifest in many different ways."

"Whatever," I sneered at him before storming out of the exam room.

I heard Dr. Ferguson call out for me to wait; I ignored him and kept walking.

It was my intent to leave the hospital, but that plan changed when I made it back out to the emergency room lobby and saw the directory on the wall.

I'll just go talk to him myself, I thought after seeing the sign with the arrow pointing in the direction of the intensive care unit.

"Can I help you?" the nurse sitting at the ICU desk asked as I approached.

"Yeah," I replied, trying to sound meek. "I'm looking for my brother. I was told he was brought into the hospital last night. The nurse in the ER said he was down here?"

I'd concocted the story about being his sister as I walked to the intensive care unit.

"What's your brother's name?" she asked.

"David Duncan," I said.

"Give me one second to look him up," the nurse said, turning her attention to the computer in front of her and tapping away at the keyboard.

"It does look like he's here," the nurse confirmed a moment later.

"Can I see him?"

"Let me see if he's awake and okay with having visitors." The nurse got to her feet and used her badge to enter the locked ICU doors.

Well, shit, I cursed.

I didn't expect her to go and talk to him first. If she found out I was lying about being his sister, she'd probably call security and have me kicked out of the hospital.

I considered leaving, but the nurse returned before I'd made up my mind.

"Good news," the nurse smiled. "He's awake and eager to see you."

Really? That was a lucky break.

"Follow me." She led me into the ICU and over to one of the doors. "He's in here," she gestured at the door. "I can give you 15 minutes," she said. "After that, I'm going to have to ask you to leave."

"Okay," I readily agreed.

The nurse held the door open and let me into the room.

"Fifteen minutes," she reminded me before leaving to return to the nurse's station.

David Duncan used the bed's remote to elevate himself to a sitting position when I entered the room.

Neither of us said a word. We just stared at each other for what felt like an eternity until I broke the silence.

"Do you know who I am?" I asked.

In David's lap was a dry-erase board and a marker. He picked it up and wrote something on it.

Given the nature of his injuries, I assumed he couldn't talk, and the nurses had given him the board so he could communicate with them.

He turned the board around so I could read the word "YES" that he'd written.

After showing me the board, he turned it around, erased what was on it, and wrote something else. When he was done, he turned it around again.

This time, he'd written five words.

Sorry, I had no choice, I read to myself.

"What do you mean you had no choice?" I scoffed. "You attacked me."

He quickly wrote another message and showed it to me.

I DIDN'T WANT TO, it said.

"Well, you did, and now my lips are starting to hurt, and the doctor thinks they might be swollen."

SORRY, David wrote on the board again.

"I don't want your apology," I snapped. "I want to know what you did to me."

I WAS CURSED, he wrote on the board. After he showed me the message, he erased it and wrote another one. YOU HAVE CURSE NOW.

"That's ridiculous," I said. "There are no such things as curses."

IT'S REAL, he underlined each word three times.

A sharp pain in my lips kept me from replying. David saw me wince and touch them, prompting him to write me another message.

YOU MUST KISS SOMEONE, OR THIS WILL HAPPEN TO YOU. He gestured at his face after showing me what he'd written.

"I'm not kissing anyone," I replied.

He underlined the words YOU and MUST several times.

Before I could respond to his message, the door opened and Dr. Ferguson entered the room.

"I thought I might find you here," he said.

David erased his message and began writing something new.

"Come on," Dr. Ferguson motioned for me to leave. "You know you're not supposed to be in here."

Since David wasn't making much sense with all of his talk about me being cursed, I decided not to make a scene and walk out peacefully.

As I turned to leave, David grabbed hold of my arm.

He showed me the new message he'd written, angling it so that Dr. Ferguson couldn't see it.

KISS SOMEONE EVERY 24 HOURS OR ELSE

"Or else what?" I asked.

David gestured at his face and then made an explosion gesture with his fingers.

"Let's go," Dr. Ferguson demanded. "Don't make me call security."

"I'm coming," I said.

As I walked past the doctor, I got a strange compulsion to kiss him. It was so overwhelming that I couldn't stop myself from doing it.

As soon as my lips touched the doctor's cheek, they stopped hurting. They also no longer felt swollen.

Maybe he was telling the truth. I looked back at David.

"What was that for?" Dr. Ferguson reached up and touched his cheek.

"For helping me," I smiled at him and walked out of the room.

DAMNED

"Hey, Glenn," Anna stopped me as I was about to get into my truck to leave for the day. "We just got a call from the sheriff's office about some missing campers."

Anna was the dispatcher for our ranger station.

"Where's Harold?" I asked. He was supposed to be the ranger on duty.

"He's still up at the lake dealing with that film crew," she replied, fidgeting with the piece of paper she held in her hands. "I tried calling him first, but he didn't answer. I figured since you were still here..." She didn't need to finish the thought.

"I'll check it out," I sighed, reaching for the piece of paper she had. I knew it contained all the details the sheriff had given her about the missing campers, along with the campsite they were assigned when they checked in at the station. "If you see Harold before I do, tell him he owes me one."

After I got into my truck, I glanced down at the details on the paper. According to what Anna had written down, two couples from the college in town were missing. Their last known whereabouts were the park's campground, which was situated between the lake and the densely forested mountains that were popular with hikers.

If they had gone into the mountains and strayed from the marked trails, it was possible they had gotten lost. It was easy to get turned around out there if you weren't familiar with the territory, which is why there were so many signs along the trails warning hikers about straying from the path. That didn't stop people from doing it, though.

Before I drove to the campground, I pulled out my phone and called Charlie, a local pilot who rented out his helicopter for sightseeing tours over the mountains. It was cheaper and easier to ask for his help than it was to go through the official channels to request a search and rescue helicopter. That's why I always called him first.

"Hey, Charlie," I said after he answered, "you busy?"

"Not at the moment," he replied. "Why? What's up?"

"I've got some missing campers and might need some eyes in the sky if you're available," I said.

"Just say the word and I can be there in twenty minutes," he replied.

"I'm heading out to the campground now. I'll let you know in a few."

The campground was a five-mile drive across the park. Along the way, I passed the lake and saw Harold's truck in the parking lot, along with the van used by the film crew. I considered swinging by and letting him know what was up, but decided it probably wasn't a good idea with the film crew around. The less press we had about missing hikers, the better.

When I pulled into the campground, I wasn't surprised to see the car that was registered to the group still parked in the parking lot.

I pulled up next to it and used my radio to call Anna.

"I found their car," I said as I got out of the truck. "It looks like they're still here. I'm heading up to the campsite now and will let you know more in a few."

"Copy," she replied.

The campsites at the park weren't accessible by vehicle. To get to them, you had to park in the lot and take a short hike through the woods.

Before I did that, I walked around the group's vehicle and looked inside to see if I saw anything out of the ordinary. I didn't.

I was a few hundred yards down the trail when I noticed that the woods around me were quieter than usual. There should be a variety of bird and insect sounds filling the air, but there weren't any. The only thing I could hear was the crunch of my boots on the deadfall that lined the trail.

The absence of sound unnerved me enough that I reached down and unsnapped the strap that kept my pistol secured. Whenever the creatures of the forest went quiet, it was usually for a very good reason, and I wasn't going to ignore the warning. There were plenty of bears, cougars, and wolves in the park who wouldn't think twice about trying to take a bite out of me if given the chance.

Usually, the larger predators didn't come this far into the populated areas of the park, but it did happen from time to time, and I wasn't going to take any chances. An animal attack could be the reason the group hadn't left their campsite yet. I hoped that wasn't the case, but I still had to consider the possibility.

I proceeded down the trail cautiously, scanning the woods around me while looking and listening for any sign that I wasn't alone. I did that until I was able to see the group's campsite in the distance.

I could see their tent and camping gear, but I couldn't see any sign of them. From the state of things, I got the impression that they had stepped away from the campsite, intending to return, but for whatever reason weren't able to.

"Anybody here?" I called out as I approached the tent. "My name is Glenn. I'm one of the park rangers." I didn't think there was anyone inside it, but on the off chance there was, I didn't want to startle them.

When I didn't get a reply, I unzipped the tent and looked inside. All I found were four sleeping bags and a bunch of personal items.

This isn't good, I thought as I turned around and examined the campsite, looking for any clues as to what might have happened to the four college students.

Since everything was still set up and it looked like nothing was missing, I got the impression that whatever had happened to them had happened the day before; otherwise, there would have been signs of them packing up and getting ready to leave at their scheduled time this morning.

"Hey, Anna," I said into my radio, "all of their stuff is still here at the campsite, but I don't think they've been here since yesterday. Looks like they might have wandered off and gotten lost. I'm going to walk the trails for a bit and see if I can find them. If I don't, I'm going to call Charlie and have him go up and see if he has better luck. In the meantime, could you please get in touch with Harold and let him know what's going on? You should also call the sheriff's office back and let them know what we've found so far."

"Copy that," she replied. "Keep me posted."

I started walking in the direction of the trailhead where the hiking paths into the mountains started, but I stopped and turned around at the last minute, heading toward one of the adjacent campsites instead. I decided it would be a better idea to check with the campers staying there first to see if they might have seen the missing group.

When I made it to the campsite, I was surprised to find it empty as well.

"Hello," I called out as I walked through the campsite. "Anybody here?"

There was no response.

I waited around for a few minutes to see if the campers would return, but they never did.

I don't like this.

Two missing groups of campers from two adjacent campsites was more than a coincidence. I confirmed that when I went to the next campsite and found it empty too.

"Anna," I called over the radio, "we have a situation up here."

I explained to her what I found and requested that she call in all available rangers and have them meet me at the campground parking lot.

"That might be a problem," she replied.

"Come again?" I wasn't asking her to repeat her comment; I was asking her to clarify it.

"I tried to call Harold like you asked, but I couldn't get hold of him," she explained. "So then I tried to call Burke and Sullivan, but they're not answering either."

"Isn't Burke supposed to be up in the tower?"

"Last time I checked," Anna confirmed.

We had a fire tower in the center of the park that we took turns manning during the dry months. This week, it was supposed to be Burke's turn. If he was going to leave the tower for any reason, he was supposed to call in to the station both before he left and upon his return. It wasn't like him to forget.

I sighed in frustration at being put in the middle of whatever shitstorm was brewing when I should be at home in my recliner with a beer in my hand.

"This is what we're going to do," I said. "I'm going to call Charlie and have him start looking for the missing campers. While he's doing that, I'm going to head over to the tower and see about Burke. I need you to keep calling Harold and Sullivan until you get hold of them. But first, I want you to call the sheriff's office and have them send a couple of deputies out here."

"Copy that," Anna said.

"This is ridiculous," I muttered to myself as I started walking back to my truck. On the way, I called Charlie and told him to get in the air ASAP and call me once he was overhead.

Fifteen minutes later, I was driving down the dirt access road that led to the fire tower. Before I got to it, Charlie called me to let me know he had arrived and started his search. In the distance, I could hear the whirring sound of his helicopter.

When I came around a bend in the road, I immediately knew something wasn't right. From my vantage point, I should be able to see the roof of the tower above the trees, but I couldn't see anything.

"Hey, Charlie," I said, "can you do me a favor and fly over the tower? I want you to check something for me."

"Aye, aye, captain," was his response.

The sound of the helicopter kept getting louder as I drove toward the tower.

"Holy shit!" Charlie suddenly shouted.

I got a sinking feeling in the pit of my stomach.

"What's going on?"

I could hear his helicopter hovering nearby, but I couldn't see it through the trees.

"You're going to need a new tower," he said. "Somebody knocked your old one down."

"What?"

"I'm not pulling your leg, man," Charlie insisted. "Your tower is lying on its side at the bottom of the valley."

"Any sign of Burke?" I was hoping that maybe he was somewhere near the tower, unharmed.

"I don't see anyone."

"Shit," I hissed. "I'm going to have to call you back." I hung up before he could get another word in.

"Anna," I called over the radio, "any luck reaching Harold or Sullivan?"

"Nope," she replied curtly.

"What about the sheriff's office?"

"They said they're sending someone."

"I need you to call them back and have them send an ambulance," I explained. "The fire tower has collapsed, and I think Burke might have been inside."

"Oh my god," she gasped.

"If you get hold of Harold or Sullivan, send them my way." I dropped the radio and hit the gas.

"Burke?" I called out as I approached the wreckage of the tower. I had to shout to be heard over Charlie's helicopter, which was hovering over the area.

I kept calling out his name as I climbed through the sideways door into the interior of the tower.

Where the hell are you?

I found his radio and thermos lying among the debris inside the tower, but I couldn't find him.

Where did you go?

I crawled back out and started searching around the outside, thinking he might have crawled out. When I didn't see any sign of him, I called Charlie back.

"Burke's not down here," I said. "He might have tried walking out; if he did, he'd likely follow the valley back to the road."

"Say no more," Charlie replied. "If he's out there, I'll find him."

The helicopter started moving away, heading in the direction I had indicated.

Before I left to join the search, I wanted to get a closer look at the tower to see if I could figure out why it had fallen. To do that, I focused my attention on the struts at the bottom of it. What I saw didn't make sense.

All four struts had clean cuts right through them. They looked like someone had intentionally sawed through them.

Who would do something like that?

I walked around the upper portion of the tower again, and that's when I noticed that the metal screen that covered the windows on one side had been bent outward. The way it was bent didn't look like it was caused by the fall. It looked like someone had done it on purpose.

At first, I thought maybe Burke had done it to get out of the tower, but that didn't make sense. There were easier ways for him to escape.

When I examined the bent screen closely, I could see blood along its edges. Most of it was dried, indicating that whatever had happened had occurred hours ago.

I didn't have time to ponder the mystery of what happened; I needed to start searching. Knowing that Burke would follow the valley to the road like I told Charlie, I decided to follow that route on foot. The easiest way to do that would be to follow the creek that ran through the center of the valley. I was sure Burke would have chosen that route as well, since the terrain was less rugged.

When I made it to the creek, I was presented with another mystery.

Where did the water go?

The creek, which was usually about a foot deep and flowing at a brisk pace, was nothing more than a trickle.

My phone rang. It was Charlie.

"Hey, Glenn," he said, "sorry to do this to you, but I've got to jet. Marjorie just called and said someone booked me for an evening flight. I've searched the valley floor twice, but I didn't see any sign of Burke or anyone else, for that matter."

"No worries, Charlie, and thanks for your help."

"I can come back tomorrow morning if you need me."

"Thanks," I said. "I'll let you know." I hung up and took a moment to collect my thoughts.

What the hell is going on?

I felt like the world had suddenly gone crazy on me. I had missing people from three different campsites. Several of my colleagues were also seemingly missing, as was a film crew that was supposed to be taking test shots of the lake as a potential filming site for a movie. Our fire tower had been knocked down, and now our creek was suddenly running dry.

My phone chimed, letting me know that I had received a text. When I looked at the screen, I was surprised to see it was from Charlie. This is what it said: *Saw this on my way back to the airfield and thought you should know about it.*

Below the text was an aerial picture of a panel truck in the woods near the back side of the park. A short distance away, a group of steel drums sat on the ground, their hazard symbols clearly visible.

"Goddammit," I cursed.

As if I didn't have enough issues to deal with, I now had to add illegal dumping to the list.

"This day just keeps getting better and better," I muttered.

Feeling like I was being torn in several different directions, I took a seat on a nearby boulder to reassess my priorities. After thinking it over, I decided that finding Burke was my top priority. He was likely somewhere nearby, injured. The other missing people would have to wait until I could touch base with the sheriff's department. There was only so much I could do on my own.

"Anna," I said into the radio, wanting to give her an update. I waited a minute to give her time to respond in case she was busy. When she didn't answer, I called her again.

There was still no response.

"She better not have gone missing, too," I snapped as I clipped the radio back onto my belt.

One problem at a time, I sighed, trying to focus my energy on finding Burke.

I looked up and down the mostly dry creek bed. If Burke had headed back toward the road, Charlie would have likely seen him. That meant he might have gone the other direction for some reason.

Maybe he was disoriented?

That was possible, especially if he had suffered a head injury when the tower fell.

With that decided, I headed up the creek deeper into the valley.

"Ugh," I grimaced when the wind blowing through the trees brought with it the scent of death. I knew the smell immediately because I had to clean up my share of animal carcasses from the park.

I had walked about a mile up the creek before the smell hit me. Based on its strength, I knew whatever was causing it was nearby.

Dear God, please don't let it be Burke, I said a silent prayer.

The source of the smell came into view after I climbed the slope a bit and came around a bend.

"Jesus Christ!" I covered my mouth.

About fifty yards in front of me was the most gruesome thing I had ever seen. Spanning across the creek bed and up into the valley on either side was a beaver dam. Interspersed among the logs used to build the dam were the carcasses of several animals and people.

My search was over. I had found all the people who were missing.

"ANNA!" I yelled into the radio. "If you're there, pick up."

The sound of something large pushing through the trees behind me startled me, causing me to lose my grip on my radio. As I bent down to retrieve it, I slowly turned around to face whatever it was.

When I saw the monstrous beaver bearing down on me, I reached for my pistol, but I wasn't fast enough. The large beast that had somehow grown to become twice the size of a bear barreled into me, knocking me to the ground, where my head slammed against the rocks of the creek bed. I tried to get up, but a huge paw tipped with long black nails pinned me down. Then everything went black as I lost consciousness.

When I came to, I found myself wedged between two logs next to the corpse of Harold. The smell of his putrefying body made it hard to breathe.

I've got to get out of here.

I struggled to pull myself out, but no matter how hard I tried, I couldn't get free. The weight of the logs and corpses pinning me in place was too heavy to move on my own.

I sighed in defeat. *It's hopeless.*

I was damned, and there was nothing I could do about it.

THE FORGETTING ROOM

"Which way?" Cora asked, panting between words.

I'd made the mistake of flipping off Billy Price after he'd called Cora and me lesbians while we were walking to the park. Now he was chasing us through the neighborhood, threatening to beat the shit out of us.

Cora was new to the neighborhood and didn't know it as well as I did, which is why she stopped when she reached the alley that ran behind Coughlin Street.

I took a quick look around to get my bearings.

"That way," I pointed down the alley.

"You're dead, Aimee!" Billy yelled as he ran up the street after us.

Despite being overweight and out of shape, he'd managed to halve the distance between us when Cora stopped.

"Hurry," I urged, grabbing Cora's arm and pulling her into the alley as I started running again.

We were halfway through the alley when I noticed the old, rickety fence with the missing slats on my left. Seeing the fence gave me a crazy idea. One that was sure to get Billy to stop chasing us.

I skidded to a halt and approached the nearest gap in the fence.

"Cora!" I yelled as she kept running down the alley. "Over here."

When she stopped, I waved her over as I squeezed through the gap. She quickly turned and followed me.

After Cora stepped through the fence and saw where we were, she gasped.

"Is that Coffin House?" she whispered, looking up at the back of the dilapidated house in front of us.

"Yep," I nodded.

The house's real name was Coughlin House, but everyone who knew the history of the house called it Coffin House.

Behind us, Billy had made it to the fence and poked his head through one of the gaps.

"Come on," I urged Cora, "I know a way inside." I hurried to the side of the house.

"You want to go inside?" Cora fretted as she followed behind me.

"We have to," I insisted. "It's the only way we're going to get Billy to stop chasing us."

I led her to the side of the house, stopping in front of one of the boarded-up windows that had been busted out years ago. With a little effort, I pushed one of the slats to the side and climbed into the house through the opening I'd made. Once I was through, I turned around and reached a hand out to Cora.

"Hurry," I urged. Billy had just come around the corner of the house. "He's coming." I reached out to help her.

Seeing Billy behind her helped Cora overcome her fear of the house. She grabbed hold of my outstretched hand and hurried through the window.

"You can't stay in there forever," Billy panted, out of breath from the chase. "I'll get you when you come out," he threatened while keeping a safe distance from the house. "Unless the house gets you first." He was hoping to scare us into leaving.

I leaned out through the window and gave him the finger before pulling Cora further into the house.

"What did he mean by that?" Cora asked, her eyes darting around the empty room we were in.

"Ignore him. He's just trying to scare us," I said. "It's just an empty house. It's not going to do anything to us."

"How can you be so sure?" Cora sounded worried.

"Because I've been here before," I revealed.

"You have?"

"Yep," I replied. "Shortly before you moved here, Marcia dared me to come inside. She bet me her Hello Kitty bracelet that I wouldn't do it."

My thoughts turned to that day and how I'd climbed through the same window Cora and I had used, walked through the house, and then exited the front door where Marcia and her groupies were waiting for me. When I held out my hand for her bracelet, she scoffed and said, *"You didn't stay inside long enough."*

If I'd known there was a time limit, I would've stayed inside longer. I considered going back inside, but I knew she would just come up with some other excuse not to give me the bracelet. She had no intention of ever giving it to me.

"Weren't you scared?" she asked.

"A little, at first," I admitted. "But once I saw that other people had been inside before me," I gestured at the obscene graffiti painted on a nearby wall, "I decided that it wasn't haunted."

"Really?" Cora sounded surprised by my claim of bravado.

"I think some people want us to believe it is haunted to keep the rest of us away," I added.

"Why would they do that?"

"Why else?" I said, tapping a beer bottle with my foot and sending it rolling into another, drawing her attention to the debris of cans and bottles that littered the floor.

"Ooooh," Cora replied, drawing out the word as it dawned on her what I was referring to. "I guess it's the perfect place if you don't want anyone to know what you're doing."

"Exactly," I agreed, eyeing the discarded condom wrapper lying among the rest of the trash.

Cora suddenly looked worried. "You don't think there could be anyone in here with us right now, do you?"

"I doubt it," I said. "It's too early in the morning. Most people come here at night when it's dark and no one will see them." I didn't know if that was true, but it made sense to me.

Agreeing with me, Cora relaxed.

"Do you think he's still outside?" she asked, referring to Billy.

I walked over to one of the boarded-up windows that looked out the front of the house onto the street and peered through the cracks.

"He's still there," I said, seeing Billy sitting on the sidewalk across the street with two of his friends. "And he's not alone. Pete and Edward are with him."

Pete and Edward were Billy's only friends. They weren't that bad on their own, but they became completely different people when they were with Billy.

From their vantage point, they could see the front and side of the house where Cora and I had climbed through the window.

"Is there any way we can sneak out without them seeing us?" Cora asked.

"I don't know," I shrugged.

I'd only been inside the house once and didn't stay for very long. The side window was the only way I knew how to get into the house. That and the front door, but it wasn't always unlocked. The house did have a back door, but that wasn't an option. A large piece of plywood completely covered the outside of the frame.

"Let's look around," I suggested. "See if we can find another way out."

We walked to the back of the house, going from room to room, checking all the windows. None of them provided the escape route we were hoping for. The boards covering them were all still firmly attached.

"Looks like that's the only way out," I pointed at the window. "That or the front door."

We were back where we started when we'd first entered the house.

"What about the basement?" Cora asked.

As we were searching the first floor of the house, we found a door with a series of steps leading beneath the house.

"I don't think we should go down there," I replied, recalling how rickety the wooden steps looked and how dark the stairwell was. "It's not safe."

The truth was, I was too scared to go down there.

"Maybe we should just make a run for it," Cora suggested. "We might be able to make it back to my house before they catch us." Her house was one street closer than mine.

"Maybe," I agreed, but abandoned the thought when I heard the voices of Billy and Edward approaching the window.

I held my finger to my lips, signaling Cora to be quiet as I motioned with my other hand for her to follow me out of the room.

Once we'd made it through the doorway, I stopped so I could listen.

"You're not scared, are you?" I heard Billy say.

"N-No," Edward stammered. "I-I... I just don't want to get in trouble."

I knew that was a lie. The consequences of his actions had never stopped him before. He was scared and didn't want to admit it.

That gave me an idea.

"Stay here," I whispered to Cora before creeping over to the window where Billy was trying to coerce Edward to come inside after us.

When I reached the window, I jumped up and screamed as loud as I could, scaring them.

They threw their hands up into the air and cried out before stumbling into each other as they tried to flee.

I couldn't stop myself from laughing.

Billy heard me and stopped running long enough to yell at me.

"You are so dead, Aimee!" he said.

"They're never going to let us leave now," Cora complained when I returned to the hall where she was waiting.

"Sorry," I apologized, suddenly feeling the weight of responsibility on my shoulders.

If I had just been able to keep myself from reacting to Billy's comment about us being lesbians, none of this would've happened, and we'd be at the park swinging like we'd planned. Knowing it was all my fault and that I'd made it worse made me feel bad.

That, in turn, made me feel like I had an obligation to get Cora out of Coughlin House and back home safely.

I stopped and thought for a moment, picturing the outside of the house in my mind, trying to think if there was another way out. That's when I remembered the ivy-covered trellis in the backyard next to the covered patio.

If we could get onto the roof of the patio, we could climb down the trellis and sneak out through the backyard without the boys knowing we'd left.

"Come on," I said to Cora. "I have an idea."

I led her up the stairs and onto the second-floor landing.

"Where are we going?" she asked as we walked.

I explained my plan to her.

"That doesn't sound very safe," she argued.

"It's the only way we're going to get out of here without them seeing us," I said. "If you don't want to do it, we can take our chances running out the front door instead." I gestured down the stairs toward the foyer.

Cora didn't like the sound of that.

"We should be able to reach the patio roof from there," I gestured to the open doorway at the end of the hall before I walked toward it.

Once we were inside the room, I approached one of the windows.

"You check that one," I gestured to the other window, "and I'll check this one."

The upstairs windows of the Coughlin House weren't boarded up like the ones on the first floor. Once we figured out which one was above the roof of the patio, we would be able to climb out and make our escape.

"It's not this one," Cora announced.

I looked through the empty frame and saw the weed-ridden backyard directly below me. The patio was several feet to my left.

"It's not this one either," I sighed. "We're in the wrong room."

I turned to leave, intending to go to the room next door, but I froze when I saw the transparent figure of a man blocking the doorway. He was wearing a tan suit that looked decades out of style and was just standing there staring at us.

Upon seeing the apparition, Cora rushed over to stand next to me.

"Is that?" she whispered, not needing to finish her thought.

I nodded. "It's Mr. Coughlin," I whispered back, recognizing him from some old newspaper articles I'd found online. "But he shouldn't be here."

"Well, he is," she stated.

"But he's not dead," I explained. "He's still in prison for killing his family."

The figure of Mr. Coughlin took a step into the room.

Cora clutched my arm, digging her nails into my skin. "We have to get out of here."

Knowing the windows were not an option, I scanned the room looking for another way out. Besides the door that Mr. Coughlin was blocking, there was only one other door in the room.

"This way," I said, running across the room and throwing the door open so Cora could run ahead of me.

Once we were on the other side of the doorway, I slammed the door shut.

As I stood there panting, trying to calm my racing heart, a wave of dizziness came over me. When it passed, I realized I had no idea where I was or why I was there. The last thing I could remember was Cora coming over to my house and asking me if I wanted to go to the park, but I couldn't remember anything after that.

"Where are we?" Cora asked.

She couldn't remember either.

"I..." I looked around the dirty bathroom we were in, hoping I might remember something, but nothing came to mind. "I have no idea," I admitted.

It was clear from its state that the bathroom hadn't been used in years, if not decades. Most of the paint had long peeled off the walls, the mirror that once hung over the sink now lay in pieces on the floor, and all the fixtures were covered in rust and grime.

"I don't like it here," Cora said.

"Neither do I," I admitted. "Let's get out of here."

I opened the door and stepped out into a large, empty bedroom that was even more rundown-looking than the bathroom. Upon seeing the room, an idea of where we were formed in my mind.

"I think we're in the Coughlin House," I said.

"Coughlin House?" Cora sounded surprised.

I nodded.

That was the only abandoned house that I knew about in our neighborhood.

"How did we get here?" Cora asked. "The last thing I remember was going to your house and asking you if you wanted to go to the park."

"That's the last thing I remember," I said.

"What do you think happened?"

"I don't know," I shrugged. "We should probably worry about that once we get out of here."

"Yeah," she agreed.

We walked toward the door that led to the hallway but stopped when the figure of a man materialized in the doorway. There was something familiar about his appearance.

Cora gasped. "Is that what I think it is?"

The ghostly figure stepped into the room.

"Run!" I grabbed Cora by the arm and dragged her back into the bathroom.

Once we were inside, I slammed the door shut and pressed my back against it.

Another wave of dizziness overcame me, once again taking my memories with it when it passed.

I did not recognize the bathroom we were in or how we'd come to be there.

"What's happening?" Cora asked. "I can't remember anything after this morning."

"I can't either."

Confused, we made our way out of the bathroom only to be blocked by the apparition of Mr. Coughlin when we tried to leave the bedroom.

Fearing for our lives, we retreated into the bathroom, where our memories were wiped away again.

That process happened repeatedly until the light coming through the windows dimmed.

"I'm so thirsty," Cora said moments after we'd fled into the bathroom and realized we couldn't remember where we were or how we'd gotten there. "And my throat hurts."

"Mine too," I said. "And I'm really hungry." I placed a hand on my stomach.

"How long do you think we've been here?" she asked.

All I could do was shrug.

"I wonder if this still works." She walked over to the bathroom sink and turned one of the knobs.

Nothing happened for a few seconds, then, all of a sudden, something in the wall behind us rattled, creating a loud clatter as a rush of stale, dusty air came blasting out of the faucet.

"Turn it off," I pointed at the sink. "Hurry."

Cora quickly turned the knob, quieting the racket.

"What was that?" she asked with a worried look on her face as she stared at the wall behind us.

"I think it was the pipes," I explained. "That happens at my grandparents' house sometimes, but not that loud. My dad said it was because there was air trapped inside them."

"That sounded like more than just pipes," she commented.

Seemingly in response to her comment, there was one final clattering sound. It started near the ceiling and then slowly made its way down the wall, stopping when it was level with the floor.

Curious, and thinking it might just be an animal, I walked over to the wall and kicked it.

"Oops," I said when my foot went right through the rotted drywall, knocking a large hole through it.

When I pulled my foot out, a small skull, covered with bits of flesh and small patches of hair, rolled through the hole, wobbling on the bathroom floor for a moment before coming to a stop near the sink. Cora hopped out of the way with a squeal to prevent it from touching her foot.

"Is that real?" she asked.

"Looks real to me," I said.

"I'm outta here," she declared, throwing open the door and running out of the bathroom.

I followed her through the bedroom, down the stairs, and out the front door. When we got outside, we were both surprised to see that it was nighttime.

"How long were we in there?" Cora asked, looking back at the house from the safety of the street.

I didn't answer her because I was too busy staring at the little boy who was looking down at us with a smile on his face from one of the second-story windows. I was about to say something to Cora about him, but he disappeared before I could get the words out.

"Come on, let's go home," Cora said, gently tugging my arm as she pulled me down the street.

"Where the hell have you been?" my mom snapped when I opened the front door and stepped into the house.

I ignored her question and instead said, "Call the police."

"What? Why?" Her anger suddenly turned to concern. "Did something happen to Cora?" She'd assumed the worst when I didn't return with my best friend.

"Cora's fine," I replied. "She went home."

"Then why do you need me to call the police?" she asked.

The further Cora and I got away from Coughlin House, the quicker our memories returned until we were able to recall everything that had happened to us while we were trapped inside. I knew I couldn't tell my mom everything that had happened, so I left out the parts about the ghostly image of Mr. Coughlin and how Cora and I kept losing our memories every time we ran into the bathroom.

I blamed Billy for our disappearance, saying he threatened to beat us up, so we hid inside Coughlin House until he and his friends left.

"And that's when we found the skull," I finished, telling her we'd just stumbled upon it while trying to find another way out of the house.

"A real skull?" I could tell from her tone that she didn't believe me.

"Yes!" I snapped in frustration.

"Stay here," she instructed before walking into the kitchen to retrieve her phone. A moment later, I could hear her talking to my dad, telling him everything that I'd told her.

"Well?" I heard my mom say to my dad once he'd finally returned to the house an hour later.

I was sitting in the dining room, finishing the last of the dinner my mom had reheated for me.

"It's real," my dad replied. "The police found the rest of the skeleton in a crawlspace behind the wall. They think it might be the body of the missing Coughlin boy."

"To think that man killed his son and stuffed his body behind the wall is unthinkable," my mom said. "What kind of monster would do something like that?"

"They don't think he was murdered," my dad revealed. "I overheard the coroner talking to one of the detectives. She said it looked like the boy may have gotten stuck in the crawlspace and couldn't get out. The entire time he was missing, he was right there above his parents' heads."

"So, Mr. Coughlin didn't kill his son?" my mom asked.

"Doesn't look like it, according to the police," my dad said. "They also think that maybe he was telling the truth about his wife committing suicide. There's at least enough evidence to get him a new trial."

The next day, I told Cora what I'd overheard my parents talking about.

"If Mr. Coughlin didn't kill his son, why did we keep seeing him in the doorway?" she asked. "That kind of makes him seem guilty to me."

"Not to me," I said. "I think his son just wanted to be found and was using the image of his father to keep us from leaving. That's why he let us go after we found his skull. He knew we'd tell someone."

I thought back to the previous night and recalled the specter of the boy standing in the window and the way he smiled at me. I think that was his way of saying thank you.

SUBDIVISION

"Mom? Dad?" I called out.

I'd woken up and gone downstairs, expecting to find my parents at the table eating breakfast, but they weren't there.

When they didn't respond to my repeated calls, I walked over to the fridge and checked the dry-erase board to see if they'd left me a message about where they were going, but they hadn't. The only thing written on it was a list of things my mom needed to pick up at the grocery store.

"Elaine?" I called out, realizing I hadn't seen my little sister either.

Most mornings, she'd be parked in front of the television, eating cereal and watching cartoons, but she wasn't in her usual spot either.

Thinking they all might have left the house without me, I went into the garage to see if either of the cars were missing. They weren't.

Where is everyone?

It wasn't like them to up and leave the house without telling me.

Maybe Dillon knows.

I went back upstairs and knocked on my older brother's bedroom door.

"Dillon?" I called out softly. "You awake?"

He didn't answer.

"Dillon!" I knocked louder, hoping he wouldn't be in a bad mood for being woken up.

He still didn't answer.

Ignoring the *Keep Out* sign on his door, I opened it and stepped into his room only to find that he was gone, too.

Downstairs, someone rang the doorbell.

When I opened the door to see who it was, I was surprised to see Lucy standing on my porch.

"What are you doing here?" I asked.

Although we were the same age, attended the same middle school, and lived on the same street, we rarely spoke to each other.

"Are your mom and dad home?" Lucy asked.

"No, why?" I replied.

"Neither are mine." She sounded worried.

"What about your sisters?" I asked, wondering if her entire family was missing like mine was.

"They're gone, too." She looked like she was about to cry. "Everybody's gone," she added, casting a glance at the houses behind her. "I thought I was the only one here until I saw you in the window." She gestured to the second floor, where Dillon's window looked out on the street.

"Have you tried calling them?" I didn't own a cellphone, but I knew Lucy had one.

"I tried calling them and texting them, but my phone doesn't seem to be working." She pulled her phone out of her pocket and showed me the screen. On it were several text messages. Beneath each message, written in red, were the words *Not Delivered* along with an exclamation point in a circle.

In the distance, someone suddenly started blaring calliope music, the kind you'd typically hear at a circus or carnival.

"What's that?" Lucy asked.

I shrugged and shook my head.

"ATTENTION CHILDREN OF THE WHISPER HILLS SUBDIVISION," a man's voice rose above the music, "PLEASE MAKE YOUR WAY TO THE PARKING LOT IN FRONT OF THE POOL FOR ORIENTATION."

Lucy and I looked at each other.

"What's that supposed to mean?" she asked.

"I have no idea," I shrugged again.

I knew as much as she did about what was going on.

The man repeated his message.

"Should we go?"

"I don't think we have a choice," I replied.

I'd been to enough orientations to know that they were not usually optional.

Seven minutes later, we reached the pool parking lot. From the look of things, Lucy and I were the last to arrive. A dozen kids were standing around, ranging in age from eight to 14. All of them had the same look of confusion on their faces. I recognized most of the kids, having seen them around the neighborhood.

"This is weird," Lucy said.

She was gazing at the small stage that had been set up in front of the pool's entrance. Standing on the stage was a tall man wearing an expensive-looking black suit. His hair was perfectly styled, and his teeth were the whitest I'd ever seen. In his hand was a megaphone. Behind him was a calliope blaring music.

Something about the man looked familiar to me.

"Do you recognize him?" I asked Lucy.

"No. Why?" she replied.

"I feel like I've seen him before."

I couldn't shake the feeling that I knew who he was.

"Ah!" the man said into the megaphone when he saw Lucy and me standing at the edge of the parking lot. "It looks like the last of our participants have arrived!"

Everyone turned to look at us.

"Gather round," the man motioned, drawing everyone's attention back to the stage. "Gather round."

Lucy and I joined the rest of the kids, staying at the back of the group.

"Let's get to it, shall we?" he announced, smiling behind his megaphone.

None of the kids in the group shared his enthusiasm. Most of them continued to look around, confused, trying to get a sense of what was going on.

The calliope music suddenly cut off.

"My name is Mr. Gin," the man said, placing a hand on his chest.

I didn't recognize the name.

"And I will be the host for today's demonstration." He paused for a moment. "You lucky kids," he swept his hand across the crowd, "have been chosen to represent everything that Whisper Hills has to offer."

"What if we don't want to?" Marcus, one of the older kids and the neighborhood bully, called out.

From the murmured agreements and other comments that followed, it seemed everyone else was thinking the same thing.

"I'm afraid you don't have a choice," Mr. Gin replied. "You will participate whether you want to or not."

"Where's my mom?" Harper, one of the eight-year-olds, asked.

"Your parents and the rest of your families have been moved to a safe location," Mr. Gin said. "As have your pets," he added as an afterthought, knowing that was likely going to be the next question.

"When can I see her again?" Harper pressed for more information.

"That depends on you," he pointed at her, "and how well you do during today's demonstration."

Other kids started shouting questions, but Mr. Gin ignored them, using the megaphone to drown them out.

"Settle down! Settle down!" he said, making a downward motion with his hand. "We don't have time for any more questions. We need to get started." Once everyone had quieted down, he continued to speak. "Thank you. Now... Today's demonstration is a free-for-all." He paused for dramatic effect. "A fight to the death."

"Is he serious?" Lucy whispered.

"I hope not," I murmured.

"Before we begin, I need to go over the rules," Mr. Gin said, "of which there are only two." He held up two fingers. "The first rule is to kill or be killed. Look around you," he gestured at us. "The kids you see are no longer your friends or neighbors; they are your enemy. If you want to survive, you need to kill them before they kill you."

Lucy and I exchanged a look. I could tell from the look in her eyes that she was thinking the same thing I was.

I don't want to kill anyone.

"The second rule," Mr. Gin continued, "is that you cannot leave the subdivision. If you try to leave, you will be shot."

As he spoke, several men wearing black body armor stepped out of the pool area and walked over to the stage, where they formed a line in front of it. The kids closest to the stage took several steps back.

"In a few minutes, these men will escort you back to your homes. Once you are safely back inside, you are to wait until you hear this sound." Mr. Gin pointed his finger in the air.

A loud siren sounded from outside the neighborhood.

"Once you hear that, you are free to begin," he said with a smile. "Any questions?"

"Is this for real?" Marcus asked. "You really want us to *Hunger Games* each other?"

"That's exactly what I want you to do," Mr. Gin said.

Marcus looked around at all the smaller kids, smirking.

"Why?" I blurted out.

Everyone's eyes turned to me.

"As I've already explained," Mr. Gin answered, "this is a demonstration. A demonstration to show people what you kids are capable of and how far you'll go to survive. Does that answer your question?"

"Not really," I said.

"Well, I'm afraid that's the only answer you're going to get. We've wasted enough time." He looked down and addressed the men lined up in front of the stage. "Get them into position," he said.

The men dispersed into the crowd, ordering us to return to our homes.

Nobody protested. We silently turned and started walking back to our respective houses.

"I'm scared," Lucy said once we reached our street.

I looked back to see that only one man was escorting us home.

"So am I," I admitted.

"You don't think any of the other kids are actually going to try and kill us, do you?" she asked.

"Marcus will," I replied.

I'd seen the way he looked at all the younger kids as we dispersed from the pool parking lot. He was sizing everyone up, trying to find the easiest targets.

"And I'm sure he's not the only one," I added.

Marcus was friends with Chad, another one of the older boys who lived in the neighborhood. Chad wasn't that bad on his own, but he became an asshole whenever he hung out with Marcus, and I'd seen the two of them talking as they walked away, likely plotting who they were going to go after first.

"What should we do?" Lucy asked.

I thought about it for a moment and quickly came up with an idea. I stepped closer to her and started whispering in her ear, not wanting the armed guard behind us to hear me.

"When you hear the siren," I said, "get to Mr. Allen's house as fast as possible. I'll meet you there."

Mr. Allen lived a couple of houses down from Lucy and across the street from me.

"Why there?"

"Our houses are the first place anybody is going to come looking for us," I explained. "We can't stay there."

Seeing that we'd reached her house, I stopped walking. I could tell that she didn't like the idea of leaving the safety of her home.

"Trust me," I said. "They won't know where to find us if we're not at home. That will give us more time to figure out how to get out of here."

"Okay," she agreed. "I'll meet you at Mr. Allen's house. And you better be there." She jabbed her finger at me.

"I will," I assured her.

"Get inside the house now!" the armed guard snapped at Lucy.

She moved to obey, but I stopped her. "Look for anything you can use as a weapon and bring it with you," I said.

She nodded her understanding, then turned and ran into her house.

"Keep walking!" The guard motioned for me to move.

Once I was inside my house, the first thing I did was run into the kitchen and grab the biggest knife I could find.

As I tested the weight of the blade in my hand, I decided it wasn't right for me. I didn't think I'd be able to use it. The thought of stabbing someone, all that blood, made me feel a little bit queasy.

I need to find something else.

I scanned the area around me, searching for something I could use to defend myself, but I didn't see anything. I did, however, see a pair of Dillon's sneakers lying next to the front door, and that gave me an idea.

I ran up the stairs and into my brother's room. From his closet, I grabbed an aluminum baseball bat.

This is perfect.

I gave it a test swing.

Knowing that I didn't have much time before the siren went off, I made my way out into the hall and over to the stairs. As I did, I passed by the room my father used as his office. The door was closed like it always was.

I reached out to test the knob, expecting it to be locked like it always was, but it wasn't. The knob turned, and the door swung open.

I'd been inside the office many times, but my father was always with me during those visits. It looked like a standard home office. A large antique desk stood in the center of the room, accompanied by bookcases filled with books and other work-related materials.

I stepped inside and walked over to the desk, surprised to see that my father had left his laptop on it. It wasn't like him to leave it out like that.

I was even more surprised to see a stack of folders sitting next to the laptop. It wasn't like him to leave his work folders out where Dillon and I could see them either. Curious, I opened the top folder to see what my father was working on. Inside was a stack of papers, the top of which was adorned with a strange geometric logo and the words PROJECT CHIMERA.

What's this all about?

I reached out to dig deeper into the file.

Outside, the siren blared, announcing the start of Mr. Gin's demonstration.

I jerked my hand back, startled by the loud sound.

Time to go!

I turned and started to leave the office, but I didn't get very far. One of the framed photographs sitting on the nearest bookcase caught my attention. It was a picture of my father receiving an award from a very familiar-looking man.

That's Mr. Gin!

I knew I'd seen him before. He was my father's boss.

The siren finally cut off.

Knowing my time was limited, I ran out of the office, down the stairs, and out of the house. When I made it to the sidewalk, I saw Lucy run onto Mr. Allen's porch.

I ran to catch up with her.

"This way," I motioned for Lucy to follow me around the side of Mr. Allen's house and into his backyard.

She stayed close to me, constantly checking behind her to see if any of the other kids had seen us.

"Where are we going?" she asked once we were safely behind Mr. Allen's house.

In answer, I walked over to one of the potted plants on the patio. After setting my bat down, I lifted the plant and retrieved the key that was hidden beneath it.

"How did you know that was there?" she asked.

I picked up the bat and walked over to the back door. "Mr. Allen once paid me to take care of his plants while he was out of town," I said. "This is how I got into the house." I held the key up.

"Hold this for me," I held the bat out to Lucy so I could unlock the door. Once I'd gotten it open, I stepped aside and let her enter the house before me.

"Here," she tried to hand the bat back to me. That's when I noticed she wasn't carrying her own weapon.

"Maybe you should keep it," I suggested. "You need something to defend yourself."

Lucy reached into her pocket and pulled out a small black spray vial. "I've got this," she said, showing it to me.

"What is it?" I'd never seen anything like it before.

"It's my sister's pepper spray," she explained. "My parents bought it for her once she got her driver's license."

Pepper spray was a good thing to have, but I didn't think it was going to be enough to protect her from the likes of Marcus and Chad.

"I still think you should keep the bat," I said.

"What are you going to use?" she countered, returning the pepper spray to her pocket.

I scanned the surrounding area, looking to see if Mr. Allen had anything lying around that I could use as a weapon.

"I'll use that," I pointed across the living room to the fireplace. Sitting next to it was a rack of wrought-iron tools, one of which was a fire poker.

I walked over and retrieved it.

"What now?" Lucy asked.

"Now we try to think of a way to get out of the neighborhood," I said.

"But Mr. Gin said they'd shoot us if we tried to leave the neighborhood," Lucy said.

When she mentioned Mr. Gin, it reminded me of the photo I'd seen in my father's office.

"I know who Mr. Gin is," I blurted out.

"You do?" she asked, sounding surprised.

I nodded. "Our dads work for him at the research center," I explained. "That's why he looked familiar to me."

"Are you sure?"

"I'm positive," I assured her. "My dad has a picture of him in his office."

"Why is he doing this to us?"

"I have no idea," I shrugged.

But my father might, I thought, recalling the stack of folders on his desk.

I was about to tell Lucy about the folders when the sound of someone yelling for help interrupted us.

We crept over to the nearest window that faced the front of Mr. Allen's house and peeked through the blinds.

"Looks like they found their first victim," I said.

Outside, Marcus and Chad were chasing Josiah down the middle of the street and getting close to catching him. Being only eight years old, Josiah had no hope of fighting off the two older boys.

They caught him right outside Mr. Allen's house, knocking him down onto the sidewalk.

Josiah started crying and blubbering for his mother.

"Get up!" Chad yanked Josiah to his feet, holding him in place for Marcus.

Marcus pulled a kitchen knife out of his back pocket and held the blade up to the smaller boy's face.

"We have to do something," Lucy said.

"There's nothing we can do," I replied. "Not if we want to make it out of here alive."

Together, we might have been able to take on one of the older boys, but there was no way we'd be able to fight both.

Lucy stepped away from the blinds, unable to watch what happened next. I, on the other hand, found that I couldn't turn away.

Outside, Marcus drew his knife hand back.

Knowing what was about to happen, Josiah struggled to break free from Chad's grip but couldn't.

"Time to die," Marcus grinned, plunging the knife into Josiah's chest not once, but three times.

Chad released the smaller boy, letting him fall to the ground.

Blood poured from Josiah's chest as he struggled to get to his feet. Even though he was dying, he still tried to get away.

He didn't get very far before he collapsed face down on the ground in a spreading pool of blood.

"Is he dead?" Chad asked.

"Looks like it," Marcus replied, nudging the body with his foot.

"Come on," he said a moment later, turning to leave. "Let's go find one for you."

Smiling, Chad followed behind him. "Let's see if we can find Brittany," he said. "I want to pay her back for squealing on me in math class."

Behind them, Josiah began to move.

"He's not dead," I whispered.

Lucy heard my comment and returned to the window to peek outside.

The two of us watched in surprise as Josiah pulled himself to his feet.

Marcus and Chad continued to walk away, oblivious to the fact that Josiah was still alive.

"What is he doing?" Lucy asked.

Josiah was just standing in the middle of the street.

I shook my head. "I have no idea."

"We have to help him," she said, "before Marcus and Chad see him."

Lucy turned away from the window and started to walk toward the front door.

"Wait," I stopped her. "Something's happening."

She quickly returned to the window where the two of us watched in horror as Josiah began to change.

It started as a violent series of tremors that encompassed his whole body. When it began, I thought he was going into shock, but that wasn't the case.

Once the tremors ceased, Josiah dropped onto his hands and knees. That's when the changes started.

His arms and legs began to lengthen and fill out before sprouting a thick coat of gray fur. Long black claws sprouted from the tips of his fingers. His skinny body swelled, becoming more muscular. The last thing to change was his head, which elongated into the snout of a wolf.

The entire metamorphosis from boy to wolf happened in less than thirty seconds. When it was complete, the Josiah wolf lifted its head and howled. That's when Marcus and Chad stopped and turned around.

"What the hell is that?" Chad yelped upon seeing the large wolf standing in the center of the road.

The Josiah wolf started advancing toward the two boys, picking up its pace as it went, a growl building in its throat.

"Run!" Marcus shouted.

He and Chad bolted up the street, running as fast as they could, but they weren't fast enough.

The Josiah wolf leaped into the air, covering an impossible distance before landing on Chad's back, knocking him to the ground.

Chad rolled over onto his back and tried to fight the wolf, but he was no match for its strength and size. All it took was one snap of the wolf's jaws on Chad's exposed throat, and the fight was over.

Marcus continued to run away, turning down the street that led to the pool. Satisfied that Chad was no longer a threat, the wolf gave chase. Lucy and I watched until both of them were out of sight, but we could hear what happened when the wolf finally caught up to him.

"Oh my God, look!" Lucy was staring at Chad's body. "He's starting to change, too."

Chad's body was undergoing the same metamorphosis that Josiah's had. In less than a minute, he too had become a wolf.

"Get away from the window," I hissed, motioning her to step back.

Once the Chad wolf had gotten to its feet, it had turned in our direction, ears erect, listening. A moment later, it lifted its nose into the air and started sniffing like it was searching for a scent. That's when I told Lucy to get away from the window.

"Do you think it heard us?" Her voice trembled as she whispered.

I took a quick peek outside.

The Chad wolf, with its nose still in the air, was slowly walking down the street in our direction.

I nodded.

"What do we do?" she mouthed the words.

I had no idea.

There was no way we'd be able to outrun the Chad wolf, and we'd surely lose if we tried to stand our ground with the meager weapons we had. Hiding also wasn't an option, not if it could track us by scent.

Scent?

That last thought triggered an idea.

"Come on," I whispered, motioning for Lucy to follow me.

I led her across the house and into Mr. Allen's bathroom. Once we were both inside, I closed the door and locked it.

"Why are we in here?" Lucy asked, doing her best to keep her voice as low as possible.

I ignored her question and held out my hand. "Give me the pepper spray," I said.

Lucy reached into her pocket, retrieved the spray, and handed it to me.

The sound of glass breaking came from somewhere in the house.

"I think it's inside," Lucy said.

We could hear nails clicking on the hardwood floor as the wolf walked through the house searching for us.

"Cover your nose," I warned Lucy as I sprayed a steady stream of pepper spray all around the door frame.

I kept spraying until it was empty.

The smell was overpowering in the confines of the small bathroom, making me regret what I'd done.

Our eyes started to water and our noses began to sting, but we both remained quiet, knowing the wolf was in the house.

Please work, I silently begged when I heard the wolf stop right outside the bathroom door.

There was a moment of silence, which was broken when the wolf sneezed. The sound was so loud that it caused Lucy and me to jump.

On the other side of the door, the wolf whined and snorted, but it didn't leave.

Lucy looked over at me, the expression on her face projecting her unspoken thought of *What now?*

The wolf pawed at the door.

I lifted the fire poker over my shoulder, readying it.

The pawing became more persistent.

Just when I thought the Chad wolf was going to break through the door, a blood-curdling scream echoed through the neighborhood, drawing its attention away from us.

We could hear its nails clacking against the floor as it ran out of the house to investigate the sound.

"We need to get out of here." Overwhelmed by the smell of the pepper spray, I coughed the words out.

Lucy didn't protest.

We rushed out of the bathroom and back into the living room, where the window we had used to look outside was a shattered mess across the floor and furniture.

"Why is this happening?" Lucy sounded like she was on the verge of crying.

"I don't know," I said, "but I think I might know how to find out." I was looking across the street at my house as I spoke.

"Here," I handed Lucy one of the Project Chimera files on my father's desk. "See if you can find anything in there." I took a different file and started flipping through it.

After we left Mr. Allen's house, we raced across the street to my house and immediately went to my father's office.

"Look at this," Lucy pulled a sheet of paper out of her file and held it out to me. "It's got all of our names on it."

Every kid at the pool parking lot was listed on a sheet of paper, along with their addresses and dates of birth.

"That's not all that's in here," she continued. "This file is full of information about us."

"I think I know why." I handed her a document from my file titled *Surrogate Mothers*.

Listed on it were a series of names along with something called an embryo code. Next to every embryo code, in quotation marks, was a name. The names of all the kids who were at the pool parking lot were listed.

"Does this mean what I think it means?" she asked.

I nodded. "They may have given birth to us, but those aren't our real mothers," I gestured at the sheet. "I think we're an experiment."

I set the folder I was holding back onto the desk and grabbed another. Inside it, I found a bunch of documents detailing the creation of something called the Chimera genome.

"What's a Chimera?" I asked Lucy.

"It's a monster from Greek mythology," she explained. "It has the head of a lion, the body of a goat, and a snake for a tail."

At first, I didn't see how that related to what was going on in our subdivision. It wasn't until I thought about it in broader terms that it made sense.

"That must be what we are," I blurted out.

"You think we're Chimeras?" Lucy asked.

"Yeah," I replied, "but not the kind you're thinking of." I showed her a document that had a diagram of the Chimera genome with a bunch of scientific terms on it, many of which I couldn't pronounce. "We're this kind."

Lucy took the document and started looking it over.

"*Canis lupus*," she read one of the words that was on the document.

"What's that?" I asked.

"It's the scientific name for wolf," she answered. "It's listed on here several times along with other canid species I don't recognize," she ran her finger down the document.

"That must be why everyone is turning into wolves," I said. "We were created to become monsters. That must be what Mr. Gin's whole demonstration is about."

Outside, somebody screamed.

Lucy and I set down the papers we were holding and retrieved our weapons, which we'd left lying on the desk. Then we walked over to the window and peeked outside.

"It sounded like it came from a couple of streets over," Lucy said.

"Yeah, it did," I agreed.

"We should probably get back to finding a way out of the neighborhood," Lucy announced, "while the wolves are distracted."

"That sounds like a good idea," I agreed.

I started to turn away from the window, but something caught my eye, drawing my attention back to it.

"Wait!" I said. "Look over there." I pointed into my neighbor's backyard, where Greta, another one of the eight-year-olds, was peeking her head out of the doghouse where she'd presumably been hiding.

"We can't leave her there," Lucy declared. "We have to take her with us."

I knew I wasn't going to be able to talk her out of it, so I just said, "Okay," and followed her down the stairs.

After Lucy and I left my house, we crept over to my neighbor's fence and used the gate to gain access to the backyard.

"Go get her," I motioned with my head. "I'll stay here and keep watch."

I kept the gate open a few inches so we wouldn't have to unlatch it again when we left. The gap also allowed me to keep an eye on the street in front of the houses.

"Okay," Lucy agreed, quietly making her way around the house to where the doghouse was.

I watched her go until she disappeared around the corner of the house.

Somewhere nearby, someone began calling for help. A few seconds later, the cries were abruptly cut off.

Please hurry, I silently urged Lucy. At the rate the kids were dropping, the neighborhood was going to be overrun with wolves soon.

I waited several minutes for Lucy to return before deciding to go and see what was taking her so long.

As I was rounding the corner of the house, Lucy and Greta were coming from the opposite direction. My sudden appearance startled Greta, causing her to yelp and point her arms in my direction.

A moment later, there was a loud bang and something punched into my chest, knocking me off my feet.

As I fell, I felt an intense pain in my chest, and I was finding it hard to breathe.

"Oh my God!" Lucy rushed over and knelt beside me.

"What happened?" I moaned, unable to find the strength to get up.

Behind Lucy, Greta kept saying, "I'm sorry, I'm sorry, I'm sorry."

"You've been shot," Lucy said, her eyes filling with tears.

I looked over at Greta, and lying on the ground at her feet was a pistol.

That's what she was pointing at me.

A violent shudder wracked my body, and I began to feel like I was on fire.

Oh no, I'm changing.

"You have to go," I warned Lucy, gritting my teeth against the rising pain shooting through my limbs. "It's not safe."

She stood up but didn't leave.

"GO! NOW!" The words came out with a snarl.

Lucy reached out and grabbed Greta by the hand, pulling her through the gate and out into the street.

With great effort, I managed to roll over onto my hands and knees.

The world started spinning as strange thoughts began to intrude upon my mind. It felt like something was trying to take over my body. I tried to fight it, but I couldn't; it was too powerful. In a matter of seconds, it overwhelmed me, making me forget who I was. All that remained was the primal instinct of the wolf.

The sound of my alarm clock going off startled me awake.

I threw off the covers and sat up.

Where am I?

The last thing I remembered was being shot and turning into a wolf.

I lifted my shirt and examined my chest, looking to see if there was any kind of wound there. There wasn't.

I sighed in relief. *It was just a dream.*

There was a knock on my bedroom door. A moment later, it swung open, revealing my father.

"Hey, Kiddo," he said. "You feeling all right? I heard you cry out earlier."

"Yeah," I got to my feet. "I'm fine. Just had a bad dream."

"What about?" he asked.

"Nothing," I waved off the question. "It was stupid."

"Okay," he said. "If you're hungry, breakfast is ready." When he was done speaking, he turned and left, closing the door behind him.

I got dressed and went downstairs, where I ate three helpings of sausage and eggs along with two huge glasses of orange juice.

"Someone was hungry," my mother remarked when she came to clear the table.

"I guess I was," I replied. I had no idea what had come over me. Once I started eating, it was hard to stop.

As I got up to help my mother clean, someone rang the doorbell. A moment later, my brother Dillon called out from the foyer.

"Hey butt-munch," he said, using one of his favorite nicknames for me. "Your girlfriend is here."

Girlfriend?

I didn't know what he was talking about. I didn't have a girlfriend.

When I went to the door to see who it was, I was surprised to see Lucy standing on the porch.

"I had the strangest dream last night," she said.

FAMILY MATTERS

"Isn't there anyone else who can take him?" Ms. Perry asked. "I'm not really set up to care for an eight-year-old."

Before she knocked on the door, Mrs. Fitzsimmons, the social worker assigned to my case, told me that Ms. Perry was my dad's older sister, which made her my aunt. I was surprised to hear about her because I didn't know my dad had a sister. He never mentioned her to me or my mom.

"You're the only living relative we could find," Mrs. Fitzsimmons replied.

When Ms. Perry didn't respond, Mrs. Fitzsimmons said, "I could put him into foster care if that's what you prefer, but it will take me some time to find a family who can take him."

"How long?" Ms. Perry asked.

"A week, maybe two," Mrs. Fitzsimmons said. "Could you at least let him stay here until then?" She didn't want to take me back to the group home where I'd been staying since the day my parents died.

Ms. Perry looked down at me. "I suppose," she said, her features softening into a smile. "Come inside." She motioned me into the house.

"Go on." Mrs. Fitzsimmons gave me a gentle push as Ms. Perry stepped aside so I could walk through the doorway. "I'll go grab his things." She gestured over her shoulder at her car parked in the driveway.

"You look just like Lawrence did at that age," Ms. Perry commented as she brushed a stray lock of hair out of my eyes.

Lawrence was my dad's name, but everyone I knew called him Larry.

Mrs. Fitzsimmons walked into the house a couple of minutes later, carrying two suitcases, both of which used to belong to my parents. Inside them was everything I owned.

She set the suitcases on the floor in the foyer and then reached into the pocket of her jacket to retrieve a business card.

"If you need anything," she held the card out, "call me anytime, day or night."

Ms. Perry took the card and put it in her pocket.

"The same goes for you, too, Jamie," Mrs. Fitzsimmons turned and said to me. "Okay?"

"Okay," I replied.

Mrs. Fitzsimmons started to leave but stopped when she remembered something.

"I almost forgot." She reached into a different pocket and withdrew three $50 gift cards, which she handed to Ms. Perry. "For groceries and anything else Jamie might need until I can find a foster family for him."

Before Mrs. Fitzsimmons left, she hugged me and whispered in my ear, "Be good, okay?"

I nodded.

She said that to me because she was hoping that I could somehow convince Ms. Perry to let me stay with her.

"I'll call you next week," Mrs. Fitzsimmons said to my aunt before leaving.

Once she was gone, I started to feel out of place and didn't know what to do.

"Are you hungry?" Ms. Perry asked.

I was hungry but didn't want to feel like a burden, so I just shrugged.

"Do you like peanut butter and jelly sandwiches?" she asked.

I nodded.

"I figured you would," she smiled. "Your dad loved them too. Come on," she nodded, "let's go into the kitchen and I'll make us some."

As we ate, Ms. Perry asked me basic questions about myself—things like what grade I was in, what my favorite color was, and what I liked to do for fun. The questions kept coming until she got to the one that she really wanted to know the answer to.

"Did they tell you what happened to your parents?" she asked with genuine concern.

Mrs. Fitzsimmons didn't give Ms. Perry the specifics of my situation. All she told her was that my parents were dead.

I nodded.

She waited patiently for me to respond.

"They were in a car accident," I said, unable to look her in the eyes when I spoke.

I didn't tell her how they were supposed to pick me up after school that day and take me to the pizza place where we were going to have my birthday party, but they never arrived. Instead, a police officer came to the school after they couldn't get a hold of anyone to pick me up. The officer stayed with me until Mrs. Fitzsimmons arrived and told me what had happened to my parents.

That happened a month ago.

Seeing my eyes start to tear up, Ms. Perry grabbed a napkin and handed it to me.

"Are you thirsty?" she suddenly changed the subject.

I nodded.

She got up, opened the fridge, and said, "I've got orange juice, milk, water, or soda."

"Can I have a soda?" I asked. My parents didn't let me drink soda very often, and the group home only let us have it on special occasions.

"You can have whatever you want." Ms. Perry grabbed two cans of soda and brought them back over to the table.

"Thank you for letting me stay with you, Ms. Perry," I said as I opened my can.

I was glad I wasn't going to be staying in the group home, even if only for a little while. There was no privacy there, and the other kids weren't very nice.

"We're family," she said, giving me a weak smile. "Call me Aunt Evie."

When we were done eating, Aunt Evie got up and started to clean off the table. Wanting to be helpful, I got up and gave her a hand.

"I guess we should take your stuff upstairs and get you situated," she declared when we were done.

I followed her out to the foyer, where she grabbed my suitcases and started walking up the stairs. Once we reached the second floor, she walked down the hall and stopped in front of a door with an old sign taped to the front that read "KEEP OUT." It was so old that the edges were flaky, and it had started to turn yellow.

"I thought you might like to stay in here," Aunt Evie said before swinging the door open.

She motioned for me to go inside and then followed behind me.

"This used to be your dad's room," she explained, setting the suitcases on the bed. "I think he'd want you to stay here too."

The room looked like it hadn't been touched since the '90s. Old movie posters like *Jurassic Park* and *Terminator 2* covered the walls. In the corner was a TV stand with an original PlayStation on it, along with a stack of over a dozen games. The TV the console was connected to looked like a big box. There were also various action figures and comic books lying around.

Aunt Evie watched me as I looked around the room.

"You don't have to worry about any of this stuff," she eventually said while motioning at my dad's things. "I was planning on getting rid of it soon, so you can have whatever you want."

"This was really my dad's room?" I asked.

The room looked like a time capsule that Aunt Evie and I had just opened for the first time in decades.

"It was," she replied. "Until he was sent away." She got a faraway look in her eyes when she said that last part.

Why was he sent away? I wanted to ask, but it was clear that whatever my aunt was thinking about weighed heavily upon her, and that stopped me from saying anything.

"Everything is exactly as it was the day he left," Aunt Evie continued.

If that was true, it meant my dad hadn't been in the room for a very long time.

"I come in here from time to time to clean, like my mother used to, but I don't mess with any of Lawrence's things when I do."

That explained why the room wasn't covered in dust or cobwebs.

"How come he never came back?" The question was out of my mouth before I could stop myself.

If that were my room, I wouldn't want to leave all my stuff behind like that. I'd come back for it if I could.

Aunt Evie sighed. "That's a long story, and one I'm not sure you're ready to hear just yet," she said, forcing a smile. "Let's just forget I said anything about it and get you unpacked."

She leaned down, unzipped one of my suitcases, and flipped the lid open. When she saw what was inside, she gave a little gasp and then paused to look at me.

"Are those what I think they are?" she pointed at the urns sitting on top of my clothes.

I nodded.

"I guess I should've expected something like that." She quickly regained her composure, picked up one of the urns, and set it on the dresser after pushing a stack of comic books to the side. "Is that okay?" she asked after setting both urns side by side.

"It's fine," I replied.

Mrs. Fitzsimmons had arranged the cremation of my parents for me and had been holding onto the urns until she found a place for me to stay. She'd mentioned it to me on the drive over to Aunt Evie's house, but I'd forgotten about them until I saw them in the suitcase.

"You can put them wherever you'd like," she seemed a little uncomfortable talking about them. "Why don't I just let you put everything where you want?" she blurted out before pulling open one of the dresser drawers. "Your dad's clothes are still in here, but you can just toss them in the closet to make room." To illustrate her point, she retrieved the socks and underwear from the drawer and tossed them into the closet, leaving the door open when she was done.

"I'll go ahead and give you some privacy so you can get settled," she said, walking over to the door and starting to leave. "If you need me, I'll be downstairs."

"Okay," I said. "And thanks again for letting me stay."

I really meant that. I was looking forward to getting to sleep in a room by myself. At the group home, I had to share a room with three other boys, one of whom snored very loudly.

Aunt Evie responded with a smile and then shut the door.

After my aunt left, I wandered around the room, examining the things my dad had left behind. I was surprised to see that he had more books and toys than I ever did. At first, that made me think he was a hypocrite because he didn't want me to own a bunch of junk, as he called it. But the more I thought about it, the more I realized he'd probably said that because of what he'd gone through.

I'm sure my dad didn't view all the stuff he'd left behind as junk. I could tell from the way everything was prominently displayed that he cared a great deal for it all.

He must've decided it was all junk once he realized he was never going to see any of it again. That was probably the only way for him to sever any emotional ties he had to it. That must have really hurt him, which is why he kept me from amassing my own collection of junk.

I wonder what happened to him.

I hoped my aunt would tell me.

In the meantime, I started snooping around the room to see what I could find that might give me more insight into what my dad was like when he was my age.

I found what I was looking for shoved behind his nightstand. It was an old sketchbook filled with random drawings of things like dinosaurs, superheroes, and spaceships, at least until I reached the last few pages.

Did my dad really draw this?

I stared down at the drawing of a mutilated animal that looked like it was supposed to be a cat or a raccoon. Standing above the animal's body was a boy and an odd-looking creature that looked like a cross between a frog and a hairless monkey. Seeing it reminded me of how Gollum looked in the original cartoon adaptation of *The Hobbit*, one of the few movies I'd watched with my dad.

The drawing on the next page was like the one before it. It featured some poor animal, a dog, I think, lying dead on the ground while the boy and creature stood over it with big smiles on their faces.

When I turned the page and saw the last drawing in the sketchbook, I quickly closed it and put it back where I found it. In that final drawing, the animal on the ground was replaced with the body of a girl, her abdomen exposed and her guts sticking out.

I couldn't get the image out of my mind and wished I'd never seen it.

Hoping to distract myself, I cleaned out the dresser and put my clothes away. When I was done, I put my suitcases in the closet, along with the old clothes from the dresser, and shut the door. Then I sat down on the floor in front of the TV to see if I could figure out how to work the PlayStation.

Two loud knocks on the bedroom door startled me.

"You okay in here?" Aunt Evie asked as she opened the door and walked into the room.

I paused the game I was playing and turned to face her.

"I'm okay," I replied.

"I'm surprised that old thing still works," she gestured at the PlayStation.

I didn't think she expected a response, so I remained quiet.

"I just came up here to see if you were hungry," she said. "I was going to make spaghetti for dinner and wanted to see if that was okay with you."

"Spaghetti sounds good," I replied.

"Okay, spaghetti it is," she smiled. "Which is a good thing because I don't have the ingredients to make anything else."

I reached out and turned the game console off.

"You didn't have to do that," Aunt Evie frowned.

"It wasn't that fun," I explained. "I was going to turn it off anyway."

"You can come help me in the kitchen if you want," she suggested.

"Okay," I agreed. I'd spent enough time alone in the room and was ready to do something else.

As I got to my feet, I happened to glance at the nightstand, which reminded me of the sketchbook that was hidden behind it. I'd considered keeping it a secret, but I decided that wasn't a good idea. If I didn't talk to someone about it, it was going to haunt me. I also thought that my aunt should be aware of this.

"Can I show you something first?" I asked her.

"Sure," she hesitated before responding.

I walked over to the nightstand, reached behind it, and pulled out the sketchbook.

"I found this earlier," I held it out to her.

Aunt Evie took the sketchbook and ran her fingers across the cover. "I always thought he took this with him," she said, more to herself than to me. "Your dad was always drawing something in here." She lifted her head to look at me. "He said he wanted to draw comics when he grew up."

She opened the sketchbook and started flipping through the pages, smiling at what she saw. "He was really good," she said.

She only looked at a handful of the earlier pictures before she closed the book and tried to hand it back to me.

"You should keep it," she said.

"I don't think I should," I replied.

"Why not?"

I took the sketchbook from her, opened it to the last few pages, and then handed it back to her.

"That's why." I pointed at the gruesome scene depicted on the page.

Aunt Evie gasped when she saw it.

"There's more," I grimaced.

When she got to the last page, the one with the mutilated girl on it, she covered her mouth with her hand. "Oh my god," she whispered. "That's me."

Before I could say or do anything, she let go of the sketchbook, letting it fall to the floor before rushing out of the room. I heard her footsteps go down the hall towards her bedroom, and then I heard a door click shut.

Not knowing what else to do, I picked up the sketchbook and stood in the doorway, staring at the closed door of her room, listening to her sob.

That was not the reaction I was expecting.

I wish I hadn't shown it to her.

I wanted to throw the sketchbook away, but I didn't know if I should, so I opted to put it in the closet instead. When I opened the door and tossed it inside, I was surprised to see that both of my suitcases were open and lying on their sides.

That was not how I left them. They should've been standing upright against the wall.

I also noticed that the pile of old clothes I'd taken out of the dresser was no longer stacked in a pile; it was now strewn about the closet floor.

That's weird.

Before I could dwell on what had happened, the sound of my aunt returning pulled my attention away. When I heard her enter the room, I closed the closet door and turned to face her.

"I'm sorry you had to see that," she apologized. "I wasn't expecting to see something like that."

"I'm sorry too," I replied, still feeling bad about showing her the sketchbook.

"You have nothing to be sorry about," she quickly countered. "You did the right thing by showing it to me."

It didn't feel like the right thing.

"Do you still want to know why your father was sent away?" she suddenly asked. "I'm sure you've already guessed most of it by now."

After seeing the drawings, it wasn't hard to piece together.

"Did he really do those things?" I was referring to the pictures in the sketchbook.

It was hard to picture my dad doing those things. Not once did I ever see him act in a way that would suggest that he was capable of such violence. He rarely yelled at me, never hit me, and was quick to come to my defense when I'd done something to upset my mom.

"He did," Aunt Evie nodded. "All except for the last one"—the one that showed her, she clarified—"obviously."

Based on that one drawing, I assumed my dad had drawn the pictures before each act was committed. Probably as a way to better visualize the dark thoughts that were brewing within his mind at the time. The only question I had was *why*.

"Why?" I repeated the thought out loud. "Why did he do it?"

My aunt shrugged. "Nobody knows. When he was asked about it, he insisted he didn't do it. He said the dearg did it." Despite the weird spelling, she pronounced it *Jar-ick*.

"What's a dearg?" I asked.

"According to Lawrence, it was something that lived in his closet and fed on blood like a vampire."

As I looked over at the closet, the image of the odd-looking creature I'd seen in the drawings flashed through my mind.

"In the closet…" I repeated. Hearing that made me change my mind about wanting to stay in the room, especially after I'd opened the closet door and found a mess of things inside.

"Oh." Aunt Evie suddenly realized the effect her words had on me. "I probably shouldn't have said that," she frowned.

"It's okay," I tried to reassure her that I wasn't really scared, even though I was.

"The dearg isn't real," she insisted. "It was something your dad created to take the blame for the horrible things he'd done. I know this because your grandmother caught him in the act. Plus, I've lived here my entire life and been in and out of this room hundreds of times, and I've never seen a monster."

"Do you understand?" she asked after giving me a moment to process what she'd said.

I nodded. That didn't make me feel much better, though. Knowing that my dad did those things still cast a pall over the room. All the cool stuff he'd left behind now felt tainted.

"You don't have to stay in here if you don't want to," Aunt Evie said. "You can stay in one of the other empty rooms if you prefer." She hooked her thumb over her shoulder.

"Okay," I said.

I didn't know what to do. I didn't want her to think I was being a big baby, but I also didn't want to stay in the room. Thankfully, my aunt picked up on my indecision and offered me a reprieve.

"Why don't we go downstairs and have dinner," she suggested, "and then you can make up your mind about which room you want to stay in later? Sound good to you?"

I nodded.

"Alright, let's go," she motioned for us to leave.

"How's the spaghetti?" Aunt Evie asked.

We'd kept to ourselves while we ate until she asked me that.

"It's good," I replied.

"Did you have spaghetti often at home?" I could tell she was just trying to make conversation and didn't really know what to say to me.

"Not really," I said.

"Your grandmother would make it for Lawrence and me at least once a week. It was by far your father's favorite meal."

That was news to me. My mother only made spaghetti on nights when my father was working late and wouldn't be having dinner with us. I got the impression from her that he didn't like eating spaghetti.

What happened to change his mind?

As soon as the thought entered my mind, an image of one of the drawings from the sketchbook flashed before my eyes. When I looked down at my plate, the mass of noodles and sauce reminded me of the exposed blood and guts my father had drawn. That comparison quickly killed my appetite.

I wonder if that's why he stopped liking spaghetti.

I pushed my plate away. "I'm full."

"Do you want me to save it in case you get hungry later?" she eyed my half-full plate.

"No, thank you," I shook my head. "I've had enough."

I got up, intending to take my plate to the sink, but my aunt stopped me.

"You can leave it there; I'll take care of it," she said as she got to her feet. "Why don't you go upstairs and decide which room you want? I'll be up in a few minutes."

"Okay," I agreed.

I'd already decided I was going to switch rooms, so I was glad she said that without me having to say anything first.

When I got to the top of the stairs, I stopped and looked down the hall. The house had four bedrooms, two on either side of the hall. My dad's old room was the first one on the right, and my aunt's bedroom was the second one on the left. That left me with two options: the one next to my dad's or the one across the hall.

I chose the one that was next door because of its proximity to the bathroom. I didn't like the idea of having to walk down the hall in the dark if I needed to get up in the middle of the night to go pee.

Aunt Evie came upstairs to check on me as I was moving the last of my things into the new room.

"This used to be my room," she said while standing in the doorway.

I figured that was the case from all the white furniture in the room, most of which was covered with stickers featuring fantasy creatures like fairies and unicorns.

"You can take the blanket from the other room if you don't want to use that one," she gestured at the floral comforter that covered the bed.

"It's okay," I said. The pattern didn't bother me.

Not having anything else to say, she stood there awkwardly for a moment before her phone rang.

She quickly pulled it out of her pocket and looked at it.

"Crap," she muttered. "I have to take this." She stepped across the hall into her bedroom. "I'll be right back."

I couldn't really hear what Aunt Evie was saying, but I could tell from her tone of voice that she was not happy with whoever she was talking to.

Once the call was over, she came back into the room and said, "What do you say about taking a quick drive with me?"

"Where?"

"I have to run into work and help them with something," she explained. "It shouldn't take longer than half an hour or so."

I didn't want to feel like a burden, so I said, "I can wait here."

"I don't think leaving an eight-year-old home alone is legal," she contested.

I didn't know if it was legal either, but I did know that my mom would frequently leave me alone while she went to visit one of the neighbors or run up to the store to pick up groceries.

"It's okay," I insisted. "I was just going to read some of those." I gestured at the stack of comics I'd taken out of my dad's old room.

"Are you sure?" she asked. I could tell she was relieved that I offered to stay home but was still unsure if it was a good idea.

"I'm sure."

"I won't be gone long," she said. "I'm going to write my cellphone number on the pad next to the phone in the kitchen. If you need me, call me, okay?" She fixed me with a stern gaze.

"I will," I promised, before grabbing the top comic off the stack and climbing on the bed to read it.

Aunt Evie hesitated in the doorway for a moment before finally deciding it was okay to leave.

"I'm going now," she called up from the bottom of the stairs a few minutes later.

"Okay," I called back and then returned to reading the comic book.

Halfway through reading my second comic, my stomach started grumbling, which reminded me that I hadn't finished my spaghetti earlier.

Maybe there was still some left.

I hopped off the bed, intending to make my way down to the kitchen to see if my aunt had saved any of it. There was plenty left over, and she didn't seem like the type of person who would just throw it all away.

As I was passing the doorway of my dad's old room, I heard the closet door creak open. I recognized the sound from when I had opened it earlier.

I froze in the middle of the hall.

"Lawrence?" something hissed. There was a brief pause before it spoke again. "I know you're here. I can smell you." It growled.

I dared not make a sound.

"Did you really think you could come back here after all this time and everything would be okay between us?"

I could hear the soft tread of its footfalls as it started to make its way slowly across the room toward the hall.

As quietly as I could, I started walking backward toward my new room. When I reached the doorway, I saw a pale hand with long black fingernails reach out and grasp hold of the doorframe of my dad's old room.

I turned around and ducked into my room right before the thing that had come out of my dad's closet stepped out into the hall.

"We made a deal, Lawrence," the creature said as it approached.

I frantically looked around the room searching for a place to hide.

"You don't even like your sister," the creature continued. "You were the one who called me out of the ether to help you get rid of her. *You*, not me." It emphasized the word *you*. "All you had to do was end her life, and then I would've taken care of everything else. I could've made it like she never existed. Instead, you were weak and got caught."

The creature's shadow preceded it into the room.

Having nowhere else to hide, I ducked down and crawled under the bed as the creature stepped through the doorway. It stopped and sniffed the air.

"That can't be," the creature hissed. "I smell you, but I also smell death."

It walked over to the dresser and lifted the lid off one of the urns, then leaned forward and sniffed the contents.

"NO!" it yelled. "WE HAD A DEAL!" With a backhanded swipe, it launched the urns containing my parents' ashes across the room, spilling the contents all over the floor.

The creature continued its tirade, pulling all the drawers out of the dresser and smashing them against the wall. When it ran out of drawers to smash, it tipped the dresser over and then jumped up and down on top of it, yelling, "WE! MADE! A! DEAL!" Each word marked a jump.

When it was done, it stood amongst the wreckage panting. Then it suddenly sniffed the air.

"I still smell life in you," it sounded confused. "Why is that? How can you be both alive and dead?"

Oh no! It knows I'm here!

I was doing my best to hold in the fear that was overwhelming me, but I couldn't do it any longer. My bladder released, emptying its contents. Urine soaked my pants and then started seeping into the carpet.

The creature sniffed the air.

"I smell fear," it said.

With one hand, the creature lashed out and lifted the corner of the bed off the floor, peering underneath it. That was the first good look I had gotten of its face. If I hadn't already pissed myself, I would have done so upon seeing its hideously misshapen head with its bulbous fish-like lips and cataract-covered eyes.

"A child!" it declared, its fetid breath washing over me. "One who smells like Lawrence but isn't." It sniffed the air again.

Frozen with fear, I stared at the hideous creature, unable to look away.

"Lawrence was your father, wasn't he?" the creature asked.

I forced myself to nod.

"I thought so," it smiled, showing its yellow teeth. "Your father and I had a deal. As his heir, his debt falls to you... and I will get what is owed." It reached out to grab me.

Before its hand could close around my arm, I pushed myself up from the floor and started running for the door.

The creature dropped the bed and started to pursue me.

Without looking back, I ran down the stairs and out the front door. I didn't stop running until someone grabbed me, preventing me from running into traffic at a busy intersection.

A few hours later, after a trip to the local police precinct, I was sitting in the back of Mrs. Fitzsimmons's car in the driveway of my aunt's house while the two of them talked on the porch. When they were done, Mrs. Fitzsimmons came back over to the car and opened the door.

"Let's go inside and talk to your aunt," she said.

"I don't want to."

"I think you owe her an explanation about why you destroyed her room," she replied.

"I already told you what happened."

Mrs. Fitzsimmons sighed. "We've been over this, Jamie. There are no such things as monsters. You're just overreacting to that story your aunt told you." She gave me a moment to respond. When I didn't, she continued, "Fine. If you don't want to talk to her, you don't have to. But we're not leaving until you go inside and clean up the mess you made."

I looked up at the second-floor window of my dad's room. Peering out of it with its face pressed against the glass was the creature. It had a smile on its face as it waved at me.

FINAL REPORT CARD

"All right, class," Mr. Howard announced. "It's that time of year."

He held up the small stack of envelopes in his hand and waved them in the air as he walked from his desk to the front of the class. Inside the envelopes were our final report cards for the year.

There were six students in the room, including me. The teachers at Phillips High School handpicked all of us to attend Mr. Howard's class of last resort—a special after-school class for behaviorally challenged teens who frequently found themselves at odds with the traditional academic experience the school offered.

"Before I hand these out," Mr. Howard continued, "I just want to say that in the ten years I've been teaching this class, you lot have been the worst." He gestured at us with the envelopes in his hand as he paced back and forth. "All of you deserve to be here." He suddenly stopped in front of Darlene's desk, looking down at her with a smile on his face. "Except for you, Ms. Evans."

Mr. Howard pulled one of the envelopes from the stack and laid it on Darlene's desk.

"You're free to go," he said to her.

Darlene wasted no time gathering her things and heading for the door.

"Later, losers," she taunted as she left the room.

Ronnie, one of the school's premier metalheads and drug peddlers, raised his left hand and gave Darlene a one-finger salute.

"What a coincidence," Mr. Howard said, weaving through the desks to stand in front of Ronnie at the back of the room. "That happens to be the number of subjects you managed to pass." He pulled an envelope free from the stack and slapped it down on Ronnie's desk.

Ronnie rotated his hand, his middle finger still up, until it was facing Mr. Howard.

Mr. Howard turned his back to Ronnie and continued giving out the envelopes. He came to my desk last.

"You almost passed, Mr. Hartley," he said, sounding disappointed as he handed me the envelope with my name on it. "If you'd just done the extra credit I assigned, you could've walked out of here with Ms. Evans."

Hearing that disappointed me far more than it did him because I had tried to do the extra credit assignment. I just couldn't get through the book he wanted us to read, which was a historical text detailing how the town we lived in, Mouthsend, was founded. It was incredibly long and extremely dull. I only managed to get through the first hundred pages before I gave up.

"Are we done?" Constance sneered. "Can we go now?"

Constance was with us because she attacked a teacher. She was given the choice of going to juvenile detention or attending Mr. Howard's class.

"Not yet," Mr. Howard answered, returning to the front of the class. "I have one last lesson for you to complete."

Everybody groaned. After Darlene was allowed to leave early, we all thought we'd be allowed to leave early, too.

"Is this going to change our grades?" Shawn asked.

Shawn was forced to take Mr. Howard's class after he was caught, more than once, vandalizing school property.

"No, it won't," Mr. Howard answered. "But it might change your attitude."

"This is bullshit," Ronnie shouted as he got to his feet. "You can't force us to stay here. You already gave us our report cards for the year." He started for the door.

Mr. Howard didn't try to stop him. He didn't have to. When Ronnie opened the door, he found himself face-to-face with Officer Reed, the school's resource officer.

Officer Reed was a head taller than Ronnie and about twice as wide.

"Where do you think you're going?" Officer Reed's voice was deep and gravelly, making it sound like he was growling out the words.

"This is bullshit!" Ronnie spat, turning and returning to his seat. He knew better than to push Officer Reed.

The officer had a reputation for using excessive force. You'd think the school would have fired him for it, but the faculty didn't seem to care. Neither did the sheriff.

"As I was saying," Mr. Howard announced, "there is one last lesson you need to complete before you can leave." He waited to see if there were going to be any more outbursts before continuing. "This lesson will be administered individually, starting with you, Mr. Whitaker." He fixed his eyes on Ronnie.

"Why me?" Ronnie griped.

"Because you're closest to the door," Mr. Howard replied.

Even though that was true, I didn't think it was the real reason he picked Ronnie first.

"Come on, let's go." Officer Reed stepped into the room and motioned for Ronnie to comply.

"Officer Reed will escort you to the testing facility," Mr. Howard explained. As Ronnie and the officer left the room, he said, "Good luck."

Ronnie replied in typical fashion by flashing his middle finger over his shoulder.

"As for the rest of you," Mr. Howard addressed the three of us who remained, "you're free to do whatever you like, you just can't leave the room until your name is called." When he was done speaking, he returned to his desk.

Not having anything else to do and not knowing how long I would be stuck there, I walked over to the bookcase on the side of the room, grabbed the town history book—the only one in the class—and took it back to my desk.

"You're such a nerd," Constance said when I passed her desk. "What're you even doing in this class?"

Knowing she was bored and just looking to cause trouble, I ignored her and continued to my desk.

"Why are you here?" Shawn asked after I'd sat down. He sounded genuinely curious.

It was common knowledge why everyone else was in the class, but none of my classmates knew why I was there.

"I don't really know why," I shrugged. "I just showed up for school one day and was told I'd be finishing the year in Mr. Howard's class."

"That's bullshit!" Shawn blurted out.

I agreed with him. It was bullshit. I hadn't done anything to deserve being put in the class like the others had, but there was nothing I could do about it. I tried to get my parents to talk to the school and have me put back in my regular classes, but they didn't seem to care. Since there was only a month left in the school year when I was moved, they told me just to *ride it out*. So, that's what I was trying to do.

"It is what it is," I said and then turned my attention to the history book.

I opened the book and began flipping through the chapters, examining the old photos it contained. Doing that was far more interesting than staring at the wall until my name was called.

I managed to get about halfway through the book before Officer Reed returned.

"You're next, Ms. Daniels," Mr. Howard announced.

Constance started to gather her things, but Mr. Howard stopped her.

"You can't take that with you," he said.

Constance scoffed but complied by dropping everything on top of her desk before following Officer Reed out of the room.

After they left, I returned my attention to the book. Fifteen minutes passed before Officer Reed returned.

Mr. Howard got to his feet and set his gaze upon Shawn. "Your turn, Mr. Mentzer," he said.

As soon as the door closed behind Shawn, Mr. Howard walked over and sat at the desk next to mine.

"Something wrong, Mr. Howard?" I asked him.

He took a deep breath and let it out with a sigh. "The others are right, you don't belong in this class," he replied.

"Then why am I here?" I've tried to get someone to answer that question for me for the past month, but everybody kept brushing me off.

"Because your parents asked for you to be here," Mr. Howard said.

"Why would they do that?" I was confused by his revelation. "I haven't done anything wrong." Not that I knew of, at least.

"Have you read the chapter on the Morton family?" Mr. Howard placed his hand on the history book as he asked his question.

"Yeah," I nodded. "They seemed like horrible people."

Outcast from England for their religious practices, the Morton family, along with families sympathetic to them, were exiled to the New World, where they founded the town of Mouthsend. When they claimed the coastal land that the town sits on, they drove out the Native American tribes who inhabited the area, killing hundreds, if not thousands, of them in the process.

"They are horrible people," Mr. Howard corrected me, "and that's why your life is in danger."

"What?" I searched his face for any sign that he was joking, but he appeared completely serious.

"I don't have much time to explain," he said, looking toward the classroom door. "So I need you to listen to me very carefully, okay?"

I nodded.

"The Morton family still controls this town," he continued.

"I thought they were all dead," I interrupted, remembering what I had learned in my original history class before I was transferred to Mr. Howard's class.

"Not quite," he answered. "That is not dead which can eternal lie."

His cryptic statement may have made sense to him, but it sounded like nonsense to me.

"I don't have enough time to explain," he said. "In about five minutes, Officer Reed is going to come in here and escort you to the catacombs beneath the school."

"The what?" Mr. Howard was starting to sound crazier by the minute.

"The catacombs," he repeated.

I could tell that having to stop and answer my questions was making him feel exasperated.

"Look, Anthony," he said, using my first name for the first time, "there is no lesson. When Officer Reed takes you out of this room, he is going to take you to the catacombs to sacrifice you to the monsters that call themselves the Morton family. That's what's already happened to Ronnie, Constance, and Shawn." His voice continued to rise as he talked. "Typically, we only do this to the worst students. Unfortunately for you," he jabbed his finger at my chest, "your parents asked the principal to make a special exception. I would've told you sooner if I could've, but I couldn't risk them finding out. If they knew I was doing this, they'd force me to join you, which is why it must look like you escaped on your own."

Mr. Howard could tell I was about to ask another question, but he stopped me with an outstretched hand.

"It's true," he insisted. "Your fellow students are dead, and your parents wanted you to join them. If you don't want that to happen to you, I need you to shut up and listen to me, okay? We are running out of time."

I nodded.

"Good." He lowered his voice to an amicable volume and pulled a folded-up sheet of paper from his pocket.

"This is a map of the catacombs," Mr. Howard explained as he held the paper out to me.

I unfolded it and set it on my desk.

"This is the quickest way out," he said, pointing at the line he had drawn through the maze of tunnels. "If you follow it, you will come out of the caves down by the harbor. From there, you need to get out of town as quickly as possible and never come back."

"What about the Morton family?" I asked.

If they were in the catacombs waiting for me, how was I going to escape without them catching me?

"Here." Mr. Howard reached into his pocket again. When he withdrew his hand, he was holding a small rock with an odd, star-like symbol etched into it. "This is an Elder Sign," he explained. "It's the only thing the Morton family is afraid of."

"What am I supposed to do with it?"

"Wield it like you would a cross to a vampire," he replied. "They won't dare come near you as long as you're holding it."

Out in the hall, footsteps could be heard coming in our direction.

Mr. Howard shot to his feet. "Put that stuff away," he gestured at the map and the Elder Sign, before hurrying back over to his desk.

I quickly obliged, shoving the paper and rock into the pocket of my jeans.

As I watched Mr. Howard rush away, something occurred to me.

"If we were all supposed to be sacrificed to the Morton family, why did Darlene get to leave?"

"Her family made a sizable donation to the police force," Mr. Howard said as he took a seat behind his desk. "That earned her a reprieve."

As soon as he was done speaking, Officer Reed opened the door and entered the classroom.

"Your turn, Mr. Hartley," Mr. Howard said to me.

As I closed the door behind me, I thought I heard him whisper, "Good luck."

"This is our stop," Officer Reed announced.

We'd walked side by side down into the basement until we came to the door that led into the boiler room.

"Go in," he gestured at the door.

I pushed the door open and walked inside. Officer Reed followed behind me.

"You're a lot quieter than the others," he remarked.

I didn't know if he was expecting a response, so I decided to keep my mouth shut. If I did try to say anything, I was afraid I might give away just how scared I was, and that might make him suspicious. I didn't want to give him any indication that I knew what was going on.

"I'm not complaining, mind you," he continued. "I just assumed you'd be as mouthy as the others. I like it. It makes my job a lot less stressful. I wish the others were like you." Officer Reed placed his hand on my back and pushed me forward. "Keep walking," he ordered.

He had me walk across the room and stop in front of a large metal door that was latched shut. It reminded me of the hatches I'd seen on some of the larger fishing vessels that were moored in the harbor.

"Open it," Officer Reed said.

I grabbed hold of the latch and yanked it up, causing it to squeal in protest. Once the latch was free, I swung the door open to reveal a set of stone stairs leading down into an impenetrable darkness.

The catacombs.

A cold, dry breeze wafted up the stairs, bringing with it the stench of dirt and decay.

How am I supposed to find my way out of that? I can't see a damn thing.

As I stood there staring, something grunted in the darkness.

"Go in," Officer Reed said. "Your classmates are waiting for you."

When I turned and looked back at him, he had a smirk on his face.

"Go," he said, more firmly this time.

I shook my head. "I'm not going." I could feel my knees start to tremble.

"Don't make me throw you down there, kid." Officer Reed took a step toward me.

I spread my arms and legs, bracing them against the door frame.

"Goddammit, kid," he cursed, striding across the room.

When Officer Reed made it to the doorway, he tried to push me through it, but I held on fast despite the pain it was causing me.

"I guess we're going to have to do this the hard way." He took three steps back before he came charging at me like a bull.

I considered trying to run around him, but I didn't think I'd make it past him. Officer Reed was a big man, and there wasn't that much room between us.

There's only one thing to do, I thought as I watched him coming at me, *and that's get out of his way.*

Right before Officer Reed's shoulder would have connected with my chest, I stepped through the doorway and flattened myself against the wall.

The move surprised him, sending him off balance and stumbling down the steps into the darkness. As soon as he was out of sight, a flurry of activity sounded below me.

"STAY BACK!" I heard Officer Reed yell. This was followed a second later by a gunshot.

The loud sound echoed through the catacombs, startling me in the process.

Before I could recover my senses, Officer Reed appeared at the bottom of the stairs. His clothing was covered in blood, but I couldn't tell if it was his or not.

His face was a mask of fury as he started running up the stairs.

"You're so dead," he growled, pointing his pistol at me.

Unable to get my legs to move, I closed my eyes and waited for the shot that would end my life.

BANG!

I jumped, expecting the bullet to punch into me, but it never happened.

I opened my eyes and saw why.

As Officer Reed was lining up his shot, one of the things in the catacombs grabbed hold of his ankles and knocked him off his feet. That caused his shot to go wide and his pistol to fly out of his hand, landing on the steps between us.

Do I dare? I stared at the pistol, wondering if I should grab it.

It was only a few feet away.

Do it! I screamed at myself.

I raced down the steps and reached for the pistol. As my hand closed around it, the long, bony fingers of one of the Morton family creatures wrapped around my wrist and started pulling me toward it.

I tried to line the pistol up with its hideous fish-like head so I could shoot it, but I couldn't get a clear shot.

If I didn't do something fast, the creature was going to drag me into the dark, where the rest of the monsters were waiting to tear me apart.

That's when I remembered the rock Mr. Howard had given me, the Elder Sign.

I jabbed my free hand into my pocket and fumbled the rock free, almost dropping it in the process.

Please work! I begged, thrusting the rock into the creature's face.

As soon as it saw the Elder Sign, it hissed, releasing its hold on my wrist to cover its face with its hands.

Finally free, I ran back up the steps, closed the door, and latched it.

"Anthony?" Mr. Howard was surprised to see me.

After I returned from the basement, I found Mr. Howard in the hall, leaving the classroom.

"What're you doing here?" His eyes moved to the pistol I was holding by my side. "And what are you doing with that?"

"You don't get to ask the questions," I said, raising the gun and pointing it at him. "I do."

"I tried to help you, Anthony," he said, raising his hands with his palms out.

"What about all of the others you could've helped?" I snapped. "How many kids did you send to their deaths before your conscience finally caught up to you?"

"I didn't have a choice, Anthony," Mr. Howard insisted.

"You always had a choice," I said, letting the sound of the gun punctuate my statement.

The bullet struck him in the abdomen, doubling him over.

I closed the distance between us and pointed the gun at his head.

"What're you doing, Anthony?" he whined.

"Something that should've been done a long time ago," I replied right before I shot him between the eyes.

From there, I walked home.

DOUBLE VISION

"We've got a problem, Dr. Paulson," my assistant, Noel, said as she barged into the women's restroom.

"What kind of problem?" I asked as I continued to scrub the blood from my hands.

"The serious kind." She sounded worried. "One of the security guards saw what you did and called the police. They'll be here any minute."

"I thought you sent the guards home," I said, walking over to the towel dispenser to dry my hands.

"I did," Noel said. "But one of them left something at the guard station and came back to retrieve it, and that's when he saw you." She was so nervous that she was wringing her hands. "The security cameras recorded the whole thing."

"I thought you said you turned the cameras off." I felt myself starting to get annoyed but pushed those feelings aside because that wasn't going to help either of us.

"I did that too, I swear." Noel was clearly flustered. "But the guard turned them back on when he returned to the desk and saw that they were off."

I took a deep breath and exhaled, using the time to collect my thoughts. What should have been an evening to celebrate had turned into a potential public relations nightmare.

"Calm down," I said to Noel, trying to take my own advice. "It's not as bad as it seems."

"What are we going to do?" There was an annoying whine in her voice. "I can't go down there and talk to the police without making things worse."

"You're not going to do anything about this," I said, placing a hand on her shoulder. "What you're going to do is go back down to the lab and finish cleaning up."

"But..." Noel tried to protest.

I cut her off with a raised hand. "No buts. I'm the one who created this problem, so I'm the one who's going to deal with it. To do that, I'm going to need you to finish cleaning up the lab ASAP."

"Okay," she relented and turned to leave the restroom. "Call me if you need me."

"I will," I replied as I watched her walk out.

Once she was gone, I checked my appearance in the mirror, staring at the blood splattered across the front of my blouse.

Nothing I can do about that now, I thought.

Five minutes later, I walked out of the elevator and into the lobby, where several police officers were gathered around the guard station.

They were so busy watching the surveillance video of me murdering someone that they hadn't heard me approach.

"Is there something I can help you with, gentlemen?" I asked to announce my presence.

They all whirled around to face me.

"That's the woman from the video," one of the officers said, pointing at me.

"Keep your hands where I can see them," another man said, drawing his pistol and pointing it at me.

I assumed he was a detective from the suit he was wearing and, therefore, the highest-ranking officer of the group.

"This is all just a big misunderstanding," I said to the detective, raising my hands. "I assure you I can explain."

"Cuff her," the detective said to the officer closest to him.

"If you want to keep your job," I warned, "I suggest you let me explain before you take me down to the station."

The officer who was coming to cuff me stopped and looked back at the detective to see if he should proceed.

"What's there to explain?" he replied. "I've seen the security footage."

"If you'll follow me down to my lab," I gestured at the elevators, "I can prove that what you think you saw didn't happen the way you think it did."

"Save it for your lawyer," he snapped. To the officer, he said, "Cuff her."

"The woman you think you saw me kill on that video is not dead," I said. "She's alive and well and waiting for us in my lab."

When the detective didn't respond, I said, "I can show you. If you'll let me." I gestured at the guard station.

The detective called off the officer who was about to cuff me and holstered his gun. "You've got five minutes." He motioned for me to approach the guard station.

Once I was standing in front of the cameras, I instructed the guard to pull up a specific camera feed from the basement hallway and rewind it.

"There she is," I pointed.

The video showed Noel exiting the bathroom after she'd warned me that the police were coming.

"Look at the time stamp," I pointed at the bottom of the screen.

"Is that the same woman?" the detective asked the guard.

"It looks like her," the guard admitted.

"What the hell is going on here?" he asked, looking from the guard to me.

Confused by the contradicting videos showing Noel alive after I'd killed her, the guard shrugged.

"I have no idea," he said.

"I can explain it to you," I said. "But we're going to have to go down to my lab before I can."

"Fine," the detective agreed. "Let's go."

He started to lead his men to the elevator, but I stopped him.

"This is a government-funded laboratory," I said. "What I'm about to show you is for your eyes only." I pointed at the detective. "They're going to have to wait up here." I swept my hand toward the other officers.

"Wait here," he said to his men. "Don't let anyone in or out until I get back," he instructed.

Once we reached the basement, I led the detective to the doors of my lab. Before I could use my badge to open them, the detective stopped in the hall and looked around.

"This is where it happened," he said. "Isn't it?"

He stopped and began to examine the area where he'd seen the murder take place on the security video.

"You did a good job cleaning up," he said. "But not good enough." He looked up and pointed at the drop of blood clinging to the ceiling.

"That won't matter once I've explained." I held my ID badge up to the electronic lock.

The lock beeped, and I opened the door to the lab.

"After you," I gestured for the detective to enter before me.

"Ladies first," he countered.

I obliged and walked into the lab.

"Where is she?" the detective asked after looking around and not seeing anyone.

I figured Noel must have hidden when she heard the door open, so I called out to her.

"It's okay, Noel, you can come out," I said.

The door to one of the supply closets creaked open, and Noel stepped out.

"Noel," I said, "this is Detective... I'm sorry, I didn't catch your name." I turned to look at him.

"Barlow," he replied. "Detective Barlow."

"This is Noel," I gestured, "the woman you saw on the video. As you can see, she is alive and well, just as I said she would be."

"How is this possible?" He stepped up to Noel and walked around her, staring at her as if she were some kind of freak. "I saw you die."

Noel chose to keep her mouth shut and instead looked to me for guidance.

"As I said, I could explain," I replied. "But I seriously doubt you'd believe me. That is why I'm going to have to show you instead."

I started walking to the center of the lab, where a large, sealed chamber housed a sleek-looking machine that rose all the way to the ceiling.

"Follow me," I instructed, unlocking the door and motioning for the detective to follow me into the chamber.

Once we were inside, I walked over to the machine in the center of the room and powered it up.

"You might want to get your gun ready," I warned him.

"Why?" he asked.

"Because you're going to need it."

Even though Detective Barlow had a look of disbelief on his face, he still drew his pistol.

"Here we go," I smiled.

I pushed the button and started the machine. A few moments later, there were several flashes of light, and then two people appeared before us.

The light from the machine was so blinding that it was hard to see the people, but we could easily tell one was a man and the other a woman by their silhouettes.

When the man raised his arm and pointed at us, Detective Barlow's instincts took over.

"He's got a gun," he cried out, pulling the trigger of his own gun and shooting the man before he could get a shot off.

The man collapsed to the floor.

The woman then lunged for the gun.

"Watch out," I yelled, but Detective Barlow was already aware of the new threat.

He fired two shots. Both hit the woman in the center of her chest, knocking her to the ground.

"Where the hell did they come from?" he turned to face me.

By then, the machine had begun to power down, and the lights had shut off. Our vision was starting to return to normal.

"They didn't come from anywhere," I explained. "We did. When I turned on the machine, it sent us exactly two seconds into the past, where we encountered the past versions of ourselves. You know what happened then." I gestured at the bodies.

"The same thing happened when Noel tested the machine for the first time," I continued. "Unfortunately, the past version of herself managed to make it out into the hall before I could stop her. Knowing that two versions of her could not be allowed to exist, I had to kill her."

"You're insane." Detective Barlow stared at me. Then he considered it for a moment. "Wait. Wouldn't that cause a paradox? How could you kill the past version of Noel without it affecting the future one?" He looked at our bodies again as he realized the same thing applied to us. "We should all be dead."

"We're not dead because time isn't a straight line," I replied. "This machine proves that. When we used it, we created a branch in time. That's how two versions of us could exist in the same place at the same time—two different versions of us, each with separate timelines."

"You make it sound like we became different people," he pointed out.

"I suppose that's technically true," I said.

"If that's the case," the detective pulled out his handcuffs and slapped them on my wrist, "then you murdered an innocent woman. It didn't matter if she was from the past or the future; she was still a human being."

"Did you forget what you just did?" I scoffed at the idea of being arrested for murdering Noel after the detective had just shot and killed the two of us.

"That was self-defense," he replied. "If I hadn't shot them, they would've shot us first."

Three years later.

"All right, Paulson, come with me," the warden opened my cell and motioned for me to follow him.

He led me across the prison to a wing I'd never been in before.

"Where are we going?" I asked.

"Your time's up. You've won your appeal. You're getting out of here," the warden said as he unlocked a door and held it open for me.

I'd been tried and convicted for what the press referred to as the world's first temporal murder. I was sentenced to life in prison without the possibility of parole, but my lawyer had been fighting that verdict for years. I was shocked to hear that we'd actually won.

"I'm actually free?" I couldn't believe what I was hearing.

"Well," he smiled as I stepped into the room and saw a familiar-looking machine, "technically speaking, you're not free. The judge decided that you still needed to pay for your crimes, so he came up with a clever solution. We're going to use your machine to create a temporal double of you. That version of you will get to go free, while this version"—he gestured at me—"has a date with the gas chamber."

TYPEWRITER

A knock on the door announced the arrival of my guest. After looking through the peephole to make sure he was alone, I unlocked the door and swung it open.

"Mr. Sutton?" I asked, making sure he was the man I was expecting.

"Yes," the man replied, "but you can just call me Travis."

Travis was a slender man who appeared to be in his mid-to-late thirties. The tweed suit he was wearing made him look like a college professor.

"You didn't tell anyone you were coming here, did you?" I asked. "Because if you did, the deal is off."

"I didn't tell anyone," Travis replied. "I swear." He held up a hand as if taking an oath.

"Is that your car?" I nodded toward the vehicle that was parked a few houses up on the opposite side of the street.

"No," he shook his head. "I took the bus and walked here like you told me to."

He was lying. I knew it was his car because I had watched him pull up and get out of it. But I wasn't bothered by that. At least he'd had the presence of mind to park farther up the street instead of in front of my house. If he had parked in front of the house, I would have told him the deal was off and to go on his merry way.

I knew I was being overly cautious, but I was only doing that because I didn't want anyone to find out why he was at my house.

"Did you bring the money?"

Travis nodded. "But I'm going to need proof that you really are Simon Lamb's daughter before I hand it over."

Simon Lamb, my father, was a horror author who'd written over 40 best-selling novels before he passed away. He had millions of fans around the world, but none of them knew I existed. And that's the way my father wanted it. He was a very private man who went to great lengths to keep his life out of the public eye. He never gave interviews, never went on book tours, and despite his publisher hounding him, he never supplied them with a picture of himself for any of his books. Instead, he sent them a photo of the typewriter all his books were written on.

I didn't even know my father was Simon Lamb until a few weeks ago, when the executor of his estate read his will to me. Up until that point, I'd known him as Walter Lawrence, my embarrassing and often overprotective father. To say I was shocked to hear that he was also a world-famous author would be an understatement.

I had no idea if my mother knew my father's secret or not, and I couldn't ask her since she'd passed away a decade before him.

"I have the typewriter," I replied to his demand for proof. "Isn't that proof enough?"

"How do I know it was really his?" he countered.

Having tried and failed to sell the typewriter before, I was ready for his skepticism.

I reached into my back pocket and pulled out a thin, paperback copy of the last book my father had written. I turned the book around and held it up so Travis could see the black-and-white photo of the typewriter displayed on the back.

"This is all the proof you're going to get," I held the book out to him. "Once you compare the picture to the real thing, you will see that it's authentic."

Travis took the book and looked at the picture.

"Satisfied?" I asked.

"Not really," he replied, handing the book back to me. "But I guess it'll have to do."

"If you don't think it's the real thing, you don't have to buy it," I said, taking the book and putting it back in my pocket. "There are plenty of other people out there who'd be happy to take it off my hands."

Before Travis, I had tried to sell the typewriter to three other people, but none of them were confident enough that I was selling the real thing. One of them was so certain that I was a fraud that she reported me to the local police.

I thought for certain the family secret was going to come out then, but it didn't, thanks to my father's lawyer, who was now my lawyer.

"Do you want to see it or not?" I asked, giving him a chance to back out before I wasted any more time on him.

"Yeah," Travis nodded. "I do."

"Then show me the money," I said. "I'm not letting you in until I know you're serious about buying it."

Travis stared at me for a moment, clearly thinking about whether he wanted to proceed, before reaching behind his back.

His hesitation made me think he wasn't really serious about buying the typewriter. He probably just wanted to touch it so he could say he laid hands on the typewriter used by Simon Lamb.

Just another crazy fan, I thought, *he probably doesn't even have the money.*

I considered closing the door in his face but decided to give him the benefit of the doubt and see if I might be wrong about him.

When I saw Travis's hand again, it was not holding a wallet as I expected. It was holding a small black pistol.

I should've closed the door.

I took a step back and pushed on the door, thinking I might still have time to close and lock it before he could get through the doorway.

"Don't," Travis warned, lunging forward to put his foot in the way of the closing door.

Since that didn't work, I turned to run but didn't make it very far. Travis pushed his shoulder against the door, forcing it open and catching me in the back in the process. The blow knocked me facedown onto the floor of the foyer.

"Get up," Travis said, stepping into the house and closing the door behind him.

It took me a moment to gather my senses and comply.

"Hurry up," he snapped.

I had to reach up and use the banister at the bottom of the steps to help myself to my feet.

"Where is it?" Travis stood in the foyer, looking through the archways on either side of the entryway.

The archway to the right led into the dining room. The one to the left led into the sitting room. I couldn't stop my eyes from flicking over to the sitting room after he asked me where the typewriter was.

Travis saw my reaction and motioned me in that direction with his gun. "Let's go," he said.

I slowly walked through the foyer and into the sitting room. From there, I crossed the room until I reached the door on the far side.

As I walked, I considered grabbing a lamp from one of the end tables and using it as a weapon, but I quickly decided that wasn't a good idea. I'd have to grab the lamp, then turn around and swing it at Travis. I didn't think I could do all of that before he was able to pull the trigger, so I decided to wait and see if a better opportunity would present itself.

"Open it," Travis said, referring to the door in front of me.

I reached into the pocket of my jeans, pulled out an antique house key, and used it to unlock the door of my father's office. Even though he was gone, I kept the door locked the way he always did when he wasn't using it.

"The typewriter is in there," I gestured through the open doorway, hoping Travis would go in before me.

The door to the office was one of the old ones that required a key to lock and unlock it from either side. If I could get Travis to go in, I might be able to pull the door shut and lock him inside. Unfortunately, that's not what happened.

"Show me," Travis motioned me into the office with the gun.

I took two steps inside the room, keeping close to the door in case I got the opportunity to run. Travis followed close behind me.

"There it is," I pointed at the typewriter sitting covered on the large mahogany desk in the center of the room. "Take it and go."

Travis walked around the desk and stood in front of the typewriter. With his free hand, he unlocked the clasps of the case and lifted the top free, setting it down next to the typewriter. Then he reached into the inside pocket of his jacket and pulled out a photograph.

While he stood there, looking from the photograph to the typewriter, I started inching my way to the doorway. I was just about to bolt through it when he stopped and looked in my direction.

"Did your father ever tell you how he got this typewriter?" Travis gestured at it with the hand holding the gun.

"No," I shook my head. "I didn't know it existed until after he died."

It was the truth. After reading my father's will, his lawyer gave me a set of keys for a storage unit across town after informing me that my father had one condition that must be met before his estate would be released to me. When I asked what that condition was, the lawyer pointed at the keys and said, "That's for your father to tell you."

When I went to the storage unit, the only things I found inside were a foldout table, the typewriter, and a stack of unpublished manuscripts. Taped to the front of the typewriter was a handwritten note from my father informing me that his estate would not be released to me until I had sold the typewriter to another writer and presented proof of the sale to the lawyer.

It was an odd demand, but one I was ready to abide by. I had no use for an antique typewriter, but I did have a use for all that money my father had squirreled away.

"He stole it," Travis's words cut through my thoughts, bringing me back to the present.

"How do you know that?" I asked.

"Because he stole it from my grandfather." Travis handed me the photo he'd been holding.

The black-and-white photo showed a man, who looked familiar, leaning against a desk with an even more familiar-looking typewriter sitting next to him.

"That photo was taken months before my grandfather disappeared," Travis explained.

"Why are you so sure that's the same typewriter?" I asked.

I agreed that it looked like my father's typewriter, but there were probably hundreds of the same model of typewriter out there. It wasn't like the manufacturer only made one.

"Look at the keys," Travis instructed.

I held the photo closer to my eyes so I could see the typewriter better.

"Some of the keys are missing," I said once I'd figured out what I was looking for.

"The same keys are missing from this one," he gestured at the typewriter on the desk.

"That still doesn't prove it's the same one," I said. "Those keys could have been defective for all models of that typewriter." I knew that was a stretch when I said it, but I was grasping at straws to prove him wrong.

"There's also this," Travis reached into the inside pocket of his jacket again, pulling out a folded-up piece of paper that he held out to me.

"What's this?" I asked.

"Read it," he replied.

I unfolded the piece of paper and looked at it. It appeared to be a photocopy of an old police report. As I read the report, two names jumped out at me. One belonged to my father, the other to a famous horror author—a man credited with revolutionizing the genre.

"Your grandfather was Harold Holt?"

"He was," Travis confirmed. "And according to that," he pointed at the police report, "your father was the last person to see him alive."

Anybody who is a fan of horror knows some version of the story surrounding Harold Holt's disappearance. Some of the stories are simple, like he just didn't want to write any longer and called it quits, choosing to step out of the spotlight in a sensational way, and some are works of elaborate fiction. The most popular of which says the author became a victim of the otherworldly monsters he often wrote about. The only thing the stories all agree on is that one day, he just up and vanished without a trace.

Reading that my father might somehow be involved in Harold Holt's disappearance added a new story to the mix.

"Where did you get this?" I asked.

If my father really was the last person to see Harold Holt alive, why was this the first time I was hearing about it? Information like that would have been woven into the stories that were circulating about his disappearance.

"I found it among my grandmother's things," Travis replied, "along with the photograph."

"How come nobody's mentioned this before?" I didn't want to believe it was real. "Have you seen the original? Are you sure it's not fake?"

Maybe you faked it yourself, I thought.

Travis ignored my questions and asked a couple of his own. "Don't you think it's just a little bit suspicious that the typewriter my grandfather used to own ends up in your father's possession? Isn't that proof enough that there's some credibility to the report?"

"If you really believe all of this, why didn't you just tell me instead of pulling out a gun?" I flicked my hand at the pistol he was holding by his side.

"I didn't think you'd believe me," he said, "and with the price you were asking for the typewriter, I didn't think you'd just hand it over if you did believe me."

"You don't know me very well then," I said. "If my father stole that typewriter from your grandfather, then I want nothing to do with it."

I didn't want to acknowledge that he probably killed the older man to get it, so I left that part unsaid.

The more I thought about it, the more disgusted I became. As much as I didn't want to believe the evidence before me, I had to accept the fact that my father was somehow involved in the disappearance of Harold Holt. Even if he wasn't directly involved, he likely knew who was and kept that information to himself.

As far as I was concerned, this revelation tainted his entire legacy. I was happy that only a handful of people knew who he really was.

"How much money do you have on you?" I blurted out.

"What?" Travis was confused by the question.

"How much money do you have?" I repeated. "According to the terms of my father's will, I have to sell the typewriter to get the deed to this house and access to all his financial holdings," I explained. "It didn't say how much I have to sell it for."

Travis reached into his back pocket with his free hand, pulled out his wallet, and fumbled it open.

"I have four dollars." He pulled the bills out and tossed them onto the desk.

"Now we just have to make it official," I announced as I picked up the money.

"What do you mean?" Travis asked.

"The executor of my father's estate has to approve the sale of the typewriter; otherwise, I won't get my inheritance."

On the far side of my father's desk was an old touch-tone phone. I took a step toward it, reaching out for the handset.

"What are you doing?" Travis raised the gun and pointed it at me.

"Calling the lawyer," I replied, my hand hovering over the phone. "You want the typewriter. I need to sell the typewriter. This gets us what we both want without you needing that," I nodded toward the gun.

"It's not a trick," I insisted when he didn't lower the gun. "If it'll make you feel better, you can dial the number for me."

"Go ahead and call," Travis finally lowered the gun, but he didn't put it away. He kept it by his side, ready to use.

Not wanting to worry him, I slowly picked up the handset and dialed the number.

The phone rang three times before Mr. Emory, the lawyer, answered.

"Hi, Mr. Emory, it's Lily," I said. "I was wondering if you could come over and validate the sale of the typewriter for me?"

"Of course," he replied. "I'll gather my things and be over shortly."

"Thanks," I said before hanging up.

"He's on his way," I said to Travis. "You can put that away now," I gestured at the gun.

Travis turned the gun in his hand, staring at it for a moment before sliding it back into the waistband of his pants.

"I was never going to shoot you," that was his way of apologizing. "It's not even loaded."

"Don't worry about it," I waved off the apology. "Let's just get through this, and then we can both forget it ever happened."

"How long will it take for him to get here?" Travis asked.

"Ten minutes or so," I replied. "He lives just up the road."

Mr. Emory was a friend of the family from the neighborhood. Even though he was retired from practicing law, he'd promised my father he'd oversee his estate and stay on long enough to help me through the process.

Not knowing what else to say, Travis began looking around the room, trying to keep himself from looking awkward. After he'd seen everything there was to see in the office, he turned his attention to the typewriter.

"What are you going to do with it?" I asked.

"Take it back to where it belongs," he said, reaching out to caress the keys with his left hand.

I assumed he was referring to the home of his grandfather, Harold Holt, which had been turned into a small museum celebrating the life of the acclaimed horror writer. I thought that would be a great place for it. Unfortunately, Travis never got the opportunity to take it there.

As soon as his fingers brushed against the keys of the typewriter, the true nature of the device was revealed.

Travis cried out as the keys came to life, lashing out like metal tentacles to wrap around his outstretched fingers.

He struggled to free his hand but, in the process, got his other hand snared by the keys.

"Help me!" he pleaded as the keys started pulling him into the typewriter.

In shock, I just stood there watching as the flesh of Travis's arms was shredded as they were forced through the narrow openings between the keys. As the typewriter ate him, it made a clacking sound, as if someone were typing away at the keys.

No matter how hard Travis struggled, he couldn't free himself. Despite his frantic attempts, the typewriter never moved, seemingly stuck to the desk as if it were bolted down.

Travis continued to beg for help until the keys were able to wrap themselves around his neck, turning his pleas into choking gasps for air.

That's when I closed my eyes and waited for it to end.

I stood there like that until I heard someone knocking on the front door.

I opened my eyes and looked at the desk.

The typewriter was still sitting there. The only sign that Travis had been in the house were the four dollar bills that were in my pocket.

"Lily! Are you in there?" Mr. Emory called out from the front porch as he knocked on the door again.

"Be right there," I called back, reaching up to wipe the tears that had fallen from my eyes as I stood there and did nothing to save Travis.

Once I felt composed, I walked into the foyer and opened the door. "Thanks for coming," I said to Mr. Emory, "but I'm afraid the buyer changed his mind."

I didn't know what else to say to him. I didn't think he'd believe me if I told him that the typewriter ate Travis.

"That's a shame," Mr. Emory replied.

"Sorry I wasted your time," I said.

"It doesn't have to be a waste of time."

"What do you mean?" I had no idea what he was implying by that.

"I've been thinking," he explained, "and I've decided that I will buy the typewriter from you. There is nothing in your father's will that precludes me from doing so, and this will save you the hassle of trying to find another buyer."

I was surprised and horrified by his offer.

"I... I don't think that's a good idea," I said.

"Really?" He was surprised that I didn't jump at his offer. "Why not?"

"I... I'm thinking about keeping it," I blurted out. That was the only thing I could think to say.

"Okay," he replied. "Well... if you change your mind, you know where to find me." He turned to leave.

"Sorry, Mr. Emory," I apologized again as he walked away.

"It was no bother," he said, waving off the apology.

I watched him walk out of sight before closing the door.

"Now what?" I said to myself, wondering what I should do with the typewriter. I knew I didn't want to touch it, which would make getting rid of it that much harder.

The sound of the typewriter's keys clacking drew my attention back to the office.

Cautiously, I walked across the sitting room until I was standing in the doorway of the office. To my surprise, I found the typewriter furiously spitting out page after page of text, shooting them into the air where they fluttered to the ground in a haphazard pile.

I reached down and picked up the nearest page, reading the typewritten words upon it. From what I could tell, it seemed to be a story of some sort.

I waited until the typewriter finished before picking up all the pages and organizing them by page number.

Blood Money, I read the title of the 400-page novel the typewriter had spat out. Below that were the words: Written by Lily Lawrence.

I dropped the novel and left the office, closing and locking the door behind me as the implications of what my father had done came crashing down on me.

He wasn't Simon Lamb, the typewriter was.

Then I thought about all the books my father had published.

Did each book require a sacrifice?

I avoided the office for a week before finally getting up the courage to go back inside. When I did, there was a single piece of paper sticking out of the typewriter. I reached over and pulled it out as quickly as I could.

There were only two words typed out on the page: FEED ME.

MOM

I walked into the house, dropped my bookbag on the floor next to the door, and announced my presence.

"Mom," I called out, "I'm home."

She always made a big deal about letting her know when I got home from school so she wouldn't worry about me.

I waited for her typical "Okay," which was usually followed by information about what and when we were having dinner, but it never came.

"Mom?" I repeated, making my way to the kitchen where she usually was at that time of day.

When I crossed through the entryway, a gruesome sight awaited me.

Lying on the floor in a growing pool of blood was my dad, and standing over him with a knife in her hand was my mom.

"This is not what it looks like," my mom insisted as she took a step toward me.

I backed away from her and bumped into the wall.

She continued to walk toward me with the knife in her hand.

I scooted along the wall, maintaining the distance between us.

"Please," she begged, "let me explain."

I looked at the knife.

She followed my gaze and acted like she didn't know the knife was in her hand.

"I'm not going to hurt you," she said, setting the knife on a nearby counter. "See?" She held her hands out in a placating gesture while still moving toward me.

Not wanting her to get too close, I stepped to the side and circled the island in the middle of the kitchen.

"I didn't kill your father," she insisted, "your mother did."

"You are my mom," I replied, confused.

She stopped and looked down at herself. "I only look like your mother on the outside," she said. "Inside"—she placed a hand on her chest—"I'm... someone else."

She sounded crazy.

"If you give me a moment, I can explain," she continued.

Not wanting to provoke her in any way, I decided it was best to play along with her until I could get out of the house and call the cops.

"Okay," I said. "I'm listening."

My mom relaxed her posture.

"My name is Mumizal," she said, "and I'm a demon."

We stared at each other as I processed what she had said.

"You're a demon?" I scoffed. "That's the story you're going with?"

"I know how crazy that must sound, but I swear to you, I'm telling you the truth," she insisted.

"Then prove it." I folded my arms across my chest. "If you can."

"Okay," Mumizal replied.

As I watched, my mom's eyes turned solid black and she levitated toward the ceiling.

"I can also speak in tongues and projectile vomit if you need more proof," the demon said as she lowered herself back to the ground.

"That won't be necessary," I backed away, putting as much distance between me and the demon as I could while looking for a way out of the house.

"You can relax," Mumizal said, holding out a hand. "I have no desire to hurt you."

"Then what are you doing here?" I asked. "And why did you kill my dad?" I gestured at his body lying a few feet away on the floor.

I figured if I could keep the demon talking, that would give me more time to figure out a way to escape.

"I already told you I didn't kill your father." Mumizal sighed in frustration. "Look," she said, trying to level with me, "your mother summoned me." She pointed to an old leather-bound book lying open on the island counter. "Well, she tried to, anyway. Her Latin was a bit rusty, and her blood circle was a bit off." The demon looked down at the badly drawn pentagram on the floor, which I had missed when I first entered the kitchen.

"Instead of binding me to the circle as she'd intended," Mumizal continued, "she accidentally bound me to herself, forcing me to inhabit her body." The demon gestured at herself.

"Why would she do that?"

That didn't sound like her at all. My mom was your typical *Donna Reed-inspired* housewife. Committing murder and summoning demons did not seem like something she'd be capable of.

"Do you really want to know the answer to that?" Mumizal asked.

"I do," I replied, "but it's not like she can tell me." I gestured at the demon.

"She can't," Mumizal agreed, "but I can. I have access to all her memories." The demon tapped her head with her index finger.

"Like I'm going to trust you to tell me the truth," I replied.

"I could have just left, leaving you to deal with all this," she swept her hand across the kitchen, "but I didn't. I also could've killed you the moment you entered the room. But I didn't. That has to count for something."

"You're still a demon," I argued.

"As surprising as it may sound to you," Mumizal huffed, "not all demons are alike."

"I find that hard to believe," I said.

"And you're basing that opinion on what?" the demon asked. "What you've seen on television?"

"That and the fact that you're from Hell," I countered. "Doesn't that make you inherently evil?"

"Evil, yes," the demon agreed, "but that doesn't mean I'm incapable of telling the truth. In fact, as a dealmaker, I make it a point to be upfront and honest about the terms of all deals I make. Most people are so eager to accept that I don't need to lie about what's at stake."

"Dealmaker?" That one word stuck out to me. "Are you saying my mom summoned you to make a deal?"

"That was her intent, yes," Mumizal confirmed, "until she bungled the job."

"What kind of deal was she going to make?"

"She wanted to switch bodies with you." The demon pointed at me.

"Why would she want to do that?"

"Isn't it obvious?" Mumizal glanced over at my dad's body.

"Not really," I admitted.

"Seriously?" the demon scoffed. "Her motivation couldn't be more apparent."

"Well, it's not to me."

As far as I was aware, my mother was the perfect wife who didn't have a care in the world. Demon summoning and murder were not things I thought she was capable of. Therefore, her motivation for doing so was not as apparent to me as Mumizal thought it should be.

Taking pity on my ignorance, the demon sighed and explained, "By swapping bodies with you, your mother would get to start her life over as a teenager. All she had to do was get rid of the two people holding her back. Her plan was simple: kill your father, swap bodies with you, and then let you take the blame for her. You'd go to prison trapped in her body while she got to take over your life."

"Why would she do that to me?"

I thought we got along great. All my friends considered her the cool mom because of how lax she was with the rules when they were around. She let me stay out late, have the occasional drink, and even let me pick out my clothes and wear my makeup the way I wanted to.

The more I thought about it, the more I realized she acted more like an older sister to me than she did a mother.

"She did it because she despised you," Mumizal answered.

"You're lying," I blurted out.

"Am I?" The demon gave me a patronizing look. "I thought we'd already gotten past that."

"If she despised me, why was she always around?" I pointed out.

Mumizal shook her head, pitying me for not being able to see something that should have been obvious.

"She was always around because she wanted to be part of the group," the demon explained, "she blamed you for cutting her childhood short and was trying to relive her teenage years by insinuating herself into your group of friends."

The more I thought about it, the more the demon's comment made sense. That explained why she always offered to act as a chaperone whenever we wanted to go out, and why she always allowed me to have get-togethers at our house.

"That's not even the worst of it," Mumizal revealed, "she also slept with your ex-boyfriend, Keith."

Hearing that made me sick to my stomach.

I often wondered why Keith would come over to my house and wait for me to get home from soccer practice. Now I knew.

"She also..." the demon started to say, but I cut her off with an outstretched hand.

"I don't want to hear any more," I said.

Mumizal was about to tell me anyway, but a knock on the door stopped her.

The two of us looked at each other and then down at my father's body.

"Was my mom expecting company?" I asked.

"No," Mumizal replied with a shake of her head. "Were you?"

"No," I replied.

"Stay here." The demon gestured for me to wait in the kitchen. "I'll go see who it is."

As Mumizal went to answer the front door, I decided to make a break for the back door and get the hell out of there.

I was halfway there when I stopped and looked back at my dad's body lying on the floor. As I stared at him, an idea popped into my head.

If Mumizal had the power to switch people's bodies, maybe she could bring my father back.

"Change your mind about leaving?" the demon asked when she returned.

"Who was at the door?" I ignored her comment.

"Nosy neighbor," Mumizal replied, "she heard your mother arguing with your father before she killed him and wanted to make sure everything was all right."

"What did you tell her?"

"I told her to mind her own business; otherwise, something unpleasant was going to happen to her," the demon gave a wicked smile as she answered. When she saw the shocked look on my face, she said, "Calm down and give me a little credit. I'm not stupid. I told her everything was fine and thanked her for her concern."

"I don't think you're stupid," I tried to apologize.

"You might be, though," Mumizal quipped, "why didn't you leave when you had the chance? Any sane person would've been out that door and down the street if they were in your shoes." She gestured at the back door as she spoke.

"I want to make a deal," I said.

"You want to make a deal with me?" She pointed at herself.

I nodded.

"What kind of deal?"

"I want you to bring my dad back." The tears I'd been trying to hold back finally escaped from my eyes.

In a weird show of compassion, Mumizal walked over to me and put her arm around my shoulders to comfort me.

"I'm afraid that's not possible," she said.

"Why not?" I pulled away.

"Because I don't have the power to resurrect the dead," the demon explained. "Nobody does."

Hearing that made me cry even harder.

"What am I supposed to do now?" I sobbed.

My entire world had been flipped upside down.

"I have an idea," Mumizal said. "An informal deal of sorts," she clarified, "it won't fix the damage that's been done, but it will allow you to live your life almost as if nothing's happened."

I wiped my eyes and waited for her to elaborate.

"I'm in no hurry to go back to Hell," she said, "so I was thinking I could stick around and play the part of your mother until this body can't sustain me any longer."

"How long would that be?"

The demon held up her arms and examined them. "A decade or so," she said.

"What about my dad?" I pointed at his body. "How are you going to explain his absence?"

"After the fight he had with your mother, he decided he didn't want to be married to her any longer, so he left."

"And you think people will believe that he just up and left everything behind? His job? His friends?"

"We'll make them believe that," Mumizal said.

"We who?" I asked. "I'm not good at keeping secrets."

"I'm not the only demon up here," she revealed, "there are thousands of us scattered around the world. We can easily make it look like your father skipped town. In fact," she paused to think for a moment, "I think there's another of my kind already here in town."

"Seriously?"

Mumizal nodded. "If I recall correctly, I think she might be a principal at one of the schools. I'll give her a call, and we can get this whole situation sorted."

"What are you going to do with his body?"

"What would you like us to do with it?" Mumizal replied.

"I think he should be buried," I said. "Here at home."

"I don't think that will be a problem," she said. "Anything else?"

I thought about it for a moment, then shook my head.

"Do we have a deal then?" the demon held out a hand.

"Yeah, Mom." I shook her hand. "We have a deal."

MUD MOUTH

"Can I go outside and play with Andrew and Julian?" I asked.

"That depends," my mom said.

"On what?"

"On whether or not you finished cleaning your room like I asked."

"It's clean," I insisted, which was a half-truth.

I did gather up all my dirty clothes and put them in the laundry basket like she wanted, but I didn't pick up the toys that were scattered around the room. I didn't see the point. They were just going to end up back on the floor again later.

My mom gave me a knowing look, signifying that she knew I was lying, but she thankfully didn't call me on it.

"Go ahead," she shooed me toward the door. "Just be back in time for lunch."

"Okay," I agreed, racing to get outside.

"And stay out of the swamp!" my mom yelled right as I was closing the door behind me.

I didn't respond because the swamp was exactly where Andrew, Julian, and I were going that morning.

The swamp, as everyone called it, wasn't really a swamp. It was a lightly wooded area next to our neighborhood that tended to retain a lot of water whenever it rained, making the area swampy for days.

"Robbie!" my friend Andrew called to me from the street corner, waving his hand in the air. "Over here."

"Where's Julian?" I asked, walking over to meet him.

"He had to help his dad with something before he could come outside," Andrew replied. "He told me to wait for him here."

The stop sign at the corner of the cul-de-sac we lived on was our agreed-upon meeting place whenever one of us was waiting for the others.

We didn't have to wait long before Julian showed up. He came walking up the sidewalk a few minutes later, carrying a large empty pickle jar.

"What's that for?" Andrew pointed at the jar.

"In case we find anything we want to catch," Julian replied.

I was content to leave the animals we found in the swamp where they belonged. Julian, on the other hand, always talked about wanting to bring them home and make pets out of them. The jar meant that he was finally going to do it.

"Let's go," Julian declared, walking across the street to where the swamp began.

Andrew and I followed behind him.

"Where do you guys want to go?" Andrew asked once we'd walked down the embankment that marked the edge of the swamp. "The rocks or the pond?"

"It doesn't matter to me," I said, not caring where we went. I was content just being outside.

"Let's go down to the pond," Julian decided. "See if we can find any frogs."

That day, the swamp wasn't much of a swamp because it hadn't rained in a couple of weeks. The ground was still soft; it just wasn't muddy. If it were swampy, we wouldn't have been able to make it down to the pond because the surrounding area floods badly, making the mud like quicksand. I almost lost my shoes last time we went to the pond after a rainstorm. My mom was pissed when she saw how dirty they were. That was one of the reasons she didn't like me playing in the swamp.

It took us about 15 minutes to make it to the reed-enclosed area that marked the boundary of the pond. As we walked toward it, I started catching whiffs of a strong chemical odor that got worse the closer we got to the pond.

"Do you smell that?" I stopped walking, not wanting to go any farther until I knew where the stench was coming from.

"Yeah, I do," Andrew replied. "It really stinks."

"I thought it was you." Julian turned and looked at Andrew with a smile on his face.

"I thought it was your mom," Andrew sneered.

"Maybe we should go to the rocks instead," I suggested before their ribbing could escalate.

Whatever was causing the area to stink couldn't be healthy.

"If you can't handle the smell, you can go to the rocks," Julian said. "I'm staying. I don't think it's that bad."

I looked over at Andrew, hoping he'd side with me.

"We're already here," Andrew said. "Might as well stay."

Outvoted, I dropped the issue and followed them to the edge of the pond.

Once we were standing next to the water, it was clear the smell was coming from it.

"What the heck happened here?" Andrew gasped.

He was looking down at the dead minnows bobbing among the reeds along the shoreline. There were hundreds of them.

"I think someone poisoned the water," I said.

"How can you tell?" Julian asked.

"The smell," I answered. "It smells like chemicals to me."

The smell emanating from the water was so strong that it overpowered the scent of all the dead fish.

"Look over there." Andrew was pointing at the far side of the pond where a wide section of reeds had been flattened.

"Let's go check it out." Julian had started walking around the pond before he'd finished speaking.

When we made it to the other side of the pond, it was easy to see why the reeds were crushed. Someone had driven a vehicle down to the water's edge, leaving behind two muddy ruts in the ground.

"Those tracks look fresh," Andrew said.

I followed the tracks from the pond to a nearby fire access road.

"They probably came out here last night," I guessed. "Dumped something in the pond and then left."

"Why would they do that?" Julian asked.

I shrugged. "Probably didn't have anywhere else to dump it."

"But they ruined the pond," Julian complained.

"I don't think they care," Andrew replied.

"We should probably go tell our parents," I suggested.

"Wait a minute," Julian suddenly blurted out. "There's something still alive in there." He was pointing to an area near the shoreline where the water was bubbling.

"It won't be for long," Andrew said.

"Maybe we can save it," Julian declared.

He took the lid off his jar and approached the edge of the water.

"I don't think that's a good idea," I said.

"We have to try," Julian insisted.

"There's no we about it. You're on your own." Andrew raised his hands, palms out, while taking a step back. "I'm not going anywhere near that water."

Ignoring our concerns for his safety, Julian squatted on the muddy shoreline and slowly lowered the jar into the water, holding it by the lip so as not to get any water on his hand. A moment later, he stood up and carried the half-full jar over to where Andrew and I were waiting for him.

"I got it!" Julian smiled, setting the jar on the ground next to his feet.

"What is it?" Andrew stared into the murky water. Something was clearly moving around inside the jar, but he couldn't discern what it was.

"I don't know," Julian answered. "I didn't get a good look at it."

He got down on one knee and peered into the jar, trying to figure out what he'd caught. The closer his face got to the opening at the top of the jar, the more agitated the thing in the water became.

"It doesn't seem very happy," Andrew said.

Julian opened his mouth to respond, but whatever he was about to say was cut off as a thick, viscous mass of slimy mud launched itself out of the jar and attached itself to his face, covering his nose and mouth.

Startled, Julian fell backward and started clawing at the thing clinging to his face, desperately trying to pull it off, but his hands kept passing through its amorphous body.

"What the fuck is that?" Andrew cried out.

I was too stunned to do anything except stand there and stare at my friend as he rolled around on the ground, fighting to breathe. It sounded like the thing was suffocating him.

"Don't just stand there," Andrew yelled at me. "We have to do something."

He knelt next to Julian, trying to assess how best to help him.

"Robbie!" Andrew backhanded me across my thigh to get my attention. "Help me!"

The stinging pain of the slap snapped me out of my paralysis.

"What do we do?" I asked as I knelt next to Andrew.

"We have to get that thing off of him," he replied.

"How are we supposed to do that?"

Julian was doing his best to get it off his face, but he couldn't get it to budge. I didn't see how we were going to be able to do anything different.

"Go get help," Andrew pointed to the line of rooftops in the distance.

He didn't have to tell me twice. I jumped to my feet and started running toward our neighborhood as fast as I could. I was halfway around the pond before I heard Andrew calling my name.

I stopped and looked back.

"Robbie!" Andrew yelled while motioning for me to return. "Come back."

I hurried back over to where he was, surprised to see that Julian was sitting up, spitting mud from his mouth.

"You got it off?" I panted, trying to catch my breath.

"I didn't do anything," Andrew replied. "It fell off on its own."

Next to him, Julian started coughing.

"Where is it now?" I didn't see it lying on the ground anywhere.

"It went back into the water," he nodded toward the pond.

"Is he okay?" I gestured at Julian.

"I'm fine," Julian croaked, then started coughing again. "I just need to get home so I can wash my mouth out with soap." He cleared his throat and then spat a huge wad of muddy phlegm onto the ground. "Help me up." He reached his hand out.

Andrew helped him get to his feet.

"Are you sure you're okay?" he asked.

Once he was on his feet, Julian started swaying back and forth, looking as though he was about to collapse.

"Julian?" Andrew sounded concerned.

"He doesn't look okay," I said. He looked pale to me.

"Julian!" Andrew repeated.

Julian slowly turned his head and stared at Andrew with a vacant look in his eyes.

"Are you okay?" Andrew asked.

Julian didn't answer; instead, he opened his mouth and vomited a stream of mud right into Andrew's face. There was so much mud coming out of Julian's mouth that it covered Andrew from head to toe.

"What the fuck!" Andrew jumped back, trying to wipe the mud off his face. A few seconds later, he started gagging. "Oh my god," he retched. "It got in my mouth."

Julian stared at Andrew for a moment before he turned and faced me. When I saw his mouth start to open, I took off running.

I ran until I made it to the other side of the pond, stopping to look back at my friends.

The two of them were slowly following behind me, walking side by side, their steps in sync.

I started running again, screaming for help once I got within earshot of the neighborhood. When I made it to the street that runs along the swamp, I saw Mr. Johnson outside mowing his lawn.

I ran over to him, yelling and waving my arms in the air. He didn't hear me until I was standing in his driveway.

"Hey, Robbie," he said after he'd turned off the mower. "Are you okay?"

I shook my head, pausing to catch my breath.

"Something . . . happened . . . to . . . Julian . . . and . . . Andrew," I panted out the words. "At . . . the . . . pond." I waved my hand toward the swamp.

Sensing the urgency of my words, Mr. Johnson started walking toward the swamp.

"Go inside and tell Mrs. Johnson to call 911," he pointed at the front door of his house.

"Okay," I nodded, running onto the porch and into his house.

"Mrs. Johnson? Mrs. Johnson?" I called out from the foyer.

"Robbie?" she poked her head out of the kitchen. "What are you doing here?"

"Mr. Johnson said to call 911," I blurted out.

"What?" she gasped, walking toward the front door. "Is he okay?" She thought something bad had happened to her husband.

"He's fine," I said. "It's Julian and Andrew," I clarified.

Mrs. Johnson opened the front door and looked outside.

"They look fine to me," she turned and looked back at me. "Just a little dirty. See?" She opened the door all the way so I could see outside.

Walking across the street, side by side, were Mr. Johnson, Julian, and Andrew. All three of them were covered in mud and walking in sync.

"I hope you don't think you're coming in here looking like that," Mrs. Johnson called out to her husband.

He didn't respond. He just kept walking, making a beeline for the house.

"Run!" I shouted at her, jumping off the porch and sprinting across the lawn toward my house.

When I looked back, I saw that Julian and Andrew had started following me while Mr. Johnson kept walking toward his wife.

A minute later, I heard Mrs. Johnson's cries of revulsion as Mr. Johnson vomited mud all over her.

"Mom! Mom! Mom!" I yelled as soon as I was through the front door.

"What's wrong?" she stepped out of the laundry room and grabbed hold of me by the shoulders.

"You have to call 911," I was speaking so fast that my words were running together. "Something's wrong with Julian and Andrew. They're sick and throwing up on people, and then those people are getting sick and throwing up on people."

"Slow down," she said. "What do you mean they're sick?"

"Something happened down at the pond," I started to explain, but that was as far as I got before she started chiding me.

"You went out to the swamp after I explicitly told you not to?" she snapped.

Before I could respond, I was interrupted by the sound of the front door creaking open. When I turned around, I saw Julian and Andrew standing in the doorway.

"You boys can't come in here looking like that," my mom pointed out. "Get back outside."

They ignored her and stepped into the house.

"We have to go," I tried to tug on my mom's arm to get her to leave, but she pulled away and stood firm.

"Leave! Now!" she yelled at them, but they kept coming.

"I said leave!" She took a step toward them.

They stopped and opened their mouths.

"Watch out!" I threw my body against my mom, knocking us both into the adjacent living room, where we tumbled to the floor.

Behind us, two streams of mud spattered across the floor where we were standing.

"What the hell is going on?" my mom cried out.

"I can explain," I said, helping her to her feet. "But not right now."

I looked back and saw that Julian and Andrew had repositioned themselves in the entryway to the living room.

"Right now, we need to run." I grabbed my mom's arm and led her out of the living room and into the kitchen.

I was hoping to make it to the garage so we could get in the car and leave, but that wasn't going to be possible. Julian and Andrew had split up to block our path.

"This way," I led her up the stairs, the only available escape route, and into her bedroom, where I slammed the door shut and locked it.

Content that we were safe for the moment, I told my mom everything that had happened when we went to the pond. At first, she didn't want to believe me. It wasn't until she looked out the bedroom window and saw what was happening to our neighbors that she accepted the truth.

Now that she agreed it was time to escape, it was too late; most of our neighbors had been affected and were now making their way into our house.

"Maybe they'll go away if we're quiet," I whispered to my mom.

The bang that suddenly rattled the door told me I was wrong.

GOOD TIMING

"If you're here for a reading, you're going to have to come back tomorrow," I said as the man walked into my shop. "I'm about to lock up for the night."

"Oh, I'm not here for a reading," the man replied with a hint of menace. "I'm here to get a refund."

His holey clothing looked to be about two sizes too big, and he smelled like he hadn't bathed in a week.

I sighed. *Oh great. Another addict looking for money.*

I knew his type well. My shop was in a low-income district known for its high crime rate. Most of the people you saw on the street were either on drugs or selling them.

Normally, the locals left me alone. As a psychic medium—a title I hate, by the way—most of them were scared that I would put a curse on them if they did anything to upset me. That helped keep them at a distance. On the few occasions I did talk to someone, they were usually overly kind and eager to stay on my good side.

It was an arrangement that worked well for me, as I couldn't afford to relocate my business to a better part of town.

Despite my *fearsome* reputation, occasionally, I'd get a guy, like the one who'd just waltzed in, thinking he could push me over and get some easy cash to score his next fix.

"I don't recall doing a reading for you," I said.

"It wasn't for me," he revealed. "It was for my mother." He started to approach me. "She asked you to speak to my stepfather earlier this week to find out where he hid his money, but you lied to her."

I remembered her. She brought in an old knockoff Rolex and asked me to use it to channel her dead husband so she could talk to him. She even offered to let me keep the watch when I was done as part of her payment. I, of course, declined and informed her that the watch wasn't real. From her reaction, I could tell she was shocked to hear that.

"I didn't lie to her," I said, taking a step back for every step he took forward. "Your stepfather did."

Just because the dead spoke through me, it didn't mean they were always going to tell the truth. I made sure his mother was aware of that before I agreed to help her.

"I just want a refund," he said, taking another step toward me. "And then I'll leave."

I hooked my thumb over my shoulder at the NO REFUNDS sign hanging on the wall behind me.

"Your mother knew what she was paying for," I said. "Now, if you don't leave, I'm going to call the cops."

The man reached into his pocket, pulled out a small revolver, and pointed it at me.

"I'm trying to be reasonable here," he said. "I just want back what my mother paid you."

"Okay." I raised my hands to keep him calm. "Let me see if I have that much on me." I turned and slowly started to walk behind the counter.

"Don't move." He jabbed the gun in my direction.

I froze.

"I was just going to get my purse." I gestured behind the counter.

Keeping the gun aimed at my head, he walked around me and moved toward the counter. That's when the door to the shop opened, and another man walked in.

"What the hell's taking so long, Scott?" the new guy asked before he'd taken stock of the situation.

He was short and stocky and just as raggedly dressed as the man with the gun.

"I told you to wait in the car, Kevin," Scott snapped at him.

"What the hell are you doing?" Kevin said after he'd seen the gun in Scott's hand. "You said you were just coming in here to get a refund. You didn't say anything about robbing the place."

"This isn't a robbery." Scott looked back at me. "She refused to give me a refund, so I had to change her mind with this." He jiggled the gun while keeping it aimed at me.

"I want no part of this." Kevin threw his hands up and started to leave, but he stopped when Scott yelled at him.

"You're not going anywhere!" He moved his arm so the gun was pointing at Kevin. "You're going to help me get my refund."

Kevin didn't say anything; he just froze in place.

"Go behind the counter and get her purse." Scott motioned with his gun. "Hurry up!" he yelled when Kevin didn't make a move to obey.

"I'm going, I'm going," Kevin blubbered before walking around the two of us to get behind the counter. He looked around for a moment and then said, "Where is it?"

"It's in the drawer beneath the display case." I pointed at the glass case that was full of crystals, tarot cards, and other new-age items.

Once Kevin retrieved my purse, he put it on the counter near Scott and said, "Here it is."

"Get her wallet," Scott instructed.

Kevin reached into my purse and started pulling out items until he found my wallet.

Trying his best to remove himself from the situation, Kevin held the wallet out to Scott and said, "Here."

"Open it," Scott replied.

Kevin undid the latch and looked inside.

"How much does she have?" Scott asked.

Kevin pulled out two ten-dollar bills and held them up. "Twenty bucks," he said.

"Where's the rest of it?" Scott jabbed the gun at me.

"In the bank," I said.

The majority of my clients paid with credit cards, so I didn't need to have a lot of cash on hand. If I ever found myself with more money than I felt comfortable with, I'd deposit it into my account as soon as possible. Since his mother paid me in cash that day, that's what I did.

"Give me the wallet." Scott reached his hand out to Kevin.

That's when I saw the knockoff Rolex on his wrist. I knew it was the same one his mother had brought in with her because of the crack in the glass covering the face.

Once Scott had the wallet, he looked through it until he found my debit card.

"Looks like we're going to the ATM." He tossed the wallet aside and held the card out to me.

I reached out, making him think I was going to take the card, but that's not what I did. Instead, I grabbed the fake Rolex and pulled it off his wrist. Once it was in my hand, I cleared my mind as best I could and called out to the spirit attached to it.

"Give that back!" Scott jammed the gun in my face.

I closed my eyes and ignored him, projecting my thoughts out into the ether: *Come, let me be your voice. I have someone here who wants to speak to you.*

When I felt a chill settle over my body, I knew my summons had been answered. As soon as I felt its presence, I relinquished control of my body.

Scott tried to yank the watch out of my grasp, but the spirit now inhabiting my body pulled my hand away.

"This doesn't belong to you, boy." The voice that came out of my mouth was not my own; it was the voice of Scott's stepfather.

Even though I wasn't in control of my body, I was still aware of everything that was happening around me.

Scott was stunned to hear the voice of the dead man.

"How are you doing that?" His voice was barely more than a whisper.

"Did you really think you could come here and get me to tell you where the money is?" his stepfather sneered. "I didn't tell your mother, and I'm damned sure not going to tell you."

The last time I channeled the dead man, he'd lied to his ex-wife and sent her on a wild goose chase, looking for a fortune that didn't exist.

When I channeled a spirit, I was often privy to certain thoughts the dead person had surrounding the question they'd been asked. That's how I learned that while Scott's stepfather was alive, he'd convinced them that he had a million dollars hidden away. He didn't, though. The truth was that he was nothing more than a swindler making his money running cons. His last con was making them believe he was rich so they'd let him be a part of their family.

"This isn't real," Scott said, placing the barrel of the gun against my forehead.

"You don't have the guts to shoot me," his stepfather said, making no move to get away.

"You're dead," Scott said as he used his thumb to pull back the hammer of the pistol.

"And you're still a worthless piece of shit," his stepfather spat at him.

The insult must have hit a nerve because a tear fell from Scott's eye.

"And a pansy," he added when he saw the tear.

The two stared at each other for what felt like an eternity before Scott's stepfather reached up and took the gun out of his hand.

"Go run home to your mommy." His stepfather pushed him toward the door. "And don't ever come back here again."

Scott stumbled back a few steps before recovering his footing and quickly turning to leave.

"That goes for you, too." The stepfather gestured at Kevin with the pistol.

Kevin didn't need to be told twice. He hightailed it out of there as fast as he could.

Thank you, I said to the spirit.

"It was my pleasure," he replied before leaving.

THE HOLLOW WEEN

"All right, class," Mr. Adamson announced after the final bell had rung. "That's all there is for today. Be safe tonight, don't eat too much candy, and don't forget to leave a bowl of treats out for the Hollow Ween. We don't want him to go hungry."

The fifth-grade class rose as one and bolted for the door. Everyone was eager to get home so they could start getting ready for the night's Halloween festivities.

Once I was out in the hall, I felt a tap on my shoulder. I turned and found Leonard, one of my classmates, falling into step beside me.

"What's up?" I asked, wondering why he'd tapped me on the shoulder.

Leonard was the newest kid in class. On his first day of school, Mr. Adamson tasked me with showing him around the campus. I did that and thought that was the end of my association with him, but it wasn't. The next day, Leonard decided we were friends and started hanging around me at lunch and recess.

I didn't really like him. He was too arrogant and bragged a lot about stupid stuff. I would've told him to get lost a long time ago, but I couldn't. Some of the other guys I hung out with seemed to genuinely like Leonard, which forced me to tolerate his presence.

"What was Mr. Adamson talking about?" Leonard asked.

I had no idea what he was referring to. Mr. Adamson talked about a lot of stuff that day.

"You're going to have to be more specific," I replied.

"The Hallow Ween bowl," Leonard clarified. "What's that all about?"

"It's Hollow Ween," I corrected him. "Not Hallow... And it's just a local tradition. It's not important."

I tried walking faster, weaving around the other kids in the hall, hoping to put some distance between the two of us, but he kept pace with me.

"Come on, man, tell me what it's all about," he insisted.

Knowing I wasn't going to get rid of him until he got the information he wanted, I gave him an abbreviated version of the legend of the Hollow Ween.

"The Hollow Ween is a monster that comes every Halloween looking for treats to eat, and if it comes to your house and you don't have a bowl of treats out for it, it will eat you instead," I explained hurriedly. There was more to the legend than that, but that was the gist of it.

"Seriously," Leonard scoffed. "That sounds so stupid."

I ignored him and kept walking, hoping he'd go away now that I'd told him what he wanted to know.

"Wait a minute." Something suddenly occurred to Leonard. "Are you saying that people put out bowls of candy and just leave them there overnight because of some made-up monster?"

"Yep," I said, not wanting to talk about it any longer.

"What do you do with the candy the next morning?" he asked.

"What do you think we do with it?" I snapped at him.

I thought the answer was obvious, but apparently it wasn't to him.

"I don't know," Leonard snapped back. "That's why I'm asking you."

"We eat it," I huffed. "What else do you think we do with leftover Halloween candy?"

"What happens if there isn't any candy in the bowl the next morning? What do you do then?" Leonard had a smile on his face when he asked the question.

"I don't know," I shrugged. "That's never happened."

I've heard stories of other kids claiming their bowls were empty the next morning, but the bowl my family put out was always full of candy the next day.

"Well." He threw his arm around my shoulders. "It might just happen tonight." He grinned at me before rushing up the street toward the neighborhood we lived in.

As I watched him go, I suddenly realized what his final comment meant.

He was going to steal the candy that was left out for the Hollow Ween.

I was sure of it.

I hope he gets caught, I thought as I continued walking home.

Or better yet, I hope the Hollow Ween eats him. I smiled at the last thought. *If only it were real.*

When I got home, I asked my mom what would happen if someone went around stealing the Hollow Ween candy.

"Honestly, honey," she replied, "I doubt anything would happen. I'm sure a lot of the Hollow Ween candy gets stolen every year. But most people don't care. It's put outside so the Hollow Ween can take it, so there's really no point in getting mad if it does get taken. Why do you ask?"

"I think one of the kids from my school is going to steal the Hollow Ween candy," I told her.

"If he does, he does," she said. "I wouldn't waste any time worrying about it. Anyone who cares that much about their candy doesn't have to leave a bowl out. Mr. Gardiner across the street has never left a bowl outside, and I'm sure he's not the only one."

"Mr. Gardiner is a grumpy old man," I blurted out.

"Don't be mean," my mom chided me. "I think he's just lonely. He hasn't been the same since Mrs. Gardiner left him."

"Mr. Gardiner was married?" I was surprised to hear that. I didn't think it was possible for anyone to like him.

"He was," my mom confirmed. "A long time ago. You don't remember because you were just a baby when Mrs. Gardiner left. She was such a sweet lady." My mom got a faraway look in her eyes as she remembered Mrs. Gardiner.

"Why did she leave?" I asked.

My mom shrugged. "I have no idea. We were all shocked when it happened."

"Maybe she finally realized he wasn't a nice person," I said. I knew I shouldn't have said that as soon as the words were out of my mouth, but I couldn't help myself.

"That's enough," my mom chided me. "Go upstairs and start getting ready for dinner." She pointed at the stairs. "And don't worry about that kid from school. If he wants to steal the Hollow Ween candy, let him. Hopefully, he'll get a stomachache when he eats it all."

I hope it makes him puke his guts out, I thought to myself as I made my way to my room.

After dinner, I put on my zombie astronaut costume and went trick-or-treating with my next-door neighbor, Gabriel, and his older brother, Sam, who was a senior in high school. I was supposed to go with my friends from school, but my mom wouldn't let me because they didn't have a chaperone. I tried to convince her that I was old enough to go trick-or-treating on my own like my friends were allowed to, but she wouldn't let me. When I tried to continue the argument by reminding her that she let me walk home from school by myself, she told me that was different and then threatened to ground me for the night if I didn't stop pushing her.

I had more fun than I thought I would. Sam wasn't as strict as I thought he was going to be, and he even took us into the neighboring subdivision, where we'd heard rumors that they were far more generous with their candy than our neighborhood. If my mom knew he'd done that, she'd have given him an earful.

By the time I arrived back home, my bag was full of candy, and my arms were starting to hurt from carrying it.

"How was it?" my mom asked before I was fully through the front door.

"It was okay," I replied, not wanting to give her the satisfaction of knowing I had a lot of fun with Gabe and Sam. Plus, I didn't want to get Sam into any kind of trouble for taking us out of the neighborhood.

"Let's see what you got," she said, reaching for my bag, which I gladly handed over.

As I followed her over to the dining room table, I stripped out of my costume and left it lying on the floor.

"You'd better not leave that there," my mom warned as I sat in the chair next to hers.

"I won't," I promised. "I'll take it with me when I go upstairs."

She knew I was eager to get my hands on some of the candy I'd gotten, so she didn't press the issue. Instead, she said, "You'd better." She smiled at me. "Otherwise, I'm going to eat all this candy myself." She dumped the bag of candy onto the table.

Over the next thirty minutes, the two of us went through the candy, separating the candy we liked from the candy we didn't like, eating a few pieces here and there. When we were done, we had two piles. The big pile had all the good candy like Hershey bars, Reese's peanut butter cups, and bags of Skittles, while the smaller one had the not-so-good things like candy corn, Tootsie Rolls, and W hoppers.

"Go get the Hollow Ween bowl." My mom pointed to the bowl she had sitting on the accent table by the front door.

When I returned with it, she scooped all the candy we didn't want into the bowl and then handed the bowl to me.

"Go put this on the porch and then run upstairs and start getting ready for bed," she instructed.

I took the bowl outside and set it on the doormat, taking a moment to look up and down the street as I did so. All the houses I could see had a Hollow Ween bowl sitting on the porch, all of them except for Mr. Gardiner's.

I hope it's all crappy candy.

If Leonard really was going to steal the Hollow Ween candy, I didn't want him to get anything good.

It was 10 o'clock when I finally climbed into bed, but I couldn't fall asleep. I tossed and turned for thirty minutes before I got up and stood at my window, looking out at the street.

I don't know if it was the candy I ate that was keeping me up or the knowledge that Leonard was going to steal a bunch of candy and probably get away with it. I wanted him to get in trouble for it.

The more I thought about it, the more I decided to take action. I know my mom told me not to worry about it, but I just couldn't let it go. So, that's why I stood by my window waiting to see if Leonard would show up.

I figured he'd want me to know what he'd done, so he would make sure to at least steal the candy from my house. And I was right. Ten minutes later, I saw him running down the sidewalk with a pillowcase draped over his shoulder. From the way the pillowcase bulged on his back, it was obvious he'd already stolen several bowls' worth of candy.

I watched from my window as he crept from door to door, looking at the bowls of candy that were left out for the Hollow Ween. If he didn't like what he saw, he left the candy alone and moved on to the next house.

From the darkness of my room, I continued watching him until I saw him run up to Mr. Gardiner's house, disappearing into the darkness of the porch.

You won't find any candy there, I thought.

I figured Leonard would quickly realize there was no candy and move on to the next house, but he never reappeared.

That's weird.

I sat there and waited for several minutes, wondering what was going on, when a light suddenly came on in Mr. Gardiner's house, illuminating the porch enough for me to see that the front door was open.

He must've gotten caught. That's the only explanation I could come up with for his disappearance.

Turns out I was right.

As I watched, I saw Mr. Gardiner pass in front of the window carrying Leonard over his shoulder.

Leonard was frantically trying to free himself, but Mr. Gardiner held firm, which I found surprising for a man who was supposed to be in his seventies. At one point, I thought I could hear Leonard's cries for help.

Part of me thought I should do something to help him, but a much bigger part of me thought, *You deserve this.*

I honestly didn't think anything bad was going to happen. I certainly didn't think Mr. Gardiner was going to drop Leonard on the floor, grab hold of his head, and then violently twist it, but that's precisely what happened.

In shock, I just stood there staring at Leonard's limp form lying on Mr. Gardiner's carpet.

Oh my God! Oh my God! Oh my God!

I thought I had just seen the worst thing in my life, but once again, I was wrong.

As I sat there staring, paralyzed with shock, Mr. Gardiner began to change.

His body stretched and distorted until his clothes ripped apart and fell off. He continued to change until he no longer appeared human. He was now just a mass of bulbous flesh with two long, spindly arms and legs, and a mouth that took up most of his head.

It's the Hollow Ween! Mr. Gardiner is the Hollow Ween!

I'd seen enough artists' renditions of the Hollow Ween around town to know that I was looking at the real thing.

When Mr. Gardiner was done changing into the Hollow Ween, he lifted Leonard's lifeless body by the feet and started shoving it into his mouth. In less than two minutes, the body disappeared down the monster's throat.

I could feel the bile rising up the back of my throat, but I couldn't force myself to look away.

From the looks of it, Mr. Gardiner was still hungry because when he finished swallowing Leonard, he picked up the pillowcase full of stolen candy and dumped that into his mouth as well. When he was done, he placed his hands on his distended belly and turned to look out the window.

Our eyes met.

Instinctively, I rolled away from the window, but I knew I was too late. The Hollow Ween had seen me.

I was certain he was going to come across the street and eat me next because I'd discovered his secret.

That thought made me sick to my stomach.

I vomited onto the floor, then lay down and curled up into a ball as I continued to retch.

A few minutes later, the door to my room swung open. I was certain it was the Hollow Ween coming to eat me, but it wasn't. It was my mom. She'd heard me throwing up and came to help.

"Looks like someone's had a little too much candy," she said as she stroked my head.

I wanted to tell her that wasn't why I was sick, but I couldn't get the words out.

"Let's get you cleaned up." She helped me to my feet and guided me into the bathroom, where she helped me out of my dirty pajamas and wiped the puke off my face.

After she'd tucked me back into bed, I finally told her what I'd seen.

"I think you just had a nightmare," she said, completely dismissing me. "Mr. Gardiner isn't the Hollow Ween. The Hollow Ween isn't real."

"But..." I tried to insist, but my mom wouldn't let me.

"No buts about it," she cut me off. "It was just a dream."

That was the end of the conversation. She didn't want to hear any more about it.

My mom let me stay home from school the next day, which I was thankful for because I didn't sleep at all the previous night.

When she called me down to the kitchen for breakfast that morning, I asked her if she'd seen Mr. Gardiner.

"No, I haven't. Why do you ask?"

I didn't respond.

"Do you still think he's the Hollow Ween?" she asked. "Is that it?"

"No," I finally said.

"It was just a nightmare, honey," my mom insisted. "You need to let it go."

I tried to do that, I really did, and I might've succeeded if it weren't for the surprise visitor who showed up at our house that afternoon.

"Jacob!" my mom yelled from the bottom of the stairs. "There's someone here to see you."

I walked to the top of the stairs and looked down at her. "Who is it?" I asked.

"One of your friends from school," she replied.

I raced down the stairs and opened the door, expecting to see Harrison or Antoine, my two closest friends, standing there, but it was neither of them. Instead, I found Leonard.

"Hi, Jacob." Leonard raised a hand in greeting. "Can you come out and play?"

WINNY

"Mind your own business, Winny," I muttered to myself.

I said that as I crested a slight rise in the forest and came upon a boy who looked to be about twelve years old, torturing an old gray squirrel he'd trapped in a snare.

I'd happened upon him on my way back from the creek to fetch water for my cabin.

Thankfully, he was too busy with the squirrel to notice he was being watched.

Wanting to keep it that way, I ducked out of sight and took the long way home so I wouldn't risk running into him again.

As I walked, the squirrel's squeals of pain haunted me.

"If you get involved," I said, "he'll run home and tell his folks, and then they'll call the sheriff, and you don't need that kind of trouble knocking on your door."

I had to put the incident behind me.

Very few people knew I lived out in the woods, and that's the way I wanted it to stay.

Later that night, once I was sure the boy had gone home, I grabbed my lantern and returned to the spot where I'd seen him.

The body of the squirrel lay on the ground with its head twisted around and the snare still tied around its neck. Several sticks were skewered through its body, staking it to the ground.

"You bastard," I cursed the boy.

I knelt beside the body of the squirrel and removed the sticks and the snare before gently picking it up and putting it in the plastic bag I'd brought with me.

I wasn't going to leave it for the scavengers to pick apart. That seemed wrong, given the horrible way it died.

You could have saved it, the voice of guilt whispered in my mind.

"Doubtful," I replied out loud. "But I could've ended its suffering in a more humane way. I'm sorry that I didn't," I apologized to the squirrel before tying the bag shut.

When I got back to my cabin, I laid the squirrel out on my work table and examined it. There were various ways I could use its body, which, in my mind, would allow its death to serve a greater purpose.

I could add its fur to the blanket I was making, its meat would make a nice stew, and the rest of it could be ground up and used as fertilizer in my vegetable garden.

"I thank you for these gifts," I said, running my hand along the squirrel's soft fur before I grabbed my knives and started skinning it.

I saw the boy again two days later while I was collecting firewood that morning. This time, he wasn't alone. He had a friend with him.

I quickly took shelter behind a nearby boulder when I heard them coming.

"Does your dad know you have his rifle?" I heard the friend ask.

I'd seen the long-barreled gun draped over the boy's shoulder before I ducked out of sight.

"No," the boy replied. "Now be quiet. You talk too much."

"Sorry," the friend apologized.

They continued walking past my hiding place, forcing me to skirt around the boulder to prevent myself from being seen.

I waited until they were out of sight before I started following them. The trail they left behind was easy to follow.

When I caught up to them again, I found them standing next to the creek. Wanting to stay out of sight, I hid behind a fallen tree. A gap beneath it allowed me to watch them.

"Grab some of those pinecones," the boy pointed at the ground around a nearby tree, "and put them on that rock over there."

"Okay," his friend moved to oblige.

Once the kid had an armful of pinecones, he carried them over to the rock and started setting them up as best he could.

While he did that, the boy removed the gun from his shoulder and aimed it at his friend's back.

"He wouldn't," I hissed.

But he did.

The sound of the rifle being fired echoed through the woods. A second later, a large spray of blood and bone erupted from the front of his chest as the bullet tore through him.

He swayed on his feet for a moment before collapsing. Thankfully, he was dead before he hit the ground. I'd hate for the boy to suffer the way the squirrel had.

"What the hell have you done?!" I stood up and yelled at the boy.

Startled by my sudden appearance, he almost dropped the rifle.

"I-I-it w-w-was an accident," he stammered.

"That was no accident," I pointed an accusing finger as I climbed over the log to confront him. "You did that on purpose."

"It was an accident," he whined. "I swear."

"And I say it wasn't," I stood there with my hands on my hips. "Who do you think the police are going to believe, you or me?"

He hadn't counted on there being a witness.

I could see a change come over the boy's face as he thought through his dilemma. Once he'd come to a decision, he raised the rifle and pointed it at me.

"Do you really think shooting me is going to help your case?"

"It does if you can't talk to the police," he replied.

"And what's your reason for shooting me?" I asked.

"I just told you what it was." He tightened his grip on the rifle to steady his aim.

"What's the reason you're going to tell the police?" I explained. "They might buy your story about accidentally shooting your friend," I gestured at the other boy's body, "but they're not going to believe you accidentally shot two people."

He had to think about it for a moment before he came up with an answer.

"I'll tell them you attacked me," he said, sounding confident that he'd come up with the perfect solution.

"Look at me, I'm over eighty years old." I spread my arms. "I'm skin and bones. Do you really think they'd believe I'd attack someone younger and stronger than me?"

The gun wavered, signaling that I was making him doubt himself again. It was time to make my move.

"What if I told you I could bring him back?" I pointed at the body of his friend.

"What do you mean?" He had a confused look on his face.

This kid is stupider than I initially thought.

"I can bring him back to life," I explained. "Make it like you never shot him. He won't even remember it happened."

"You're lying." He steadied the gun and took a step toward me. "Nobody can do that."

"I can," I insisted. "But I have to do it soon. The longer we wait, the harder it will be."

"Okay, then do it," he nodded at the body of his friend.

"It's not that simple," I said. "I can't just snap my fingers and bring him back. There's a ritual that must be performed, and I can't do it here. We need to take his body back to my cottage."

The boy just stood there staring at me. I could tell I was about to lose his interest, so I made him an offer he couldn't refuse.

"I'll tell you what," I smiled. "If you help me take his body back to my cottage and I can't bring him back, you can shoot me."

"There's nothing stopping me from shooting you right now," he countered.

"We've already been over why that's a bad idea." I took a deep breath and sighed. "But if you really think you can handle all of this on your own, go ahead and shoot me." I spread my arms.

He lowered the gun.

"How far away is your cottage?" he asked.

"It's just over that hill," I turned and pointed.

It took the two of us thirty minutes to carry the body back to my cottage.

"We need to place him on the table," I instructed as we carried him inside.

After we did that, the boy started wandering around my home, examining the taxidermied animals I had mounted on the walls and sitting on shelves.

"Did you make these?" he asked.

"I did," I replied as I started gathering jars of herbs and the other ingredients I'd need to revive his friend.

"Could you teach me how to do it?"

"I could," I said out loud. To myself, I said, *but I won't*.

I grabbed a bucket and carried it over to the boy.

"Make yourself useful," I said, thrusting the bucket into his arms. "Run down to the creek and fetch me some water."

He looked like he was about to protest but then thought better of it.

After he left, I retrieved the spell book I kept hidden in an old tin box under the floorboards with the rest of my valued possessions. The book was given to me by my mother, who got it from her mother. It'd been handed down like that for over 300 years until it reached me.

I no longer had a daughter to give it to. The state had taken her away from me when she was just a baby. They said I was unfit to raise a child on my own.

I could've used the book to find her and take her back, but I never did. The world was changing too much, and there wasn't much place in it for people like me anymore. I decided it was better to let my daughter be a part of that world instead of dragging her into mine.

She'd be in her sixties now with children and grandchildren of her own. Thinking about her reminded me of just how old I was and how little I had to show for my life.

I can at least do one good thing before I die, I thought.

The boy returned with the bucket of water, sloshing it all over the floor as he carried it through the door. I walked over and took it from him before he could spill any more.

I set the bucket on the table and used the water to clean the blood from the dead boy's body as best I could. Then, I mixed the ingredients I'd gathered and poured them into the dead boy's mouth. When I was done, I caught the other boy flipping through my spell book, which I had left sitting on a chair.

"You don't want to mess with that," I said, slamming the book shut and picking it up.

"What is it?" he asked.

"It's none of your business, is what it is," I replied.

"Is that what you're going to use to bring Howie back?"

"Stop asking questions and get over here and help me." I carried the book over to the table and set it down next to Howie's body.

"Set your rifle down and then stand right there," I pointed at the opposite side of the table.

Thankfully, he did what I said without protesting.

I opened the book to the page I needed and then read over it, making sure I had everything I needed. Satisfied that I did, I looked up at the boy and said, "For this to work, I need you to do everything that I tell you. Do you understand?"

The boy nodded his head.

"Good. Now lean forward," I motioned him closer.

When he was close enough, I dipped my finger into the gunshot wound in Howie's chest, coating it with blood.

"What're you doing?" The boy stepped back when I reached the bloody finger out toward him.

"If you're going to help me bring Howie back, I have to anoint you," I explained. When he didn't return to the table, I said, "You do want me to bring him back, don't you?"

"I guess," he replied reluctantly.

"Either you do or you don't," I snapped. "Hurry up and make up your mind. I can't bring him back by myself."

"I do want you to bring him back," he said after thinking about it for a few minutes.

"Then get over here," I motioned again.

When the boy returned to the table, I dipped my finger in Howie's blood again, then reached out and started to draw an arcane symbol upon the boy's forehead. I could tell he didn't like having the blood on his skin from the way he closed his eyes and scowled, but I didn't care. The only thing that mattered was that he kept his mouth shut.

As I drew the symbol, I recited the words written in the book, imbuing the symbol with the power needed to fuel the resurrection spell.

I could see that the boy was about to open his mouth and say something, but I stopped him by reaching out with my other hand and pressing a finger to his lips.

"If you had interrupted me, I would've had to start all over again," I said when I was done.

"Sorry," he apologized before reaching up to touch the bloody symbol on his forehead.

"And don't touch that." I grabbed hold of his hand before he could ruin it.

"It feels weird," he whined.

"It's supposed to. That means it's working."

"What's it for?"

"It's called a Martyr's Mark," I explained. "With it, you are going to bring Howie back to life."

"Me?" he sounded surprised. "I thought you were going to bring him back."

"The magic has to come from you," I pointed at him.

"But I don't have any magic."

"Thanks to the mark I drew on your head, you do," I said. "Now get over here so we can finish the spell."

He stepped up to the table.

"What am I supposed to do?"

I held up the book and showed him a picture. "See this symbol?" I tapped the page. "You need to draw it on Howie's forehead using your own blood."

"What?" He didn't like the sound of that.

I picked up a knife and held it out to him. "Just slice your thumb," I said.

When he didn't make a move to take the knife, I lunged across the table, grabbed his hand, and cut his thumb.

"Why'd you do that?" he yelled, cradling his injured hand against his chest.

"Because it would've taken too long for you to do it yourself," I chided. "Now hurry up and draw the mark on his forehead before the blood starts to clot."

The boy glared at me but did as he was told.

"It's done, now what?"

I tossed him a strip of cloth. "Wrap that around your finger."

While he did that, I walked around the table with the book.

"See these words?" I pointed at the page. "You need to place your hand on Howie's forehead and say them."

"But..." I knew what he was going to say and stopped him.

"You don't need to understand them, you just have to say them," I said. "They are pronounced exactly as they look."

"Okay." He reached out, placed his hand on the dead boy's forehead, and recited the words. I was surprised at how well he pronounced them.

As soon as he was finished, he slumped to the floor.

"What's happening to me?" His words came out slow and drawn out.

"You're dying," I stood over him. "That resurrection spell you just performed required a willing sacrifice, and you were that sacrifice. To put it in words you can better understand, you gave up your life so Howie could have his back."

"You tricked me," were the last words he said.

"I righted a wrong," I said to his lifeless body.

On the table, Howie sat up.

"My chest hurts," he complained as he touched the huge hole that was still in his chest.

That's not right, I thought. *The wound should have healed. Unless...* I looked down at the book.

Goddammit, Winny, I chided myself, *you used the wrong spell.*

I was supposed to use the resurrection spell, but I accidentally used the reanimate one. Since they had similar requirements and names, it was easy for my senile old brain to get the two mixed up.

"That's what I get for trying to do the right thing," I muttered, retrieving the boy's rifle and aiming it at Howie's head.

GRIEF SUPPORT

"Is it me?" I leaned over to Sally and whispered, "Or has Bud put on some weight since last week?" I nodded to where Bud was standing in front of the refreshment table.

Bud Morrison was the grief counselor who ran the support group in the community center. He had been doing so for the past three months after the previous counselor retired. I'd joined the group a few weeks earlier at the suggestion of my psychologist, who thought I needed a bit more help processing the loss of my wife and daughter than she could provide.

I wasn't trying to be mean to Bud. I was just pointing out how much he had changed since we last saw him. If anything, I was concerned. Usually, when someone started gaining weight like that, it meant something was wrong.

"Maybe a little weight," Sally replied. "And I think I know why." The corner of her lip turned up in a half-smile as she gestured at the paper plate Bud was holding. On it were two donuts, while a third donut was in his free hand, headed toward his mouth.

"He does love his donuts," I remarked.

Bud brought two dozen donuts every week, and there were always plenty left over by the end of the meeting. He'd always encourage us to take some home with us. Still, most of us didn't have much of an appetite, given the emotional rollercoaster we experienced listening to each other's stories.

"I think I might grab one before he eats them all," Sally joked. "Do you want one?" she offered.

"No thanks," I shook my head. "I'm good."

"You should try to eat something," she said, eyeing me from head to toe. "Because it looks like Bud is gaining all the weight you're losing."

Her comment stung and made me feel like a hypocrite for mentioning Bud's weight. I knew I had lost some weight. I just hadn't realized how much until that moment.

I looked down at my baggy, ill-fitting clothes—clothes that used to be snug in places.

"Maybe I'll have one donut," I said, more out of shame than hunger, as I followed Sally to the refreshment table.

"Help yourself," Bud said around a mouthful of donut as we approached the table, and each of us grabbed a paper plate. "There's plenty to go around."

He stepped out of the way so we could each take a donut from one of the boxes lying open on the table. Sally grabbed a raspberry-filled while I grabbed a chocolate sprinkle. I didn't really like sprinkles, but seeing the donuts in the box reminded me of my daughter, who loved them.

"While I got you here," Bud said, his voice taking on a somber tone, "I wanted to give the two of you a heads-up that Dolores is no longer with us."

"Oh no," Sally held a hand to her face as her eyes started to tear up. "Not Dolores."

"I'm afraid so," Bud replied.

"What happened?" I asked. "She seemed okay when she was here last week."

Dolores was a widowed woman who'd lost her son a few months back to a senseless act of violence during a robbery at a convenience store. Not only did she lose her son that day, but she also lost her livelihood.

Unable to afford to live on her own after her husband passed away, she'd moved in with her son so he could help her get back on her feet. He passed away before that could happen, leaving her with nobody to care for her.

The last I heard, Dolores was working with a social worker to find a place for her to stay, and she seemed optimistic about her options.

To hear she died was like a punch in the gut.

"They think it was suicide," Bud responded to my question.

Hearing that made it so much worse. We knew she was struggling, but we thought she was making progress. That just goes to show you how well people mask their pain.

"Do you know when the service is?" I asked.

Even though I'd only known Dolores for a short time, I still felt like I should go and pay my respects.

"I don't think there's going to be one," Bud revealed. "As far as I'm aware, she doesn't have any family left to arrange anything like that."

"That's terrible," Sally said.

"We could each say a few words about her before we start the group session if you like," Bud suggested, looking from Sally to me.

"It's the least we should do," I replied.

Sally nodded her agreement.

"All right then," Bud said. "I'll give you a few moments to yourselves." He then excused himself and went to take his seat at the head of the group.

No longer interested in eating the donut, I waited until Sally started walking to her seat so I could throw it away without her seeing.

The group session ultimately focused entirely on Dolores, which I didn't mind. Everyone there shared a few words about her before Bud reminded us of all the mental health services available to us should we find ourselves in a position like Dolores's. He also told us to look out for one another and to speak up if we saw any member of the group struggling.

When he said that, I could feel Sally's eyes on me, which reminded me of the comment she'd made earlier about my weight loss.

After the meeting, Sally asked if I wanted to go to the diner on the corner, which had become the unofficial gathering place for group members who didn't want to go home after the meetings.

I was about to give her my usual excuse for why I couldn't go, but then I changed my mind.

"Sure, I'll go," I said.

Dolores always went, and that made me feel like I should go at least once to honor her memory.

"Really?" Sally sounded surprised.

I nodded. "Lead the way."

While at the diner, I managed to eat a grilled cheese sandwich and a bowl of tomato soup, which was the most substantial meal I'd had all week. When I was done, I took a sip of my coffee and then said, "We should arrange a memorial service for Dolores."

Everyone at the table stopped eating and looked at me.

"We can't just let the state discard her in some pauper's grave," I continued. "She should be properly buried."

"That sounds great and all, but who's going to pay for it?" Alex, who became a part of the group after his dog was hit by a car, said. "I barely make enough to pay my bills. As much as we all agree with you, I don't think any of us can afford to help."

The rest of the group murmured their agreement. Even Sally agreed with Alex.

"Dolores does deserve a proper burial," she said, "but I don't think she'd want us to go out of our way to help her."

"I'll pay for it," I blurted out.

I lived in the home I inherited from my parents and had plenty of money in my savings account. I could easily pay for Dolores's funeral without it affecting my livelihood.

"You don't have to do that," Sally said.

"I know." I slid out of the booth, pulled a twenty out of my wallet, and tossed it onto the table to cover my portion of the bill. "But I want to," I said before leaving.

For the first time since my wife and daughter had died, I felt like I had a purpose. Something to focus my time and energy on, if only for a little while.

The first thing I did when I got up the next day was to call the funeral home that took care of the service for my family.

I explained what I wanted, and they promised to take care of everything and call me once they had received Dolores's body.

That call came two days later.

"Sorry it took so long to get back to you," the funeral director said. "Mrs. Sherman's remains had already been turned over to a research center, and we had to send someone out of state to pick her up. She just arrived a few minutes ago."

"Is she okay?" The thought of her being used for research appalled me.

"She's fine," he assured me and then proceeded to talk about plans for the memorial service.

When I first called, the funeral director hadn't wanted to confirm any of the specifics of the service until he'd secured the body and had a chance to assess the condition of Dolores's remains. Now that he had her, he was confident we could proceed as we'd originally discussed, which was to have her buried next to her husband and son.

"There's just one last thing," he said. "Will you be providing clothing for Mrs. Sherman, or would you like us to provide something?"

I hadn't thought about that.

"I'll provide something for her," I said.

It seemed wrong not to bury her in her clothes.

"How soon do you need them?" I asked.

I had no idea how or if I was going to be able to get her clothing, but I wanted to try.

"If you still want to have the viewing on Friday, I'd need the clothing by tomorrow evening," the funeral director replied. "Also," he added, "if you have a recent picture of Mrs. Sherman, that would be helpful as well."

"I'll see what I can do," I said before ending the call.

I don't suppose you know where Dolores lived? I texted Sally.

After I got off the phone with the funeral director, I texted her, hoping she might be able to help me retrieve the dress and the picture, both of which I knew I could only obtain from Dolores's apartment.

I don't, Sally texted back. She texted a new message a moment later that said, *I think Joann gave her a ride home one night. I'll text her and see.*

Thank you, I replied.

Fifteen minutes later, Sally texted me the address. I thanked her again and then immediately set out for Dolores's apartment.

"Hi," the apartment manager greeted me with a smile when I entered the office. "How can I help you?"

"I'm here about one of your tenants," I said. "Dolores Sherman. She was staying here with her son."

The apartment manager frowned when I said Dolores's name.

"Mrs. Sherman was such a nice lady," she said. "Shame what happened to her and her son."

"Would it be possible to see their apartment?" I asked, getting right to the point.

"Why?" the manager narrowed her eyes.

"I'm in the process of arranging her funeral, and I think she'd want to be buried in her own clothes," I explained. "I also need to find a recent photo so they can present her as she'd like to be seen." I was hoping that mentioning that would appeal to her sense of decency and she'd let me into the apartment.

"Are you family?"

"No," I shook my head. "I heard she didn't have any family left to see that she was properly laid to rest, so I decided to do it myself."

"How do you know Dolores?"

"We met at a grief support group," I replied. "I recently lost my wife and daughter."

I could tell by the sympathetic look on the manager's face that I had finally won her over.

"You're not with that other guy, are you?"

I was confused by the question. "What other guy?"

She described someone who sounded a lot like Bud Morrison, but I didn't tell her that.

"No," I said. "I'm not with anyone. It's just me." When she didn't respond, I added, "If you don't believe me, you can call the funeral home yourself and verify my story."

"That won't be necessary," the manager finally said. "Truth be told, the apartment was going to be cleared out in a few days anyway. The only reason it hasn't yet is because the rent was paid up until the end of the month. I was hoping a family member might show up to claim the property inside."

"Did that other guy say what he wanted?" I was curious why Bud wanted to get into Dolores's apartment.

"He just said he was a friend of hers and that he left something in the apartment the last time he had visited and asked if he could go get it. I told him I'd be happy to go get it for him if he told me what it was, but he changed his mind and said it wasn't important."

"When was this?"

"Three days ago, I think," she replied after a moment of thought.

If she remembered correctly, that would be the day we had our last support group meeting.

What was Bud after? Did he know something about Dolores that the rest of us didn't?

After we were done talking, the manager led me across the complex to Dolores's apartment and let me inside.

"I shouldn't be too long," I said, thinking she was going to come inside and wait while I gathered the belongings I needed.

"Take your time," she replied. "I've got some stuff to do back at the office. If you finish before I get back, lock the door behind you and swing by the office before you leave."

"Okay," I agreed. "And thanks for doing this."

She acknowledged my gratitude with a smile and a nod before leaving.

Once she was out of sight, I went into the apartment and shut the door.

"Wow, that's a lot of stuff," I muttered upon seeing how many pieces of furniture were crammed into the apartment.

It was clear that when Dolores moved in with her son, she brought as much of her house with her as she could, which was a good thing for me because it made finding a photo of her easy. There were several of them scattered around the living room.

After grabbing what I considered the best photo of her, I went down the hall to find her bedroom.

It was easy to see which one was hers.

Seeing her bed all made up with the pillows perfectly arranged reminded me of how my wife would do the same thing to our bed. With that memory came the thought of how much my wife was like Dolores. That reminded me of just how much I missed her.

Needing a moment to compose myself, I sat on the edge of Dolores's bed and stared out the window. That's when I saw Bud Morrison pull into the parking lot.

I watched as he got out of his car and started heading directly toward Dolores's apartment.

What are you up to? I thought as I watched him walk out of sight around the corner of the building.

As I pondered why he wanted to get inside the apartment so badly, I remembered that I hadn't locked the front door.

I rushed across the apartment, hoping to reach the door before he did, but I was a couple of seconds too late. As I reached out for the deadbolt, the door swung open.

"Eric?" Bud was surprised to see me standing in the doorway. "What are you doing here?"

"What are *you* doing here?" I countered.

He eyed me for a moment before answering.

"I was doing private sessions with Dolores to help her manage her grief," he explained. "And the last time I was here, I left a piece of paper that had some... sensitive information on it. I was hoping to grab it before someone else found it."

"What kind of information?" I pressed, keeping myself in the doorway so he couldn't get by me.

"Nothing that would hurt anyone other than myself," Bud sighed. "Can I please come in and look for it?" He gestured at the interior of the apartment behind me.

"That's not really my call," I said.

And then, as if on cue, the office manager came walking up to the apartment.

"What's he doing here?" she snapped.

"He just showed up," I said.

"Do you two know each other?" she looked from Bud to me.

"No," we both replied, almost in unison.

"Then I think you should leave before I call the cops," she said to Bud.

"I'm going," he said, giving me one last look before walking back toward the parking lot.

Once Bud was gone, the manager came into the apartment and shut the door behind her.

"Did he say anything to you?" she asked.

"Just that he was a friend of Dolores's and that he left something in the apartment," I lied, telling her the same thing she'd told me earlier.

"Did you find what you needed?"

"Not quite," I said. "I've got the picture," I gestured to where I left the photo of Dolores on the dining table near the kitchen. "I just need to find a dress... I don't suppose you could help me with that? I'm not really sure what would be appropriate."

"I suppose I could do that," she agreed and walked toward the bedrooms.

While she did that, I started searching the apartment for the piece of paper that Bud said he was looking for. I searched everywhere without finding anything and was about to give up when I decided I should look under the couch and the other pieces of furniture in the room, just to be thorough.

I still couldn't find it.

"What do you think of this one?" the apartment manager asked, holding a white, vintage shirtdress that looked like it was from the 1950s or 1960s.

"I think that looks perfect," I replied, taking the dress and draping it across my arm when she offered it to me. "I guess I'm done here."

I turned to pick up the photo I'd left on the table. When I did, I happened to see a folded piece of paper lying on the seat of one of the dining chairs. Making sure the apartment manager wasn't looking, I quickly grabbed the piece of paper and hid it behind the photo.

"Thanks again for letting me grab these things," I said as I made my way out of the apartment.

"Don't mention it," she waved off the gratitude as she followed me out. "I was glad to help. Most people wouldn't care enough to do what you're doing."

"If you'd like to come to the service, I can send you the details," I offered.

"Please do," she replied.

After that, we parted ways. She started walking back to the office, and I started walking back to my car.

As soon as I felt I had walked far enough away, I pulled the paper out, unfolded it, and read the message that was written on it.

This is what it said:

I know what you are, Bud, and if you don't help me, I'll tell everyone.

It was signed by Dolores.

I know what you are. What the heck is that supposed to mean?

I folded the paper back up and put it into my pocket. If it was the paper Bud was looking for, I would gladly return it the next time I saw him, right after he explained what it meant.

After I left the apartment complex, I went straight to the funeral home and dropped off the dress and picture. While I was there, the funeral director and I hashed out the specifics of Dolores's funeral, which we settled on having the following day.

I didn't expect a lot of people to come to the funeral on such short notice, so I was surprised when everyone from the group showed up, including Bud.

"It was beautiful," Sally said after the service. "I think Dolores would've loved it."

"I hope so."

As we were talking, I noticed that Bud was heading to his car.

"Excuse me for a second," I apologized before running to catch up to him.

"Hey, Bud," I called out. "Do you have a second?"

Bud stopped and looked at me but didn't say anything.

When I caught up to him, I pulled the paper out of my pocket and held it out to him. "I think this belongs to you."

Before he could grab it, I yanked it back. "What did she mean by 'I know what you are'?" I asked.

He eyed me for a moment before replying. "I'll explain," he said, "but not here."

"Where?"

"Meet me at the diner when you're done here," Bud said, and then he turned and left.

I put the paper back in my pocket and returned to the funeral.

When I finally made it to the diner, I found Bud sitting in a corner booth nursing a cup of coffee.

"Do you want anything?" he asked as I slid into the booth opposite him.

"Just some answers." I pulled the note out, unfolded it, and held it up for him to see.

Bud didn't say anything; instead, he reached into the jacket of his suit and withdrew a small paperback book. He set the book on the table and slid it across to me.

"What's this?" I dropped the paper, picked up the book, and read the title.

Myths and Legends of the World.

"That belonged to Dolores," he said.

I picked up the book and flipped through it until I came to a dog-eared page. The title at the top of the page said *Penthos, Eater of Grief*. It was circled with a red pen. Written beneath the circle was the name Bud.

As I looked at the page, I noticed that one sentence was underlined. The sentence read: *If you ask Penthos to show you his grief, he must show you his true form.*

Curious, and also feeling a little crazy for thinking there was anything to what was written in the book, I looked up at Bud and said, "Show me your grief."

Bud's appearance changed instantly; gone was the nondescript, currently overweight man who appeared to be in his late thirties. In his place was a being who looked vaguely human but with gray skin and black eyes.

I gasped when I saw him.

The image remained for only a moment before it reverted to the Bud I was familiar with.

"What the hell was that?" I leaned back, wanting to put some distance between Bud and me.

"That was my true form," he explained. "I am Penthos, the grief eater. I don't know how Dolores figured it out about me, but she did."

"What did she want from you?" I pointed to the line on the note where she had demanded that he help her.

"She wanted me to take her grief away," he replied.

"You can do that?" I asked.

"I can," he confirmed.

"You mean to tell me," I pointed my finger at him, "that for all the months I've been struggling with the loss of my wife and daughter, you could've taken the pain away and you chose not to?"

"It's not that simple," Bud replied. "There are risks involved."

"What kind of risks?" As soon as the question was out of my mouth, I was able to answer it myself.

"Dolores," I answered. "That's what killed her."

Bud nodded.

"Grief is like a drug to me," he explained. "The stronger it is, the greater the high, and Dolores's grief was strong. You can see what it did to my body." He spread his arms to indicate the sudden weight he had gained.

"Why would that kill her, though?"

"Because her grief was greater than her will to live," Bud said. "It was the only thing keeping her alive, and once I took it, she had nothing left to live for."

After he said that, I started to reflect on what my life had become since I'd lost my wife and daughter. I went to work, did a half-assed job while I was there, went home, stared at the television, and ate far less than I should.

I was barely living. Planning Dolores's funeral was the most alive I'd felt in months, and that feeling was now gone.

"I want you to take my grief," I said.

"You wouldn't survive," Bud said. "I can smell your grief, and it is far greater than Dolores's."

"I know."

Bud continued to protest until I threatened him the same way Dolores had.

"If you don't," I said, "I'll tell everyone what you are."

Bud took a deep breath and let it out as a sigh.

"I'll swing by your apartment tomorrow night," he said as he slid out of the booth. "Get your affairs in order by then."

That's exactly what I did.

"Are you ready?" Bud asked.

I was surprised he came. I figured he'd try to find a way to back out of it.

I nodded.

"Sit back and try to relax," he instructed.

I leaned back into the couch.

Bud placed his hands on either side of my head. When he did, I started feeling sleepy.

"How long will this take?" I asked.

"It shouldn't take more than a few minutes," he replied.

The drowsy feeling intensified and was accompanied by a fluttering in my chest, which I assumed was my heartbeat growing weaker.

I was ready for my heart to stop beating when the door to my house suddenly opened and Sally walked in.

"I'm here, Bud," she called out. "Where are you?"

"In the living room," Bud replied.

I wanted to tell her to leave, but I couldn't get the words out of my mouth.

"Is he okay?" she asked.

"He will be," Bud said.

"What do you want me to do?" Sally asked.

"Take his hand and tell him how you feel about him," Bud instructed.

While I lay there helpless in Bud's hands, Sally poured her heart out to me. As she did, I felt my heartbeat start to grow stronger.

PHOTOGRAPH

A little bell above the door jingled as I entered the photography store. A moment later, an elderly man stepped out of a curtained doorway at the back of the shop.

"Good morning." He placed his hands on the counter and greeted me with a smile. "How can I help you?"

I cleared my throat and pulled a folded newspaper out of my back pocket. "I'm here about the ad you put in the paper," I said, holding it up for him to see.

The man adjusted his glasses and motioned for me to hand him the newspaper. "Let's have a look at that," he said.

He took the paper and laid it on the counter as he began scanning the classified ads.

"Ah, here it is," he muttered to himself. To me, he said, "I'd forgotten all about this. Where did you find it?"

"What do you mean?" I was confused by his question.

"This paper was printed over a year ago," he gestured at the date in the corner of the page.

"Oh." I felt like an idiot. "I got it at the diner on the corner," I said, hooking my thumb over my shoulder.

"That figures," he laughed. "I told Alvin he needed to clean out that bin." He was referring to the newspaper bin in the entryway of the diner where I'd gotten the paper. "This was the last edition they printed before the paper went belly up," he explained. "They've been sitting there ever since."

"I take it that means the job is no longer available." I couldn't keep the disappointment out of my voice.

He didn't respond to my comment; instead, he said, "You're not from around here, are you?"

I shook my head. "No, sir. I was just passing through when I saw your help-wanted ad."

I was traveling cross-country on a bus with no destination in mind, figuring I'd find somewhere along the route to settle down. The only reason I was there was that the bus had made a rest stop at the diner, and I had a couple of hours to kill before it left again.

"Do you know anything about photography?" he asked.

I did. Otherwise, I wouldn't have bothered answering the ad.

"A little," I replied. "I took some classes in high school and was planning on majoring in photography when I went to college, but..." I paused, wondering how much I should tell him.

"But life got in the way," he interrupted, saving me from having to go into further detail about why I never made it to college.

"Yeah," I agreed. "Life got in the way."

The old man studied me for a moment before he spoke again.

"I've been hoping to retire," he said. "But the only way I can do that is if I can find someone to run the shop for me." He folded the paper back up. "The job's yours if you want it."

"Really?" I hadn't expected to be offered the job without an interview.

"I ran this ad every week for a year," he said, waving the paper in his hand. "And in that time I didn't get a single applicant. And now, a year after I've resigned myself to working until the day I die, you show up asking about it. I call that providence." He smiled at me. "So... do you want the job or not?"

"I do," I blurted out. "But I'm afraid you might change your mind once you hear where I've been."

I didn't think it was right to keep my past from him. He was likely to find out about it sooner or later, and I'd rather he heard it from me instead of somebody else.

The old man's features softened. "I'm not some small-town ignoramus," he said. "I know an ex-con when I see one. I'm assuming you've done your time and repaid your debt to society, or you wouldn't be here looking for a job."

"I..." I started to explain why I was in prison, but the old man held up a hand, stopping me.

"It doesn't matter to me," he said. "I've always trusted my gut, and my gut says to trust you."

"Thank you." Overcome with emotion, I struggled to get the words out. I was so used to being treated like a monster that his kindness overwhelmed me. "I won't let you down."

I approached the counter and held out my hand. "I'm Simon," I introduced myself.

"Abraham," he replied, taking my hand and shaking it.

Abraham didn't just give me a job that day; he also gave me a place to stay. Most people would've scoffed at having to stay in the drafty, outdated apartment above the shop, but not me. Anything was better than the tiny prison cell I'd just spent the last 10 years in.

"Do you think you can handle the shop on your own today?" Abraham asked. "I have a few errands I need to run."

He'd stopped by the apartment about an hour before we were scheduled to open.

"Sure," I agreed. For the past five days, Abraham had been training me on how to run the shop, and while I wasn't 100% sure I was ready to be left alone, I didn't want to let him down.

"Great," he replied.

He pulled a keyring out of his pocket and held it out to me. On it were all the keys to the shop, including the one to the cashbox he kept in the office.

I took the keys, surprised that he already trusted me enough to give all of them to me. I assumed he'd just give me the key to the door and the display case. That was all I really needed to man the store while he was gone.

"I'll be back before closing time," he said. "If you need anything, you've got my number." After that, he took his leave, and I went downstairs and got things ready to open the shop.

About six hours later, the bell above the door chimed. When I looked over to greet whoever it was, I saw Abraham walking into the store carrying a large manila envelope under his arm.

"I see you haven't burned the place down yet." He smiled.

"There's still time." I returned the smile.

"How were things while I was gone?" He walked across the shop and behind the counter, setting the envelope he was holding next to the register.

"Okay," I replied. "I sold a couple of those disposable cameras this morning," I said, pointing at the display rack. "Other than that, it's been quiet."

"That's more than I sold all week."

Abraham wasn't joking. While he was training me, he didn't sell a single thing. It made me wonder how he could afford to hire me, let alone keep the shop open. Concerned, I decided to just go ahead and ask him. I didn't want to get too comfortable if he couldn't afford to keep me.

"Can I ask you a personal question?"

"You can ask me anything you want," he replied.

"How do you afford all this?" I looked around the shop at all the photography supplies he sold. "It doesn't seem like you get much business here." He'd probably do a lot better in a larger city.

"This"—Abraham raised his hand and twirled his finger in the air, indicating the shop—"is just something to do to pass the time while waiting for the real moneymaker to come through." When he said the word moneymaker, he placed his hand on the manila envelope sitting on the counter.

"You don't need to worry about your job," he continued, guessing the reason for my question. "Thanks to this, I make plenty of money," he patted the envelope. "Let's go into my office and I'll explain." He motioned for me to follow him.

Once we were seated at the desk in the office, he reached into one of the drawers and pulled out a thick leather photo album. He placed it on the desk and turned it to face me before sliding it over.

"Have a look," Abraham gestured at the album.

I leaned forward and lifted the cover, surprised by what I saw. After flipping through the first few pages, I'd seen enough and closed the album.

"These are all death photos." I pushed the album back toward him.

"They are," he confirmed.

"I didn't think anyone still did that," I said.

Death photos were a popular thing in the late 1800s and early 1900s, but that was mostly because a lot of people died without any photos taken of them while they were alive. A death photo was the last chance for a family to preserve their loved one's appearance. That's why the deceased was often posed as if they were still alive before the photo was taken.

"They don't," Abraham agreed. "This is a special service that I offer. One that I want you to take over for me."

"Me?" I replied. "I don't think I'm the right person for that."

The thought of taking pictures of dead people sounded distasteful to me.

"It's not what you think," he tried to assure me. "And I happen to think you're the perfect person for the job."

"I appreciate your confidence in me, but I think it may be misplaced."

Even if I did agree to do it, it had been well over a decade since I took any pictures; everything I'd learned about lighting, framing, and posing had been forgotten. I doubt anyone would want to pay for a mediocre photo of their deceased loved one.

"I have a session scheduled for next weekend," Abraham said. "I want you to come with me. I think you'll change your mind once you see how it's done."

"Okay," I agreed. "But I'm not making any promises."

"Fair enough," he said, taking the album and putting it back inside his desk.

"How long are we going to be gone?" I asked Abraham after he told me to pack an overnight bag in preparation for the death photo session.

"Just the one night," he replied.

"What about the shop?" I asked.

He reached under the counter and pulled out a sign. "Put this in the window," he instructed.

I looked at the sign as I carried it over to the display window at the front of the store. It said:

AWAY ON BUSINESS. IF YOU NEED ASSISTANCE, PLEASE SEE EMMA NEXT DOOR.

Emma was the pharmacist and owner of Cobb's Drug Store, which was next door to the photography store. Abraham had introduced me to her during my first week in town. Like him, she was in her early 70s. When I met her, she was in the process of training her granddaughter to take over for her.

I put the sign in the window next to the closed sign and then returned to where Abraham was packing up his camera gear.

"You're taking that?"

I was surprised to see that Abraham was packing up the vintage daguerreotype camera that was sitting on a tripod in the corner of the shop. I thought it was just there as a curiosity, like the rest of the old cameras that decorated the shop.

"It's the only camera that works for these kinds of photos," he replied, patting the case the daguerreotype was in.

"I've never used one," I said.

It would have been challenging for me to take over the death photo side of the business if I had to use a camera I was unfamiliar with.

"Don't worry about that," he waved off my concern. "It's not as hard as you think. Now run upstairs and pack. We need to be on our way." He returned his attention to packing up the rest of his supplies.

Six hours later, we arrived at our destination—a small one-story family home in the neighboring state.

"Wait here," Abraham instructed before getting out of the car and approaching the house.

I watched through the passenger-side window as he spoke to the young woman who answered the door. I figured she must've been a nurse or some other type of healthcare worker based on the green scrubs she was wearing.

The woman stepped aside and let Abraham into the house. He was in there for about 10 minutes before he came back outside.

"Help me grab the gear," he said, walking to the back of the car and opening the trunk.

I grabbed the bulk of the equipment and then followed Abraham back into the house, where he led me to the master bedroom.

While waiting in the car, I did my best to mentally prepare myself for the death photo. I'd never been in the same room with a dead body before, and the thought of having to help pose one was making me very nervous.

Before stepping into the bedroom, I stood out in the hall and took a deep breath to calm my nerves. What I saw when I finally entered the room surprised me.

I pulled Abraham to the side and whispered, "I thought we were here to take a death photo?"

"We are," he whispered back.

"But she's not dead," I said, nodding my head toward the sickly woman who was lying in the bed surrounded by several pieces of medical equipment.

While I talked to Abraham, the nurse was helping to prop the woman up into a sitting position before leaving us alone in the room with her.

"I'll explain after we take her photo," Abraham said.

He stepped away from me and began setting up the old camera.

"I'm ready when you are, Ms. Mullins," he said to the woman when he'd finished setting everything up.

"Will this really work?" Ms. Mullins sounded tired and out of breath as she spoke.

Abraham nodded. "I promise you it will."

Will what work? I wanted to ask him, but I didn't want to interrupt him as he started to adjust the position of the camera.

"Hold this for me," Abraham instructed, holding out the powder tray that was attached to a long wooden pole. Sticking out of the bottom of the pole was a long cord that ended with a small circular handle with a button on the end of it.

After I took the powder tray from him, he reached into one of his bags, pulled out a bottle of powder, and filled the tray. When he was done, he picked up the circular handle and held it in his hand with his thumb poised above the button.

"The exposure time for this camera is about three minutes," he said to Ms. Mullins. "So I'm going to need you to hold your pose until I say. Can you do that for me?"

"That won't be a problem," Ms. Mullins replied. "I can barely move as it is."

"You might want to close your eyes," Abraham warned me a moment before he pressed the button, igniting the powder in the tray.

Even with my eyes closed, the flash was incredibly bright, forcing me to turn my head away.

"All right, we're done here," Abraham announced as he started breaking down the camera and putting it away.

"That's it?" Ms. Mullins asked. She sounded disappointed. "I don't feel any different."

"You won't," Abraham replied. "At least not yet. But you will soon. I promise."

"What is she talking about?" I leaned over so I could whisper to him.

"I'll explain everything later," he whispered back. "We need to let Ms. Mullins get some rest," he nodded toward her and then changed the subject. "Take that outside and dump it in the grass," he pointed at the tray I was still holding, which contained the ashes of the flash powder. "Then come back here and help me load this stuff back into the car."

I got the impression that he wanted me out of the room so he could talk to Ms. Mullins alone, so I obliged him.

When I left them, I considered standing outside the doorway and eavesdropping to see what he said to her, but I changed my mind when I saw the nurse sitting at the dining room table looking in my direction.

"So," I said, "are you ready to explain what all of that was about?"

I'd waited until we were well on our way back to the photo shop before I said anything. I was hoping Abraham would bring it up on his own, but he didn't, and I was getting a little impatient.

"Not just yet," he replied. "First, I need to show you how to use the camera. Then I will explain everything." When he saw the annoyed look on my face, he added, "I know that's not what you wanted to hear, but I promise it's for the best. Just sit tight for a few more hours. That's all I'm asking."

"Okay," I relented. I didn't really have a choice.

Abraham changed the subject after that, choosing to talk about the town we called home, giving me a little bit of history about its inhabitants while letting me know who I could trust and who to stay away from. Overall, he made it sound like a great place to live.

"All right," Abraham pushed his empty plate away. "I guess it's time."

We'd stopped at the diner when we'd gotten back into town and had just finished eating a late lunch when he made his declaration.

He stood up, pulled two $20 bills out of his wallet, and set them on the table.

"I have a couple of fives if you don't have anything smaller." I gestured at the bills.

Our tab was only $25.

Abraham waved off my offer.

"Doris deserves it," he said, referring to the waitress who was serving us.

It was his money, so I didn't push the issue.

"Would you mind unloading the car? I need to stop by and see Carl for a moment." He gestured up the road to where Carl, the only lawyer in town, had his practice.

"I don't mind," I replied, getting up and following him outside. "Do you want me to open the shop when I'm done?" I asked before we went our separate ways.

"Not yet," he said. "We have much to discuss, and I don't want any interruptions."

"Okay," I replied. "I'll see you in a bit." I gave a brief wave and then turned and walked across the street to unload the car.

Abraham returned 30 minutes later carrying a thick folder, which he put on the desk in his office before coming back out to the sales floor.

"The first thing I need to show you is this." He walked over to the daguerreotype camera, took it out of its case, and slid the plate out after setting it on the counter.

"This can't be the picture you took," I said after he'd handed it to me.

I was there, and I saw how Ms. Mullins was posed. She was alive and had her arms folded in her lap. In the picture Abraham handed me, her arms hung limply at her sides, and she was clearly dead.

"It is," he assured me.

I opened my mouth to ask him how that was possible, but he stopped me with an outstretched hand.

"Let me show you how to use the camera, and then I will explain," he said.

Over the next 15 minutes, Abraham showed me how to set up the daguerreotype and load the film plate into the slot. Then he showed me how to focus the lens and take a picture while holding the powder tray.

"Think you're ready to give it a try?" he asked when he was done.

"Yeah," I nodded. "I think so."

He walked around the camera and stood in front of it. "Take my picture," he said.

I did everything Abraham had shown me to get the camera ready and then said, "Smile," as I pressed the button that would ignite the flash powder.

He didn't smile.

"Now we just have to wait a few minutes for the picture to develop," he said.

While we waited, I decided to ask him a question. "How much do you charge for these photos?" I gestured at the camera.

He'd told me that the death photos were where the shop made most of its money. That made me curious about how much he charged.

"As much as they are willing to pay," he replied cryptically.

"You don't have a set rate?" I was surprised to hear that.

"I'm providing a service," Abraham said, pulling the plate out of the camera as he talked. "It's up to the client to decide how valuable that service is."

"That sounds like an easy way to let people take advantage of you," I said.

"Not these people," he said, walking over to set the picture I'd taken next to the one of Ms. Mullins. "Come here and I'll explain," he waved me over to the counter. "What do you see?" he asked when I was standing next to him.

"I... uh..." I'd looked at the pictures, expecting to see the same thing I saw earlier, along with the photo I'd taken of Abraham, but that's not what I saw.

The pictures were not as they were supposed to be.

The one of Ms. Mullins, where she'd originally appeared dead, now showed her lying in bed, smiling, and looking full of life. The one I'd taken of Abraham, where he should be standing in the shop, now showed him lying on the ground with a lifeless look on his face.

"I don't understand," I said.

"Let's go into the office and I'll explain." He picked up the photos of Ms. Mullins and himself and took them into the office.

Before we sat down, he went over to the small fridge he kept in the corner, pulled out two beers, and set them on the desk.

I popped the top off mine and patiently waited for him to settle into his chair and get comfortable.

"That camera is special," he started, pointing his finger to where the daguerreotype was set up on the sales floor. "It doesn't take death photos; it suspends death. But only for a short while."

"Suspends death?" That was not what I was expecting to hear.

Abraham nodded. "When I took Ms. Mullins's picture, the camera suspended her death in this photograph." He touched the image of Ms. Mullins.

"If it suspended her death, why did the image change?"

"Because you transferred her death to me when you took my picture," he revealed. "That's why I appear dead in this photo." He touched the image of himself.

"Wait. What?" I set my beer down and leaned forward. "Why would you do that?"

"Because I don't have much time left," he said. "And it was the quickest and easiest way to show you how to use the camera so that you can take over for me."

"What if I don't want to take over for you?"

"You will," he said. "It won't be easy at first, but you'll change your mind once you see the good in what you're doing."

As he spoke, a thought occurred to me. "If you're dying, why didn't you just use the camera on yourself?" I said. "Assuming it actually does what you say it does."

"I thought about it," Abraham said. "Thought long and hard about it. But I eventually concluded that if I did, I still wouldn't have much time left. I'm old. If I skipped the death waiting for me, another would arrive shortly to take its place. On the other hand, Ms. Mullins is young; she has the potential to live a long and happy life because of me. I take comfort in knowing that, and you should, too."

When he was done talking, he grabbed the thick folder he'd brought over from the lawyer's office and set it in the middle of the desk.

"You'll have to forgive me for rushing through things, but I don't have much time left, and we still have a lot of things to go over."

He pushed the folder across the desk to me.

"This is everything I own," Abraham said. "It's all yours now. The shop, my house, the car—everything has been transferred over to you."

I was speechless.

"All I ask," he continued, "is that you use the camera to help people. People like Ms. Mullins."

That wasn't the part I had an issue with. Stopping someone from dying sounded fine. The part that bothered me was that I had to transfer that person's death to someone else, condemning them instead.

"I don't know about all this."

"It's not as hard as you think." Abraham could read the concern on my face. "There are plenty of people who deserve to live," he said, "and even more who deserve to die."

ITZPAPALOTL

"All right, everyone," the guide announced. "It's time to return to the bus."

The bus was not much bigger than a van and looked cobbled together from parts of other vehicles.

"So?" I asked my husband, Edward. "What did you think?"

I'd convinced him to go on a tour of some old Aztec ruins while we were vacationing in Mexico. I'd chosen that particular tour because it claimed to take us to sites that weren't among the most visited tourist destinations.

"It was okay," Edward replied.

"Just okay?" I scoffed. I thought the site was amazing. "How could you not be in awe standing before something this old?" I swept my arm toward the stone temple.

"History is more your thing," he admitted before starting on the path back to the bus.

"Hold up," I called out to him. "Your backpack is open."

He was about to swing his bag off his shoulder to check it, but I stopped him.

"I got it," I said, walking up behind him to adjust the zipper.

"Thanks," he replied as I fell into step alongside him.

"I can't believe you didn't like that," I said.

"I didn't say I didn't like it," Edward explained. "It's just hard for me to get excited about some old buildings carved out of stone the way you do."

"That was so much more than just an old building carved out of stone," I decided to educate him. "That was a temple to Itzpapalotl, ruler of Tamoanchan and queen of the Tzitzimimeh."

"Gesundheit," he replied, turning my comment into a joke.

After that, I just kept my mouth shut about it. I'd taken lots of pictures, intentionally excluding my husband from any of them so that I could look back and remember the visit, pretending he wasn't there.

As the bus was leaving, I felt Edward tense as he stared out the window at something. When I followed his gaze, I noticed that he was looking back at the temple.

"Did you see that?" He kept his voice low as he pointed out the window.

"See what?" I hadn't seen anything except the temple retreating in the distance as we drove away.

"The woman who was standing there." He looked back at me, studying my face to see if I was being serious. When he saw that I was, he said, "How could you not see her? She was wearing this big headdress that looked like butterfly wings." He held his hands to the sides of his head, mimicking what he had seen.

"And she was wearing a mask that looked like a skull," he continued.

What he described sounded familiar, prompting me to open my guidebook and flip through it until I found the page I was looking for.

"Did she look like this?" I showed Edward the picture of a woman dressed as Itzpapalotl.

The picture was from a local festival where villagers dressed as various Aztec gods and performed plays telling stories about the roles the gods played in daily Aztec life.

I'd gone to see it while Edward went on a night fishing excursion. It was an incredible production that didn't try to gloss over any of the darker parts of Aztec lore.

"Sort of," Edward answered as he took the book from me to get a better look. "The woman I saw was taller and thinner, and what she was wearing looked cruder," he explained.

"Who is she supposed to be?" he asked, handing the book back to me.

"That's Itzpapalotl," I replied. "The goddess whose temple we just visited."

"You really didn't see her?" he asked.

"No, I didn't."

From the way he was looking at me, I got the impression that he didn't believe me.

Edward confirmed the thought when he said, "I think you're fucking with me."

"I really didn't see anyone," I insisted.

"Okay," he said. "I believe you." The smirk on his face told me he didn't.

"I—" I didn't like that he didn't believe me and was going to keep insisting that I hadn't seen anything, but he cut me off.

"Let's just forget about it." He waved off the comment I was about to make. "It's not important."

"Okay," I agreed. "But I really didn't see anything," I repeated, needing to get the last word in.

The bus ride back into town took a little over an hour, and we changed the subject to our plans for the evening.

We settled on having dinner at the hotel and drinks on the beach.

As we got up and started disembarking from the bus, Edward suddenly stopped in the doorway, causing me to bump into him.

"Why'd you stop like that?" I asked, feeling a little irritated.

"There she is again." Edward lifted his hand and pointed to an area of dense vegetation off to the side of the hotel. "You see her, right?"

I didn't see anyone.

"What's the holdup?" a man waiting to get off the bus griped.

"We have to keep moving," I said, giving Edward a little nudge in the back to get him moving again. "We're holding up the line."

He stepped off the bus and started walking toward the hotel, keeping his eyes fixed on the spot where he claimed to have seen Itzpapalotl.

I followed behind him until he stopped and pulled out his phone.

"What are you doing?" I asked.

"I'm taking a picture of her," Edward replied, holding up his phone.

I continued walking. After being out all morning in the summer sun and touring historical sites, I was eager to get into the shower.

Edward continued to stare at the spot beside the hotel until we entered the lobby.

When I finished my shower, I came out of the bathroom to find Edward sitting on the edge of the bed, staring at his phone.

"This doesn't make sense," he said.

"What doesn't?"

"This." He held his phone out to show me something.

"Hold on," I said, making him wait. "Let me get dressed first."

He got up and started pacing the floor, waiting impatiently for me to pull out a fresh set of clothes so I could get dressed.

"All right, show me." I took a seat on the edge of the bed and held my hand out for his phone.

Instead of giving it to me, he stepped closer and showed me the most recent photos on his camera roll.

"I took a dozen photos of her," he said, "and she isn't in a single one of them." He enlarged photo after photo, showing me the same group of bushes.

"I don't know what to tell you," I said. "Maybe you're going crazy," I suggested.

"That's not funny." He sounded agitated.

"I wasn't trying to be funny," I replied. "Do you know if there's any history of mental illness in your family?"

"There's not," he snapped.

"Then why do you think you're hallucinating?"

"I didn't say I was hallucinating." He started pacing again.

"You're seeing an Aztec woman that nobody else can see. What would you call it?"

"I don't know," he replied, plopping down on the edge of the bed next to me. "Maybe I'm cursed."

"Cursed?" I couldn't help but laugh when I said the word. "Why would you think that?"

"Don't you remember what the guide said when we were at the temple?" He gestured with his hands, projecting his exasperation. "He said that people believed it was cursed."

"That's not what he said," I corrected him. "He said that people who'd taken things from the temple had died under mysterious circumstances, leading others to believe the place was cursed."

"That sounds like the same thing to me."

"Did you take something from the temple?" I asked.

"No," he protested.

"Then you should be fine," I explained. "The curse the guide was talking about only affects people who take things out of the temple. Personally, I don't believe in that sort of thing, and I'm surprised to hear that you do."

"I don't know what I believe." Edward was clearly upset. "All I know is that something weird is going on, and it started at that temple." He jabbed his finger at the balcony doors to emphasize his point.

I knew there was nothing I could say to placate him, so I just kept my mouth shut.

"Just forget about it," he sighed in defeat as he lay back on the bed and shut his eyes.

"Maybe you should take a nap," I suggested.

He sounded like he could use one.

"What are you going to do?" he asked.

"I was thinking of heading down to the market to do a little shopping," I said.

There was an open-air market in the center of town I'd been meaning to visit, and now seemed like the perfect time.

"Can you do me a favor?" Edward asked, pushing himself up the bed so his head rested on the pillows.

"Depends on what it is," I replied honestly.

"If you see any of those beaded necklaces while you're out, can you pick one up for me?" he asked. "The kind that goes across the chest." He made a sweeping motion under his neck with one hand. "Do you know the kind I'm talking about?"

"I think so," I said. "Why do you want one of those?"

"My boss asked me to pick one up for his wife," he explained.

"I'll see what I can find." I picked up my backpack and slung it over my shoulders. "I hope he's planning on paying you back for it."

Edward didn't reply.

"I'll be back in a couple of hours," I said as I exited the hotel room. "Love you."

"Love you, too," he replied before settling in to take his nap.

When I returned from the market, I was surprised to find that Edward wasn't in the hotel room.

I looked around, checking to see if he had left me a note, but I didn't find one. I did, however, find his phone lying on the bed.

Thinking he might have stepped out for a bit, I watched some television while I waited for him to return. When he didn't return after an hour, I became concerned and went down to the hotel lobby to look for him.

"Excuse me," I said to the man behind the guest service desk. "I was wondering if you've seen my husband." I described what Edward had been wearing the last time I saw him.

"No," the hotel clerk shook his head. "I haven't seen him."

"Can you check and see if anyone left a message for room 322?"

Since Edward didn't have his phone with him when he left, I thought he might have left a message for me at the front desk.

"Did you say 322?" the clerk repeated my room number.

"Yeah," I nodded.

"There's no message," he replied, "but we did get a noise complaint about that room."

"What kind of noise complaint?" I asked.

"Guests in the neighboring room said the occupant was yelling," he said.

"How long ago was that?"

"About an hour or so."

That would've been shortly after I left for the market.

"Did you send anyone to the room?"

"We did," he explained, "but nobody answered the door."

"Okay." I'd learned all I could from him. "Thanks."

I turned around and went back up to my room, where I waited a couple more hours for Edward to return. When he didn't show up by dinnertime, I decided it was time to go to the authorities.

"The last time you saw your husband was when you left to go to the market, correct?" Detective Becerra asked me.

He was the detective assigned to help me find my missing husband.

"That's correct," I confirmed.

"What did the two of you do before that?" he asked, trying to learn more about what Edward was doing before he disappeared.

"This afternoon," I replied, "when we got back from our tour."

"What tour would that be?" Becerra leaned forward, readying his pen to write in his notebook.

"Alejandro's."

When I said the name, the detective and the police officer standing next to him exchanged a look.

"Did Alejandro take you to Itzpapalotl's temple?"

I nodded. "He did."

"Did your husband take anything from the temple?"

I shook my head. "Not that I'm aware of." It was clear what they were thinking. "You don't think the temple is really cursed, do you?" I asked.

"A lot of strange things have happened around that temple," Detective Becerra explained. "That is why it is off-limits to tourists."

"Off-limits?" I repeated. "If I'd known that, I never would have gone." I was afraid I might be in trouble for admitting I'd gone there.

"Do not worry, Señora Hartley." The detective raised a hand in a placating gesture. "You did nothing wrong. Alejandro is the one who will have to answer for this trespass."

I sighed in relief.

"Is there anything else you can tell me that might help me find him?" he asked.

I hadn't planned on telling them about Edward's hallucinations, but I decided it might be important, especially after their reaction to our tour of Itzpapalotl's temple.

"There is one thing," I revealed. "My husband said he kept seeing a woman who was wearing some sort of butterfly headdress and a skull mask."

Detective Becerra and the officer exchanged another look.

"I think we have everything we need," the detective said. "Officer Reyes will escort you back to your hotel." He gestured to the uniformed man. "We'll be in touch if we find anything."

Detective Becerra quickly disappeared through a door that led further into the police precinct.

He sure seemed to be in a hurry, I thought.

"Right this way, señora," Officer Reyes said, motioning for me to follow him outside to his car.

Shortly before midnight, there was a knock on the door of my hotel room. When I looked through the peephole, I saw Detective Becerra standing on the other side.

"I apologize for disturbing you at this late hour, Señora Hartley," he said after I'd opened the door.

"Did you find my husband?" I asked before he could say anything else.

He ignored my question and instead said, "I'm going to need you to come with me."

"Okay," I replied. "Let me grab my things." I ducked back into the hotel room, grabbed what I needed, and then followed the detective to his car.

Once we were inside the car, Detective Becerra drove me to the local hospital, which was nothing more than a single-story stucco building in need of a paint job.

"Follow me," he said, leading me to the back of the hospital, where he stopped outside a set of double doors. The sign above them labeled the room beyond the morgue.

"Is he dead?" I held a trembling hand to my face.

"I'm afraid so, señora," the detective replied in a sympathetic voice. "His body was found on top of Itzpapalotl's temple."

"What happened to him?" I wiped the tears that were coming from my eyes.

"You don't want to know," Becerra said.

"Please, I have to know," I insisted.

The detective sighed and said, "Someone cut out his heart."

I gasped and held my hand over my mouth.

"I just need you to confirm that it is indeed him for our records," Becerra said. "Can you do that?"

I nodded.

The detective pushed open the door and let me enter before him.

"Señora," the doctor on the other side greeted me.

The morgue smelled of antiseptic with an underlying scent of death. In the center of the room was a table upon which was a body covered with a sheet.

Becerra nodded at the doctor, silently indicating for him to proceed.

The doctor walked up to the table and lowered the sheet far enough for me to see Edward's lifeless face.

"That's him," I confirmed.

The doctor covered Edward's head again.

"Who would do something like that?"

Detective Becerra pulled a phone out of his pocket and showed me an image of a familiar-looking idol.

"This was placed in his chest after his heart was removed," he explained. "Do you recognize it?"

I nodded. "There were several of those at the temple we toured."

"We think your husband removed one of them from the temple."

He did, I answered in my head, *but he didn't know it.*

I'd secretly slipped one into his backpack when he wasn't paying attention.

I'd been trying to find a way to get rid of my husband ever since I found out he was cheating on me with one of his coworkers. That's who he really wanted the beaded necklace for. That story about buying it for his boss's wife was bullshit.

When I heard stories about Itzpapalotl's curse, I decided to go there and find out if there was any truth to them. Lucky for me, there was.

"Can I have a moment alone with my husband?" I asked, doing my best to continue sounding like a grieving widow.

"Of course," Detective Becerra said. "Take all the time you need. We'll be right outside."

He and the doctor stepped out to give me some privacy.

Once they were gone, I pulled out Edward's phone and used it to take a picture of his corpse. I then sent the picture to his mistress with the caption: WISH YOU WERE HERE.

"I'm done," I announced as I pushed my way out of the morgue to join the two men in the hallway.

Over the next few days, I made arrangements to have Edward's body sent back home.

As far as I could tell, the police weren't doing much to investigate my husband's death, which was fine with me.

The day I was supposed to leave, Detective Becerra surprised me by meeting me at the hotel.

"Did you need something, Detective?" I asked.

"I came to offer you a ride to the airport," he replied.

"I don't think that's necessary," I said. "You've done enough already."

"Please, I insist." Becerra held the car door open for me. "It's the least I can do."

"Okay," I relented.

I got into his car while he loaded my bags into the trunk.

On the way to the airport, the detective offered me his condolences.

"We will catch the person who killed your husband," he said. "That I promise you."

I seriously doubt that, I thought. Out loud I said, "I hope so."

When we made it to the airport, Detective Becerra retrieved my bags while I got out of the car.

"Have a safe flight," he said as he handed the bags over to me.

"Thank you," I said. "For the ride and everything else you've done for me."

"Don't mention it." He waved off my gratitude. "It was my pleasure."

I waited until he drove away before going into the terminal. As I looked for my gate, I noticed an odd-looking woman in ancient Aztec clothing, wearing an ornate butterfly headdress and a skull mask.

Itzpapalotl, I gasped.

I looked down at my bag and noticed that the zipper was slightly open.

When I opened it the rest of the way, I found a stone idol sitting on top of my clothes. Attached to it with a rubber band was a note that said:

I thought you might like a souvenir of your trip.

It was signed by Detective Becerra.

HOSTAGE SITUATION

"Wake up!" a distorted voice yelled.

I cracked my eyes open and looked around, trying to figure out who was talking to me. That's when I realized I was lying on my basement floor.

"Hello?" I called out, pushing myself into a sitting position. "Is there somebody down here?" I was confused and had no memory of going down to the basement.

"Wake up!" the voice repeated, drawing my attention to the old tape recorder on the seat of a broken chair.

As I slowly got to my feet, my head started pounding, and a sudden wave of vertigo hit me. I would've fallen if I hadn't placed a hand against the wall to steady myself. That's when I heard the clanking of metal and looked down to find a chain padlocked around my left ankle.

I followed the chain with my eyes to where it was fastened to a support beam in the center of the basement.

What the hell is going on?

"Are you awake?" the voice on the tape recorder asked. "If you are, I need you to listen to me. The lives of your kids depend on it."

My kids?

"If you need a minute to compose yourself before we continue, press the pause button," the voice continued.

I approached the tape recorder and examined it, recognizing it as one of the many things my husband held on to from his childhood. I'd tried to get rid of it a few times, but he always stopped me, saying he might need it one day.

"Are you ready?" the voice said a few seconds later.

I reached out and pressed the stop button.

No, I'm not ready.

I pressed the eject button and pulled out the tape. Like the recorder, it belonged to my husband. It was one of his old mixtapes before whoever had put me in the basement recorded over it.

Is that who's doing this to me? I wondered, thinking my husband, Wayne, was still mad at me for the fight we had the previous night.

He'd been spending a lot of time with his friends on weekends, leaving me at home with the kids. It was making me feel neglected, and I'd finally decided to say something about it. In typical Wayne fashion, instead of talking about it, he turned it into a huge fight before storming out of the house.

Did he come back?

I suddenly realized I couldn't remember anything after the fight. My mind was blank.

Why can't I remember?

I reached up and touched the side of my head, something I often did when I was trying to think. As my fingers brushed against my scalp, a sharp pain exploded just above my ear.

"Ow," I hissed, gently probing the area.

Where did that come from?

There was a huge bump on the left side of my head.

That must be why I can't remember.

I looked down at the tape in my other hand.

Maybe this will explain what happened.

I slid it back into the recorder and pressed the play button.

"Your kids are safe... for now," the distorted voice on the tape said. "And if you want them to stay that way, I'm going to need you to do something for me. I'm going to need you to prove just how much you love them."

There was a brief pause before the voice continued.

"Right now, you're thinking about how horrible life would be without them and that you would do anything to save them," it said.

The voice was right; that was exactly what I was thinking.

"That's why I'm going to give you a chance to prove it," the voice continued. "Behind you is a box labeled Christmas Ornaments. I need you to open that box and remove the plastic container inside it."

I turned around and located the box. It was the only one within reach of the short chain that bound me. When I opened it, I saw one of my blue kitchen containers nestled among a bunch of Christmas lights. I removed it and carried it back to the chair. As I did, something heavy inside shifted back and forth.

The tape continued to play, but only silence came from the speaker for almost a minute.

When the voice returned, it said, "Do you have the container? If you do, open it."

I pulled the lid off the container. There were two things inside: a cleaver and a Polaroid picture.

"The picture is proof that I have your kids and that they are alive," the voice said. "The cleaver is for you to prove how much you love them."

I reached down and pressed the stop button on the tape recorder after setting the plastic container next to it. Then I pulled out the photo and held it up so I could look at it.

It showed both of my kids, bound to chairs with duct tape. Tears stained their terrified faces.

"Why are you doing this?" I spoke the question out loud. "Why?!" I yelled, which caused my sore head to start throbbing.

I had to close my eyes and take a couple of deep breaths as I waited for the pain to subside. When I opened them again, my gaze fixated on the cleaver.

I reached down and picked it up, leaving the photo in its place.

Maybe, I thought, eyeing the chain around my ankle.

I knew the cleaver was strong enough to cut through bone, and I hoped it might be strong enough to cut through the thin links of the chain.

Unfortunately, it wasn't.

I tried several times in different ways, but I couldn't even make a dent in any of the links.

Not wanting to give up that easily, I turned my attention to the beam I was shackled to.

Maybe I can cut through that.

I tried. I did make a little progress, but not much. In the fifteen minutes I hacked at the beam with the cleaver, I managed to carve a small notch in one of the corners.

I eventually had to stop because my hands were starting to cramp.

When I sat down to rest, I eyed the tape recorder.

Might as well listen to the rest.

I crawled over to the recorder and pressed the play button.

"If you're thinking about using the cleaver to escape, don't," the distorted voice said. "By the time you cut through that beam, your kids will already be dead."

I guess I should've listened to the tape first, I chided myself.

"Now, if you're ready, it's time to prove how much you love your kids," the voice continued. "To do that, I'm going to need you to cut off one of your fingers or toes. It doesn't matter which one. I'll give you thirty minutes to get it done. If I don't get what I want by then, one of your kids will die. The clock starts ticking now."

Thirty minutes? From when? Did that include the time I spent trying to cut myself free? How are they keeping track of time? Am I being watched?

Those were the questions that raced through my mind as I turned in a circle, scanning the basement, looking for any sign that I was being watched. All I saw were stacks of boxes and old furniture lined up around the perimeter of the room.

Plenty of space for someone to hide, I thought as images of a dark figure crouching in the shadows filled my mind.

"Twenty-five minutes," the voice said from the recorder.

I was so focused on the dark recesses of the basement, thinking someone was there, that the sound of the voice startled me.

A moment later, it said, "Having trouble deciding? If I were you, I'd take a pinky. It's small and its loss won't affect your ability to use your hand that much."

I looked down at the fingers of my right hand. The voice did have a point. My pinky was small, and I was fairly certain I'd be able to whack it off with one swing of the cleaver. I didn't think I'd be able to do that to any of my toes. They were too close together. I'd probably end up cutting off more than one.

Pinky it is.

I placed my hand on the cold concrete floor and splayed my fingers.

I don't think I can do this, I thought as I lined the cleaver up with the base of my pinky, thinking about how much it was going to hurt.

"Twenty minutes," the voice called out a couple of minutes later. "I know this is no easy task. Therefore, I'm going to help you by giving you a little motivation." There was a rustling sound before the voice started speaking again. "Say hello to your mommy," it said. That was followed by the sound of tape being ripped from skin.

My son wailed in pain and started crying. That made me start crying too.

"Did that help?" it asked before going silent again.

"You have to do this," I said to myself. "You have to." I kept chanting that over and over as I raised the cleaver over my head and brought it down as hard as I could, closing my eyes at the last moment.

For a fraction of a second, I thought I'd missed my finger because I didn't feel anything. But that thought was short-lived as an intense pain shot up my arm.

When I opened my eyes and held up my hand, I saw that I had not missed. I'd completely severed my pinky from my hand and managed to slice a deep gouge in the side of my ring finger as well.

There was so much blood.

I think I'm going to be sick.

I felt nauseous as the room started spinning.

The last thing I remember before passing out was falling to my hands and knees and vomiting on the floor, where it mixed with the blood.

"Wake up!" the distorted voice demanded.

I cracked my eyes open and stared at the ceiling. When I saw the light fixture from my bedroom above me and realized I was lying in my bed, I sighed in relief.

It was only a dream.

As I pushed myself up from the bed, a sharp pain in my right hand made me wince and cry out. I looked at my hand and saw it was heavily bandaged.

It wasn't a dream. I really did cut off my pinky.

"Are you awake?" the voice asked from the tape recorder that was now sitting on the nightstand.

"Fuck you," I snapped. "Where are my kids?!"

"I'm afraid I've got some bad news," the voice continued. "The finger was not enough. I really thought it would be, but unfortunately, it wasn't. Therefore, I'm going to need you to do something else for me."

"No fucking way!" I spat.

There was no way I was going to cut off another finger or do anything else to hurt myself.

I stood up and rushed over to the bedroom door. As I reached the end of the bed, a shoestring tied across my path caught my ankle, sending me falling to the floor. I tried to throw out my hands to catch myself, but I was too slow. My forehead collided with the front of my dresser, knocking me unconscious.

"Wake up!"

When I regained consciousness, I found myself in a sitting position with something covering my face, preventing me from seeing where I was.

"Ow," I groaned. My head felt like it was going to explode.

"Are you awake?"

I was really getting tired of hearing that voice.

"If you are, I need you to listen to me," the voice said. There was a brief pause before it started speaking again. "You are currently sitting in your living room with a pillowcase over your head. When you feel ready, I need you to take it off. There's something I want to show you." There was another pause. "Take all the time you need."

I didn't need any time. I immediately reached up and pulled the pillowcase off my head.

When I saw my husband's body sitting in the recliner across the room, I screamed.

Someone had slit his throat. The resulting gush of blood stained the front of his clothes and the floor in front of him.

"He'll never hit you again," the voice said. The recorder was sitting on the coffee table in front of me.

"Who the fuck are you!?" I screamed at the recorder.

"That's not the only surprise I have for you," the voice said. "I have one more waiting for you in the kitchen."

"Fuck you!"

I lashed out and knocked the recorder off the table as I got to my feet. It crashed against the wall, knocking the battery cover off. I expected the batteries to fly out as well, but there were no batteries in it.

"You can't get rid of me that easily," the voice coming from the recorder was no longer distorted.

It was my voice.

This has to be a dream! It has to!

I backed away from the recorder, heading for the entryway that led to the kitchen.

"It's not a dream," my voice said via the recorder. "Not yet."

I rushed into the kitchen and stopped when I saw the bodies of my two children at the dining table. They'd had their throats slit as well. Their blood coated the surface of the table.

"No," I shook my head.

"Yes," was the response from the recorder. "This is the way it has to be."

"Bring them back," I demanded.

"You know that's not possible."

"BRING THEM BACK!" I screamed, and I kept yelling it until I blacked out.

When I regained consciousness, I was in complete darkness.

"I know you're awake in there." It was my voice, but it wasn't me.

"Where am I?" I asked.

"You're where I was before your husband knocked me free," the other version of me answered.

The memory of my husband striking me during our argument returned.

"I tried to keep you suppressed," the other me explained, "so I could have control of the body, but you were stronger than me. That's why I had to hurt you. It was the only way to get you out of the way so I could regain control."

"You killed my kids." The image of their lifeless bodies filled my thoughts.

"I wouldn't have had to if you would've just stayed here like you were supposed to," she replied.

"This is my body!" I shouted.

"Was your body," the other me corrected. "It's mine now. And if you promise not to try to regain control of it, I'll show you how to get your kids back."

"How?"

"They're not really dead," the other me teased. "Not where you are. In there, they're still alive."

The darkness around me dissolved, replaced by a hospital room. I suddenly found myself lying in a hospital bed, giving birth to my son.

"If you stay in here, you can be with them forever and imagine the life you always wanted."

HOLY SHIT

"Hey, kid," the homeless man motioned, "come here for a minute."

I was walking several steps behind my parents, who were busy talking to our neighbors, the Winslows, when he called out to me.

The Winslows had invited us to attend their church with them after my parents expressed their dissatisfaction with our old church. They were excited because the Winslows' church was different from the other churches in town. To attend, you had to have an invitation from an existing member of the congregation. My parents loved the idea of a church with a curated membership.

The homeless man was standing to the side of a cinderblock structure that housed the church's dumpster. The way he hugged the wall and kept looking around made me think he was trying to keep anyone else from seeing him.

"It's okay," he continued. "I'm not going to bite. I just want to give you something."

He held out his hand to show me the pendant he was holding. It was attached to a long silver chain.

I stopped walking and turned to face him.

"If you're going in there," he nodded to the church behind me, "you're going to need this." He let the pendant drop from his hand, dangling it by the chain.

When I didn't make a move to approach him, he said, "Catch," and swung the pendant my way.

I managed to catch it by the chain a moment before it would've hit the ground. After I did, I looked over at my parents to see if they had noticed that I wasn't following them any longer. Thankfully, they hadn't yet.

When I looked at the pendant, I was surprised to see how ornate it was. It was shaped like an eight-pointed star and studded with red and blue gemstones. It looked expensive.

"Put it on. It will protect you," the homeless man said. "And don't let anyone see it."

"Jackson!" my dad called out. "What are you doing back there?" He'd finally noticed I wasn't behind them.

The homeless man quickly ducked out of sight.

"Nothing," I replied, quickly shoving the pendant into my pocket before jogging to catch up to them.

Once we'd made it to the church steps, I glanced back to where the homeless man was. He'd moved away from the dumpster and was now standing at the edge of the parking lot. When he saw me looking at him, he pointed his finger at me before lifting his arms and pantomiming putting something over his head.

It was clear what he wanted me to do.

I reached into my pocket and wrapped my hand around the pendant.

It will protect you, the homeless man's words echoed in my mind. That made me wonder what I needed to be protected from.

I turned around and looked up at the large wooden doors of the church. They didn't look any different from the doors of our old church.

It wasn't until Mr. Winslow opened the door and I got a look at the inside of the church that things started to feel off to me.

The first thing I noticed was that all the pews were facing backward, so when everyone was seated, they would be looking at the doors of the church and not at the priest on the altar.

The second thing I noticed was the absence of any sort of religious iconography.

At our old church, there were stained-glass windows that depicted different aspects of Jesus's life. There was also a life-sized statue of Jesus crucified on the cross that hung on the wall behind the altar. I didn't see anything like that at this church.

I tugged on the jacket of my dad's suit to get his attention.

"What's up?" he asked.

"Why are all the pews backward?" I whispered.

My dad laughed.

"Jackson wants to know why all the pews are backward," he said to Mr. Winslow.

"Well, Jackson," Mr. Winslow said to me, "they are backward so that we are facing the world outside while the priest gives his sermon." He gestured at the church doors as he spoke. "Instead of at a single man standing on the altar"—he moved his hand to gesture at the altar—"we do that to remind us that God is everywhere, not just in this building." He paused for a moment, letting me process what he had said. "Does that answer your question?"

Why not face the windows? I thought. There were two rows of them high up on the walls to either side of the altar. At least that way, everyone would be able to look outside at the sky instead of at the church doors.

I didn't say that, though; instead, I said, "I suppose," and let the matter drop.

"We have a special section for our new parishioners," I heard Mr. Winslow say to my parents. "Come on," he motioned for us to follow him, "I'll show you."

He led us across the nave to the set of backward-facing pews that were closest to the altar.

"I'll see you after the sermon," Mr. Winslow said after we'd taken our seats.

I watched him walk back a few rows to join his wife.

While we waited for the sermon to begin, I noticed that the slotted book racks that ran along the back of the pew in front of us were empty. There were no Bibles, no hymnals, nothing. They were completely empty.

I stood up for a moment and pretended to adjust my pants as I scanned the row of pews in front of me, looking to see if any of them had books in their racks. They didn't.

What kind of church doesn't have Bibles? I thought as I sat back down.

I considered asking my parents about it but decided against it. I figured they would just say something along the lines of *You don't need a Bible to worship God.*

Somewhere in the church, a bell tolled.

I looked up and watched a man walk over to the church doors and lock them.

"Why did they lock the doors?" I whispered to my dad.

"That's just the way they do things here. It's probably to keep anyone from coming inside and disrupting the priest's sermon. Now be quiet," he shushed me.

That weird feeling that something was off returned.

I reached my hand into my pocket and pulled out the pendant the homeless man had given me, doing my best to shield it from my parents' view.

It will protect you, the man's words echoed through my mind again.

It couldn't hurt, I thought, before quickly slipping it over my head and tucking it under my shirt so no one could see it.

"Stop wiggling around," my dad chided when he saw me adjusting my clothes out of the corner of his eye.

Thankfully, he hadn't seen me put the pendant on.

Another bell chimed. The murmur of conversation died down until the nave was completely silent.

I heard the creak of a door and the sound of hard-soled shoes tapping on the hardwood floor behind me. I started to turn around, but my dad stopped me.

"Keep looking forward," he instructed. "Mr. Winslow said it's disrespectful to look at the priest."

It was incredibly hard to keep myself from turning around, but I managed to do what my dad asked by keeping my eyes fixed on the church doors, thinking about how I wanted to leave.

"Let us pray," the inhuman voice of the priest on the altar behind us sent a shiver down my spine. It was deep and hollow, sounding as if it were being projected from some cavernous space.

As one, all the parishioners bowed their heads. It was creepy.

My parents copied them.

"Bow your head," my dad said when he saw me staring at the people sitting in front of us.

I did as he said, but I did not close my eyes the way everyone else had. And I'm glad I didn't.

"Let us begin," the priest's voice echoed across the nave.

There was a moment of silence before a humming sound made the air in the church vibrate. It started softly but grew in intensity.

The louder it got, the weirder I felt. It was like every cell in my body was coming apart.

Afraid, I turned to my dad for help and was shocked to see him sitting there with a smile on his face. When I leaned forward so I could see past him, I saw that my mom was smiling too.

This isn't right, I thought.

That's when I turned and looked behind me at the priest standing at the altar. Only it wasn't a priest. It was something else. Something I can only describe as a man-shaped void that was filled with stars, contained within a thick green cloak.

From within that void, dozens of long black tentacles unfolded and started reaching out across the nave, where they attached themselves to the backs of the parishioners' heads.

When several of the tentacles started heading in my direction, I slid off the pew and onto the floor. From there, I watched in horror as two of the black appendages latched onto my parents.

Thinking one was going to come for me next, I got my feet under me and prepared to run. But one never came.

That's when the homeless man's words echoed in my mind again.

It will protect you, he'd said.

I reached up and clutched the pendant through my shirt.

He knew this was going to happen. That's why he gave it to me.

Not knowing if I should stay or leave, I looked up at my parents and was shocked to see them rise into the air, suspended by the tentacles attached to their heads. When I looked around, I saw that everyone else had also been lifted into the air.

I slowly got to my feet and faced the priest-thing on the altar. Whatever it was, it couldn't see me. To confirm that, I raised my hands over my head and waved at it. Nothing happened.

It's like I'm invisible.

I walked to the center aisle and stood there, looking around at all the people suspended in the air.

What is it doing to them?

Whatever it was, they seemed to enjoy it because every single person had a smile on their face.

Should I leave or should I stay?

I looked from my parents to the doors of the church, wondering what the right thing to do was. Ultimately, I let my fear decide for me and started walking toward the doors at a brisk pace.

When I made it to the doors, I quickly unlocked them and grabbed hold of the handle, but the familiar voice of the homeless man stopped me before I could open them.

"I know you're scared," he said, "but you have to stay."

"Why?" I wanted answers.

"You're just going to have to trust me," the homeless man replied. "I'll explain everything to you later. You don't have much time. You need to relock the doors and return to your seat," he urged.

I tightened my grip on the door handle, intending to open it anyway.

"If you leave," it was like the homeless man could read my mind, "they'll know that you know, and that won't end well for you."

I didn't like the sound of that.

"Fine," I sighed, releasing the handle.

"What's your name, kid?" he asked.

"Jackson," I replied.

"You're doing the right thing, Jackson," he praised me.

"Where can I find you when this is over?" He'd promised answers, and I was going to make sure he gave them to me.

"I'll find you," he replied. "It's not safe for me here."

"How will you find me?"

When the homeless man didn't respond, I repeated the question.

He still didn't answer, giving me the impression that he'd already left.

I turned around and looked back toward the altar. That's when I noticed that the people closest to me were being lowered back down to their pews.

Shit!

I quickly rushed back to my seat, making it back seconds before my mom and dad were placed back onto the pew next to me.

That was close.

I took a couple of deep breaths and tried to calm my racing heart.

Above me, the tentacles were being withdrawn into the body of the priest. Once they'd all returned, the strange humming sound stopped, and the priest closed his cloak before walking out of the nave through a door to the side of the altar. As soon as the door closed behind him, the bell sounded again.

Everyone in the church raised their heads.

"That was incredible," I heard my dad say to my mom.

"We should've come here sooner," she replied.

They both turned and looked at me.

"What did you think?" my dad asked.

"It was awesome," I forced a smile to my lips. "I can't wait to come back next week."

My parents were pleased by my response, which I was thankful for. I was worried they would see through the lie and know I was not part of whatever happened.

"I don't know about the two of you," my mom said, "but I'm starving. What do you say we stop by IHOP on the way home and grab something to eat?"

I was surprised to hear her say that because we'd already eaten a big breakfast before we left the house this morning.

"I'm pretty hungry myself," my dad agreed.

"Let's go," I said, getting to my feet.

I wasn't really that hungry. I was just eager to put some distance between us and the church.

As we made our way out, the Winslows stopped us.

"Well?" Mr. Winslow asked.

"You were right," my dad replied. "That was amazing. I don't consider myself an emotional guy," he touched his chest, "but that sermon really moved me."

"It really was wonderful," my mom nodded in agreement. "Thank you so much for inviting us."

"We're glad you could make it," Mr. Winslow said.

"We were just about to grab a bite to eat," my dad gestured at the church doors. "Do you want to join us?"

Please say no, I thought. I didn't want to hang around the Winslows any longer than necessary. Especially if all they and my parents were going to do was talk about the church.

"I wish we could," Mr. Winslow apologized, "but we have to stay for our one-on-one sessions with the priest."

"One-on-one session?" my dad asked. "What's that like?"

Mr. and Mrs. Winslow looked at each other and smiled before returning their attention to my parents.

"It's mind-blowing," Mr. Winslow said. "If you liked his sermon, you're going to love his one-on-one talks."

"How do we sign up for those?" my mom asked.

"You don't," Mrs. Winslow answered. "Every week the priest handpicks a select group of parishioners to talk to. This week," she linked her arm through her husband's, "we're among the lucky few."

"We should get going," Mr. Winslow said. "We don't want to keep the priest waiting." He started leading his wife back up the aisle toward the altar. "Enjoy your lunch," he said as they walked away.

"Can we go now?" I asked.

"Someone's hungry," my dad ruffled my hair as we walked out of the church.

We finally made it home an hour later. Thankfully, while we ate, my parents discussed other topics besides the church. They didn't mention it once, not even in the car on the way to the restaurant. Which I thought was kind of odd. It was like they'd forgotten all about it the moment we left the church.

When I stepped out of my room, after changing out of my church attire, I noticed that my parents' bedroom door was shut. They rarely shut it. When they did, they were usually in there, and that typically only happened when they were going to bed.

"Mom?" I gently knocked on their door.

"What do you need, honey?" she replied without opening the door. She sounded like she was out of breath.

I didn't really have a reason for knocking other than to see if she was inside. But I didn't tell her that; instead, I blurted out, "Can I go outside?"

A sudden urge to leave had come over me right before I said that. It was triggered by the strange way my parents were acting. They seemed okay while we ate, so I wasn't overly worried about what happened to them in the church. Now I was.

I reached down and placed my hand in my pocket, grabbing hold of the pendant inside. I'd taken it off when I changed clothes, thinking I didn't need to wear it any longer.

Maybe I should put it back on.

I pulled it out and quickly slipped it over my neck.

"You can go," my mom replied. "Just be home in time for supper."

"Okay," I agreed, making a hasty exit.

I left the house through the garage so I could grab my bike, intending to ride it to the park. I'd seen a few of my friends hanging out there when we drove by on our way home from church.

"Hey, Jackson," Wesley waved from the swings when he saw me riding up the sidewalk. He was the only one of my friends who was still at the park when I finally got there.

I returned the wave and rode over to where Wesley's bike was lying in the grass. I dropped mine next to his and walked over to the playground. Wesley jumped off the swing and jogged over to meet me.

"What's up?" he asked.

"Nothing," I replied. "Where are Alan and Jamie?"

"They had to go home for lunch," he explained. "They said they'd come back when they were done."

I must've had a funny look on my face because Wesley cocked his head to the side as he looked at me.

"Something wrong?" he finally asked.

I wanted to tell him about what happened at the church, but the more I thought about what I was going to say, the crazier it sounded.

Eventually, I thought, *screw it*, and blurted out, "Do you believe in monsters?" As I spoke, I subconsciously reached up and touched the pendant that was hanging under my shirt.

"What kind of monsters?" Wesley furrowed his brow as he tried to figure out the point of my question.

"Any kind."

I didn't think I needed to clarify. A monster was a monster as far as I was concerned.

Wesley thought about it for a moment before replying, "I don't think I do," he said. "If monsters were real, I'd think we'd have seen some sort of evidence of their existence by now." He paused for a moment before continuing. "It would be cool if they were real, though," he smiled. "Especially werewolves."

When he saw that I wasn't as enthusiastic about his response as he was, the smile dropped from his face.

"Do you believe in monsters?" he asked.

I opened my mouth to say *yes,* but before I could get the words out, Jamie called out from behind us.

"Hey, losers," he yelled as he ran across the playground to where Wesley and I were standing.

"That was fast," Wesley said to him. "You were only gone for like ten minutes."

Jamie ignored Wesley's comment and instead turned to me, saying, "Dude," as he placed his hand on my shoulder and took a moment to catch his breath, "there's some old homeless guy looking for you at the end of the block." He stretched his arm behind him and pointed at a man who was sitting beneath a stop sign near some bushes.

Even though I couldn't see him clearly, I could tell it was the same man who had given me the pendant in the church parking lot.

"I'll be right back," I said, walking toward the man. "Watch my bike."

"I wasn't telling you to go talk to him," Jamie said. "I was warning you so you could avoid him."

I stopped and turned to face him so I could address him directly. "It's okay," I said. "I know him."

"You know a homeless guy?" Wesley asked.

"It's a long story," I said, starting to walk again. "I'll tell you about it when I get back."

"Hello, Jackson," the homeless man smiled as I approached him. "Told you I'd find you."

"How did you know I'd be here?"

"That's not important right now," he replied. "Right now I need you to return the pendant I gave you." He held his hand out.

"No," I shook my head. "Not until you tell me what the hell happened at the church."

I didn't usually curse like that, but it felt appropriate under the circumstances.

The man rose to his feet and brushed his dirty pants off. "Hell is the wrong word to describe what happened there," he said. "That thing you saw is from somewhere else. Somewhere much further away than Hell."

"Now give me the pendant," he held his hand out again.

"What is it?"

"I don't have time to explain that right now," he explained. "It's not safe."

"I'm not giving the pendant back until you do."

"Fine," he sighed in frustration, reaching into his pocket and withdrawing a folded piece of paper that he held out to me.

I took the paper and unfolded it. Written on it was an address.

"What's this?"

"That's where I'm staying," the homeless man tapped his finger on the address. "Come find me tonight after your parents go to bed and I'll tell you everything I know." He stopped speaking to look over my shoulder at the park where Jamie and Wesley were watching us. "You haven't told them anything, have you?"

"No," I shook my head.

"Don't," the homeless man warned. "The more people who know, the more risk you put us and them in. Got it?"

I nodded as I shoved the paper with the address into my pocket.

"Good, now get going," he made a shooing motion with his hand. "I'll see you tonight."

"What if I can't get out?" I asked.

I'd never snuck out of the house before and was afraid I'd get caught.

"You don't have to worry about that," the man said. "Your parents will be too busy to notice that you're gone."

He seemed awfully sure of that.

"What if they aren't?"

"Trust me," he said. "They will be. Now go. And bring the pendant with you."

I turned to leave but stopped and turned back to face the homeless man.

"Now what?" he asked.

"What should I tell my friends?" I jerked my thumb over my shoulder. "They're going to ask me why you were looking for me."

The homeless man rubbed the stubble on his chin as he came up with an answer.

"Tell them I'm your uncle," he said.

"My uncle?" I scoffed.

That sounded like a ridiculous idea.

"Yes, your uncle," he sounded a little irritated at being interrupted. "Tell them I'm broke and that I came to beg some money from you. Also, tell them that they shouldn't tell anyone we talked because you don't want your parents to get mad at you for helping me. That should satisfy their curiosity and keep them quiet."

"Okay," I agreed and started walking back to the park.

"What was that all about?" Jamie asked.

"If I tell you, you have to promise not to tell anyone," I said, looking from Jamie to Wesley.

They both promised.

"He's my uncle." I hated lying to them, but I didn't want to put them in any kind of danger.

"Your uncle?" Wesley sounded skeptical.

"Yes, my uncle," I repeated. "My parents don't want me to have anything to do with him, which is why you can't tell anyone he was here, okay?"

"What did he want?" Jamie asked.

"He was begging for money."

"Why won't your parents help him?" Wesley asked.

All the questions were starting to overwhelm me.

"They just won't!" I snapped. "Now drop it!"

"He's probably a drug addict," I heard Jamie whisper to Wesley. "That's probably why he's homeless."

I knew they weren't going to quit, so I decided it would be best if I just left.

"Where are you going?" Wesley asked when he saw me walking over to retrieve my bike.

"Home," I replied.

"But you just got here," he said.

"I don't feel like hanging out anymore," I said.

As I rode away, I could hear Wesley blaming Jamie for making me leave.

"Hey, Kiddo," my dad said as I walked through the front door. "How was the park?"

He was sitting on the couch watching TV in a T-shirt and sweatpants. I thought that was odd because he only wore stuff like that when he was getting ready for bed.

"It was okay," I lied.

"You didn't stay very long."

"Everyone had to go home," another lie.

Ever since the homeless man had given me the pendant, I have told more lies in a single day than I had all year.

"That's too bad," he tried to sound sympathetic, but I could tell he didn't care.

"Where's mom?" I asked.

She was the one who usually greeted me when I got home.

"She's in the shower," my dad said without taking his eyes off the TV screen. "Did you need something?"

"No," I replied. "I was just wondering where she was."

It wasn't like her to take a shower in the middle of the day.

I left the living room and went to my bedroom, where I spent the rest of the afternoon playing on my computer.

The next time I saw my parents was at dinnertime; their strange behavior continued.

They always sat across the table from each other, but this time they were sitting next to each other. As we ate, they would constantly stop to whisper to each other. The way they smiled and giggled at whatever was being said made them seem like children.

"Can I be excused?" I asked after I'd seen enough.

"Don't you want dessert?" my mom asked. "I made cinnamon rolls."

"Maybe later," I said as I got to my feet. "I'm not that hungry right now. I think I ate too much for lunch," I offered as an excuse.

"We did eat a lot," my dad agreed.

"I'll save you some in case you change your mind," my mom said.

"Okay."

I couldn't get back to my room fast enough.

At about nine o'clock that same evening, my mom knocked on my door and then opened it before waiting for me to respond.

"Hey, Honey," she said, standing in the doorway. "Your father and I are heading to bed early tonight. Do you need anything before we go?"

I shook my head. "I'm good."

"Don't stay up too late," she pointed a finger at me.

"I won't," I lied.

As soon as I thought they were asleep, I was going to climb out my window and head to the address the homeless man had given me.

"Good night, love you," she said as she closed the door.

"Love you too," I replied.

I waited until eleven p.m. before I crept out into the hall to see if my parents were awake. As I listened, I could hear one of them snoring.

Time to go, I thought.

I went back to my room, shut the door as quietly as I could, then went over to the window and eased it open.

Climbing out wasn't as easy as I thought it would be. It took me longer than I expected, and I made a lot more noise than I'd intended.

Once I was outside, I stood at the open window, staring at my bedroom door, waiting to see if my parents had heard me. When neither of them came to my room to investigate the noise I'd made, I assumed the coast was clear and shut the window.

I ran around to the front of the house, got on my bike, and rode away from the house as quickly as I could.

What should have been a fifteen-minute ride to the address ended up taking me half an hour.

While I was on my computer earlier that day, I'd looked up the address the homeless man had given me and plotted a route that I thought would have the least amount of traffic on it. Even though traffic was light, there was still enough of it that I had to make a few detours along the way to prevent being seen.

I figured if anyone saw a 12-year-old kid riding a bike that late, they'd call the cops, and that would not be good.

I guess this is it. I stopped in front of an abandoned house and compared the numbers on the paper to the rusty numbers affixed to the wall next to the boarded-up front door.

It made sense that a homeless man would live someplace like that.

I walked my bike up the weed-infested path until I got to the porch.

"Hello," I called out. "Anyone home?"

The scuffle of approaching footsteps startled me.

When I turned around to see who it was, I was surprised to see a priest standing on the path behind me.

"Sorry," he apologized, raising his hands. "I didn't mean to scare you."

I hadn't recognized him until he started speaking.

"You're the homeless guy," I pointed my finger at him.

He looked a lot different now that he was all cleaned up.

"That was a disguise," he explained, "something that allowed me to get close enough to the church so I could give you that," he pointed at the slight bulge of the pendant beneath my shirt.

"Why did you give it to me?" I pulled the pendant free from my shirt.

"Let's go inside and I'll give you all those answers I promised you," he swept a hand toward the small church across the street behind him.

"Okay," I agreed, pushing my bike along with me as I followed him over to the church.

I felt a lot better going there than I did about having to go into the abandoned house.

"Have a seat," the priest gestured at a chair in the small office to the side of the altar.

Once I'd sat down, he walked around the large desk that dominated the room and sat across from me.

"My name is Father Bradley," he placed a hand on his chest as he introduced himself. "To answer your first question, I gave you that," he moved his hand to point at the pendant, "because you're the only one who can help me stop the thing that has taken over my church."

"Your church?"

He nodded. "Before that thing took over, I was the priest of that church. Ever since then, I've been hiding out here," he gestured at the walls around us, "trying to find a way to stop it."

"What is it?"

Father Bradley reached into his desk and pulled out an old leather-bound book. He opened it and started flipping through the pages, looking for a specific one. When he found it, he turned the book around and slid it across the desk to me.

"It's called a Great Old One," he tapped the page. "They are beings from beyond space and time that have been trying to gain a foothold in our dimension."

I tried reading what was on the page, but I stopped after the first paragraph. Even though the words were in English, the style it was written in was hard to follow.

"Its official name is Azbycx," he said, pronouncing it az-bix. "Informally, it is known as The Many."

"Why is it called that?"

"Because it's not a single creature, it's a collective of hundreds of individual creatures living entwined as one, feeding off of each other."

"Why is it here?"

"To reproduce," he explained. "It can't create offspring on its own. It needs us to do that."

As soon as he said that, it suddenly dawned on me why my parents were acting weird and what they were doing in their bedroom.

They were having sex.

"It infects people, alters their DNA, and drives them to procreate," Father Bradley confirmed what I was thinking. "But the offspring is not human, it's one of The Many."

"How do we stop it?" The idea of my mother becoming pregnant with one of those things made me feel sick.

Father Bradley gave me a sympathetic smile. "Does this mean I can count on you to help me destroy it?"

I nodded. I had to save my parents.

"Wait here," he said. "I'll be right back."

Father Bradley got up and left the office. He returned several minutes later, carrying an old, thin box made of wood and adorned with strange symbols. He set the box on the desk in front of me and opened it. Nestled inside was a knife that was fashioned out of bone. It was about twelve inches long and didn't look to be very sharp.

"What's that?" I asked. It looked like something a caveman would make.

"This," he lifted the bone blade out of the box, "is a very special knife. It was hand-carved from a bone shard that once belonged to an Elder God." He held the blade up before his eyes.

I got the impression I should be impressed by what he was saying, but I wasn't. It looked like the knife was carved out of an ordinary bone to me.

"It doesn't look very sharp," I said, vocalizing one of the first thoughts I had about the knife.

"Looks can be deceiving," Father Bradley said.

He quickly flipped the blade around and then stabbed it into the surface of his desk. To my surprise, the knife cut through the wood like it was putty, until only the handle was visible.

"Give it a try," Father Bradley said, letting go of the knife and gesturing for me to take it.

When I grabbed the handle, I expected to have difficulty pulling the blade free from the desk, but I didn't. It slid out of the wood as easily as it had gone in.

"Be careful," he said when I raised the knife over the desk. "It doesn't take much force to use."

He was right; when I brought the blade down, it slid into the wood like butter. I was so impressed by the knife that I lifted it and brought it down again.

"Don't get too excited," Father Bradley warned. "The longer you hold that knife, the more dangerous it becomes."

"What do you mean?" I held the knife before my eyes so I could examine it better.

"Give it a minute and then you'll understand," he said.

I had no idea what I was supposed to be waiting for until the whispering started. I couldn't make out what it was saying, but it was making the hairs on the back of my neck stand up.

"Do you hear that?" I lowered the knife and looked at Father Bradley.

Before answering, he quickly grabbed the knife from me, put it back in the box, and slammed the lid shut.

"I don't hear it. But I have heard it before," he said. "Only the bearer of the knife can hear it. The longer you hold it, the clearer it becomes. Trust me when I tell you that you do not want to hold it long enough to hear what it has to say."

"Why not?"

A small part of me felt compelled to free the knife from the box again so I could listen to the whispers.

As if he could sense what I was thinking, Father Bradley placed his hand on the box and pulled it away from me.

"The last person who listened to the knife slit his own throat in the sacristy," he revealed. "That is why I keep it locked up now."

"Won't this protect me?" I grabbed hold of the pendant around my neck.

Father Bradley shook his head. "That is an Elder Sign," he pointed at the pendant, "a symbol of protection created by the Elder Gods, one of the beings whose bone was used to fashion this." He tapped his fingers on the box. "Because of that, it offers no protection against the knife's influence."

"Oh," was all I could think to say.

"Speaking of which, I think it's time you gave that back to me," he held his hand out for the pendant. "Don't worry," he added when he saw the disappointed look on my face, "I'll give it back to you next Sunday so you can send Azbycx back to where it belongs."

"How am I supposed to do that?" I asked as I placed the pendant in Father Bradley's palm. "It has over a hundred tentacles." I pictured myself using the bone knife to slice through the tentacles that were attached to the parishioners, but there were just too many for me to handle, especially if I could only hold the knife for a limited time.

"You don't need to worry about the tentacles," he explained as he opened a drawer in the desk and dropped the pendant into it. "All you need to do is close the doorway it's using to access our world."

His comment about the doorway brought to mind the image of the man-shaped void from which the tentacles were sprouting and the cloak that covered it.

"The priest is the doorway," I said.

Father Bradley nodded. "He is."

"Which means I have to kill him to close the doorway." I was okay with the idea of killing a monster, but I wasn't sure I could kill a person.

Picking up on my reluctance, Father Bradley reached out a hand and placed it on my shoulder. "I wouldn't be asking you to do this if there was any other way to stop it," he said. "I've run out of options and people who can help me. You are the last hope we have."

I didn't like the tremendous weight that was being placed upon my shoulders.

"What about the police or the military?"

Father Bradley shook his head. "The police chief is a member of the congregation," he revealed. "Any time I've tried to bring outside attention to the church, he quickly gets it dismissed. The last time I tried, he was able to get a warrant for my arrest, which stated that I was a danger to the church and the congregation." He gave me a weak smile. "Which is technically true, just not for the reasons they believe."

That explained why he had disguised himself as a homeless man when I first met him and why he was hiding out in a church that looked as if it hadn't been used in years.

"I can't force you to do this if you don't want to," he said, "but for the sake of your parents and the community, I hope you will."

"I...," I opened my mouth to voice my concerns, but Father Bradley stopped me with an outstretched hand.

"You don't have to decide right now," he said. "In fact, I'd prefer if you didn't. This is no small task I'm asking of you. Which is why I think you should take the week to think about it. Okay?"

"Okay," I agreed. That sounded reasonable to me. "How will I let you know once I've made up my mind?" I asked.

He thought for a moment. "Meet me at the park Saturday afternoon. You can tell me your decision then. Does that sound good to you?"

"Yeah," I nodded.

"Alright then, get going," he nodded toward the door.

I got home at 12:30 a.m.

When I turned onto my street, I was relieved to see that there wasn't a cop sitting in my driveway. I was even more relieved when I saw that all the lights in my house were still off. That meant my parents hadn't discovered that I wasn't in my room like I was supposed to be.

I rode my bike through the yard and parked it against the wall next to my window so I could use it to climb back into the house. As I did that, I lost my footing and tumbled to the bedroom floor, banging my knee.

Oh, shit, that was loud!

There was no way my parents didn't hear that.

I quickly jumped up, closed the window, kicked off my shoes, then threw myself under the covers and pretended to be asleep.

A few seconds later, my door creaked open.

"Jackson," I heard my dad whisper, "was that you?"

I kept my eyes shut and stayed perfectly still as I pretended not to hear him.

He crossed the room and stood over my bed. Even though I couldn't see him, I could feel his presence. He stood there for only a minute, but it felt like an hour.

"What was it?" I heard my mom whisper when my dad returned to the hall.

"I don't know," he replied. "I'm going to take a quick look around, you go on back to bed."

"Okay," she replied, "but don't take too long, I was thinking, since we're up, we could..."

Gross!

After speaking with Father Bradley, I could easily guess what she was implying, and that thought made me cringe.

Thankfully, my dad shut the door, and I didn't have to hear any more of their conversation.

It was hard to get up the next morning. I didn't make a habit out of staying up that late on a school night, so six a.m. came a lot sooner than I wanted it to.

"Did you sleep in your clothes?" my mom asked when she saw me leave my room to go to the bathroom.

I looked down at what I was wearing and tried to act surprised. "I guess I did."

"What time did you go to bed last night?" she asked, her face showing a judgmental look.

"11:30," I lied. I knew she wouldn't believe me if I told her I went to bed before ten, and I certainly couldn't tell her the real time.

She shook her head. "If that happens again, I'm going to take away your computer," she assumed, thinking I was up late playing video games.

"It won't," I said to placate her.

"It better not," she pointed a finger at me. "Now hurry up and get ready for school."

When I walked into the kitchen to eat breakfast, I was surprised to see my dad sitting at the table, still wearing his bedclothes. Normally, he was already at work by the time I got up.

"What's Dad doing home?" I asked as I grabbed the plate of eggs and bacon my mom had made me.

"He decided to take the day off so he could help me with some things around the house," she said.

I figured that was a lie and that the real reason he was staying home was so that they would have plenty of time to be alone while I was at school, time they were likely going to be spending in the bedroom.

The thought of that made me feel sick to my stomach.

"Something wrong?" my mom asked when she saw the look on my face.

"No," I shook my head. "I'm just tired."

"That's your own fault," she gestured at me with the spatula she was holding.

"I know." I didn't want to have that conversation again, so I turned around and carried my breakfast to the table, where I ate with my dad while he asked me a bunch of questions about how I was doing in school.

I didn't mind talking to him; it made everything feel routine, if only for a little while. It wasn't until he started asking me about the girls at my school and if I liked any of them that I started to feel uncomfortable.

I didn't answer him. Instead, I quickly got up and headed for the door. "Gotta go," I said, grabbing my backpack on the way. "I don't want to be late for the bus."

"What's his deal?" I heard my dad ask my mom as I walked outside.

"Can't you tell when your son is embarrassed?" she replied.

Not wanting to hear any more, I rushed outside and shut the door as quickly as I could.

———•O•———

The rest of the week was pretty much the same. My parents continued to spend a lot of time in their bedroom, and I spent as much time avoiding them as I could. By Wednesday, I'd made up my mind that I was going to do whatever I could to stop Azbycx so that I could have a normal life again.

Feeling like Saturday couldn't come fast enough, I decided to do a little research on everything that Father Bradley had told me. I booted up my computer, opened Google, and started to type out the phrase GREAT OLD ONE, but I stopped before pressing the enter key when I remembered the parental controls my parents had installed on my computer.

If they were to check my search history, they'd see everything I had seen. I thought that was too much of a risk. If anyone at the church found out that I knew about Azbycx, that would not be good for me or my parents.

I turned off the computer and decided to watch TV instead.

The next day, I decided to go to the library after school and use their computers to search, but I gave up on that idea when the librarian recognized me.

"Didn't I see you at church this past Sunday with your family?" she smiled as I approached the desk.

"Uh... yeah," I replied. "It was our first time."

I considered lying and telling her she had the wrong kid, but I decided that wouldn't be a good idea. If she was certain she had seen me and I said she didn't, that might make her suspicious.

I'm becoming paranoid, I thought.

"What did you think of the service?" she asked.

"It was... uh... awesome," I tried to sound enthusiastic.

"Right?" she agreed. "I met my boyfriend there." The librarian blushed when she told me that. "Sorry," she quickly apologized, "I don't know why I told you that. I guess I'm just happy that I found someplace where I feel like I'm a part of something bigger than myself, you know?"

"I do," I nodded—*more than you can possibly know.*

An awkward silence followed our exchange.

"Is there anything I can help you with?" she eventually asked.

"I'm good," I replied. "I was just going to go look at the comic books," I pointed at the shelf of graphic novels before heading in that direction.

I pretended to look over the selection of comics for a few minutes before randomly choosing a couple of titles to check out.

"Your books are due on the 14th," the librarian said after she'd scanned them and handed them back to me. "See you this Sunday," she said, giving me a quick wave as I started to walk away.

"See you," I returned the wave and left as quickly as I could.

After that, I spent the rest of the week close to home until Saturday finally came.

"Can I go to the park?" I'd just scarfed down a peanut butter and jelly sandwich for lunch and was heading for the door before either of my parents could answer.

"Hold up," my dad said.

I stopped with my hand on the door handle.

"Everything okay?" he asked.

"Yeah," I replied. "Why do you keep asking me that?"

"You've been spending a lot of time in your room lately," he said. "It kind of makes me think you've been avoiding us."

You've been spending a lot of time in your room, too, I thought, but I would never say that out loud.

"I'm not avoiding you," I said. "I've just been busy."

"Busy doing what?"

"Playing Minecraft," I explained. "I've been building a new world." That wasn't a lie; I had started playing Minecraft as a way to pass the time while avoiding my parents.

"Why don't you stay home and watch some TV with us?" my dad suggested. "You can go to the park another day."

"But Wesley is waiting for me." That was the only reason I could come up with for needing to leave.

"Let him go and play with his friend," my mom finally intervened. "It's better than being stuck inside the house with us. Besides…"

"Thanks, Mom." I threw the door open and rushed outside before my mom could finish her sentence and before my dad could protest.

When I got to the park, I didn't go to the playground. Instead, I rode around the block, looking for Father Bradley. I did that for an hour without seeing any sign of him before I decided to ride over to the abandoned church to see if he was there.

When I walked up the steps of the church, I noticed that the door was slightly ajar.

That doesn't look good.

"Hello?" I called out while pushing the door open a little further so I could see inside. "Father Bradley, are you here?"

The only sound was the echo of my voice across the seemingly empty building.

Maybe he left to meet me at the park. That would explain why the door was open. *He might've been in a hurry and forgot to close it all the way.*

But if that's what he did, why didn't I see him?

I was torn between going back to the park to look for Father Bradley and staying at the church to see if he came back. I stood there for five minutes before I decided to stay. It made the most sense since that was where he was staying. He'd have to return eventually.

I took a quick look around to make sure nobody was watching before I slipped into the church and closed the door behind me.

"Father Bradley?" I called out again as I crossed the nave and made my way to the office where we had talked.

He wasn't in there either, so I sat down in the chair that was in front of the desk and waited for him to return.

I sat there for about fifteen minutes before I started getting paranoid.

What if they caught him?

He did say he was a wanted man.

If they did catch him, they might know about me.

I got up and was about to leave, but I stopped when the memory of Father Bradley putting the pendant into a desk drawer flashed through my mind.

I doubted he would have left it there for anyone to find, but I decided to check anyway.

He did leave it!

It was sitting right where he left it. When I pulled it out of the drawer, I noticed there was an envelope lying beneath it. Written on the outside of it was the letter J.

J for Jackson. I bet he left this for me.

I put the pendant around my neck, opened the envelope, and pulled out the note that was inside. This is what it said:

J,

I'm sorry I couldn't be there to meet you. I'm no longer safe here and must leave town for a while. I will return if and when I can. In the meantime, I hope you've decided to help. The knife is hidden under the bench in the confessional. Good luck.

FB

I shoved the note back in the envelope and put it back in the desk drawer before going into the confessional to find the knife.

The box was right where he said it would be. When I pulled it free, I glanced inside it to make sure the knife was still inside.

When I saw the blade, I had the urge to pick it up. A strong need to feel it in my hand. I started to reach my hand into the box.

NO!

I slammed the box shut before the desire to wield it could overwhelm me. As soon as it was out of sight, the need to hold it started to go away. It never went away completely, but it became weak enough that I was able to resist its call.

I have everything I need to stop Azbycx. I need to get out of here in case whoever is looking for Father Bradley came back.

If Father Bradley wasn't safe at the church, I wasn't either.

When I made it back home, I pulled my bike to the side of the house so my parents wouldn't see that I was back yet. Then I opened the garage and started looking for a place to hide the knife and the pendant. I didn't feel safe bringing them into the house. I couldn't risk my parents finding out about them.

I found the perfect hiding place in a tub of Halloween decorations that was tucked away under my dad's workbench. Halloween was just over six months away, which meant there was no reason for my parents to look inside the tub.

That's one problem solved. Now I just need to figure out how I'm going to sneak the knife into the church.

I wasn't worried about anyone finding out about the pendant; I'd already worn it once for several hours, and nobody noticed it under my shirt. The knife, however, was not going to be as easy to hide.

"What are you doing out here?" The sound of my mom's voice startled me. She must've heard the garage door open and come out to see what I was doing.

"Uh... I am... uh... I am looking for...," I started looking around, trying to come up with a plausible reason for lingering in the garage when my eyes came upon the flat basketball that was lying on top of a box of junk. "I'm looking for the pump," I said. "I need to air up my tires."

I thought that sounded like a great excuse.

"Why don't you come inside and ask your dad?" she replied. "I don't want you out here messing with his stuff."

"Ask me what?" my dad appeared in the doorway behind my mom.

"Jackson is looking for the bicycle pump," she said to him.

My dad squeezed by her to come out into the garage and then walked over to his workbench, where he leaned down and started moving things around as he looked for the pump. One of the things he moved was the tub of Halloween decorations I'd hidden the knife and pendant in.

I must not have snapped the lid back onto the tub properly when I was done because as my dad slid it out of the way, the lid came free, partially exposing the contents inside.

I held my breath, waiting to see if my dad would notice the odd-looking box sitting prominently on top of the decorations.

Thankfully, he didn't.

"Here it is," he pulled the pump out from beneath his workbench and handed it to me before snapping the lid back onto the tub and sliding it back into place.

"Thanks," I said.

"Put it back when you're done," my dad said before returning to the house.

"I will," I replied and then waited for the two of them to go back inside.

That was close, I sighed in relief.

Dinner that night was just as awkward as it was every other night that week, which was the reason I scarfed down my food and asked if I could be excused as soon as I was finished.

"Not this time," my dad said as he pushed his plate away. "You've spent enough time in your room this week. Tonight, you're going to watch a movie with me."

"What movie?"

"That fantasy movie you've been waiting to see," he replied. "I can't remember the name of it. I saw it when I was browsing Netflix last night. The one with the dragon."

"Eragon?"

"That's it," he smiled. "What do you say we head to the living room and get it started?"

"Okay," I agreed. As a fan of the book series the movie was based on, I'd been looking forward to seeing it. Telling him I wasn't in the mood to see it would have raised too much suspicion.

"What did you think?" my dad asked as the credits started to roll.

"It was okay," I replied. "The book was better."

"They usually are," he said.

"What did you think?" I asked.

"It was okay," he said, parroting my opinion.

Not having anything else to say, both of us remained quiet until my dad pushed himself up from his chair and started heading for the kitchen.

"I'm going to go see if your mom needs any help," he said as he walked by me.

"I guess I'm going to start getting ready for bed," I said, following behind him until I made it to the hall, where I turned and headed for my room.

I wasn't really going to go to bed. Watching the movie had given me an idea about how I could sneak the knife into the church, and I was eager to get back to my room so I could get started on it.

The idea started when I saw all of the swords being held in scabbards in the movie. When I saw that, I thought a scabbard would be a good way to carry the knife. I could easily tuck it into my waistband and carry it into the church. But then I started to think about the way the knife made me feel when it wasn't in the box, so I discarded that idea.

I had to keep the knife in the box until I was ready to use it.

I need a scabbard for the box, I thought at the time, but that idea seemed silly, until I thought about it a little more. That's when I realized that I didn't need a scabbard; I just needed a place I could carry it that was hidden from view, like a pocket.

A hidden pocket.

That one thought was all it took to remind me about the suit jacket that my parents made me wear for special occasions, like our family photo. Like most suit jackets, it had a hidden pocket on the inside. It wasn't big enough to hold the box the knife was in, but it would be if I made a minor alteration to it.

That is what I started doing as soon as I arrived in my room.

Once I was finished, I went out to the garage and retrieved the knife and pendant from the tub of Halloween decorations and put them in the modified jacket. I wasn't worried about my parents catching me because they were already in their bedroom with the door shut when I left my room.

"Well, look at you," my mom was walking down the hall when she saw me getting dressed the next morning. "I thought you hated that suit."

She stepped into the room to get a better look at me.

"I do," I replied, "but I wanted to look nice for church today."

"You look very nice." She reached out to adjust my tie. "Very handsome."

Having her hands that close to the pendant under my shirt and the knife box tucked away inside my jacket caused me to tense up and pull away.

"I've got it," I reached up and fixed the tie myself.

"Sorry," she apologized. "I keep forgetting you're about to become a teenager and aren't my little boy anymore."

My thirteenth birthday was a few months away.

"It doesn't feel like thirteen years have already passed," she sighed. "It seems like only yesterday I was still changing your diapers."

I could tell from the faraway look in her eyes that she was lost in her memories.

"What's going on in here?" My dad saw us standing in the room and walked in to join us. When he saw that I was wearing my suit, he said, "What's with the monkey suit?" he pointed. "I thought you hated it."

I was glad that he showed up before my mom said anything else to make me feel awkward but I didn't like that he was making a big deal out of my suit.

"Leave him alone," my mom said, gently pushing him out of my room. "He just wants to look good for church."

"Is that right?" he smirked. "Who's he trying to impress?" He lowered his voice to a whisper, trying to keep me from hearing what he said to my mom, but I heard it anyway. "Do you think he's finally starting to show some interest in girls?"

"Stop, you're going to embarrass him," my mom replied once the two of them were out in the hall. Then she turned to me and said, "Be ready to go in about ten minutes, okay?" She reached out and started to pull my bedroom door shut.

"Okay," I said.

"Look, there's the Winslows," my dad pointed as he got out of the car.

Mr. and Mrs. Winslow were walking through the church parking lot with another couple when my dad called out to them, prompting them to stop and wait for us to catch up.

"This is the other couple I was telling you about," Mr. Winslow said to the couple he was with, gesturing at my parents. "Last week was their first time here."

As Mr. Winslow introduced my parents to the new couple, I scanned the parking lot, looking to see if I could find Father Bradley lurking around anywhere. Unfortunately, I didn't see him.

"Jackson!" I heard my dad yell at me.

"What?" I turned to face him.

"Sorry, he's been a bit distracted lately," he apologized to the couple, adding, "I was trying to introduce you to Mr. and Mrs. Carr." He nodded toward the couple. "They're new to the church like us."

"Oh, hi," I gave them a weak wave and a partial smile.

You need to run away and never come back, I thought, wishing I could tell them that for real.

"Shall we go inside?" Mr. Winslow motioned.

When everyone started walking, I lagged a few steps behind so I didn't have to listen to them talking about how great the church was.

Once we were inside, the Winslows left the Carrs in my parents' care before they took their seats in the middle of the church with the rest of the regular parishioners.

"They make all new members sit in the front," my mom explained to the couple as we walked up the aisle to take our seats in the same pew we sat in last Sunday.

Since there were now five of us in the row, I had to sit on the very end, furthest away from the altar. While we waited for the service to start, I was thankful for the Carrs' presence because they kept my parents' focus away from me.

The bell tolled a few minutes later. The same man who locked the doors the previous Sunday got up and locked them again.

The second bell chimed, and everyone but me bowed their heads.

A door creaked open, and footsteps approached the altar.

"Let us begin," the inhuman voice of the priest announced.

I wanted to turn and look at the priest, but I knew that was a bad idea. I couldn't give him any indication that I knew what was going on, so I kept my eyes forward as the strange humming sound started to fill the church.

"Let us pray," the priest said.

The tentacles of Azbycx flowed out of the priest's robes and began attaching themselves to the heads of all the parishioners.

It's now or never.

I reached into my jacket and pulled the knife box free.

You can do this.

I got to my feet and walked around to the back of the pew before making my way up to the altar. As I did, a woman cried out.

I froze and looked around to see who it was. When I saw her, I was surprised to see her lying on the ground in the center aisle without a tentacle attached to her head. She was clutching her very pregnant belly and had her legs spread wide. A large pool of blood was spreading out from the area between her legs.

The sight unnerved me.

She's having a baby.

I knew, from what Father Bradley had told me, that the baby the woman was about to give birth to wasn't human.

Confirming that thought, a long black tentacle unraveled from between her legs, dripping a viscous substance onto the floor.

That's when I turned away. I couldn't watch her any longer.

That's what's going to happen to my mom if I don't do something.

I opened the box and let it fall to the church floor as I pulled the knife from it.

You can do this, I repeated as I walked up the steps to where the priest stood at the altar.

His arms were raised high, and a thick mass of tentacles sprouted from his cloak.

He's not human, I reminded myself.

I clutched the knife in my hand and started to raise it over my head as I maneuvered behind him.

I was about to slam the knife down into the priest's back, but before I could, something yanked me off my feet, causing me to drop the knife when I hit the floor.

"NO!" I yelled when the knife tumbled out of reach.

When I looked down at my foot, I saw a long black tentacle wrapped around my ankle. At first, I thought the priest had somehow figured out what I was about to do and sent a tentacle to stop me, but that wasn't the case. The tentacle that had a hold of me belonged to the thing the woman on the floor had given birth to.

The protection offered by the pendant didn't seem to affect it.

I rolled over onto my stomach and started dragging myself across the floor toward the knife, using every ounce of strength that I could muster. It wasn't enough. My fingers brushed the handle of the knife before I was dragged several feet away from it.

"NO!" I yelled again.

I refused to give up.

I tried to pull my leg free from the thing's grasp but couldn't. It was too strong.

That's when someone grabbed hold of my shoulders and started trying to pull me from the creature's grip.

I looked back and was surprised to see the woman who had birthed the monstrosity trying to help me. But even with her help, the creature was too much for us.

"Hand me the knife," I grunted, pointing at the bone blade that was lying on the floor a half dozen feet away.

She let go of me and crawled across the floor, leaving a trail of blood and birthing fluid behind her. When she reached the knife, she collapsed. She was too exhausted to return with it.

I reached out my hand and pleaded with her to give me the knife.

"Hurry!" I said.

With the little energy she had remaining, she slid the knife across the floor with just enough force for it to reach me.

I grabbed hold of it and sliced the tentacle that was wrapped around my ankle.

The creature squealed and withdrew its injured appendage, which had started spurting a viscous green substance that looked like mucus.

"This ends now!" I jumped to my feet and ran back toward the priest.

That's when the knife started whispering to me. Even though I had no idea what language the whispers were in, I could clearly understand them.

Join me, it cooed.

I stopped to listen. I didn't want to, but I was no longer in control of my body.

Join me, it repeated. I brought the knife up to my neck.

"WATCH OUT!" the woman yelled at me, breaking the hold the knife had over me.

I turned around to find that all the tentacles that were attached to the parishioners had started to come free and were now making their way towards me.

It knows!

I started running again, leaping into the air at the last second to avoid a tentacle that was reaching for my legs. As I soared through the air, I brought the knife over my head and gripped it with both hands, bringing it down on the priest's back right as the first tentacles reached me.

A rush of wind followed a loud keening noise, and then I slammed into the floor and blacked out.

When I came to, Father Bradley was standing over me with a smile on his face.

"You did it, kid," he said.

"I don't know if I can do what you did, Father Jackson," Abigail, the 14-year-old girl sitting across from me, said.

I felt bad having to put her in the same situation I was in twenty years earlier. Unfortunately, there was no other option. I'd have gone into her church and faced Azbycx myself if I could've, but that was no longer an option. It was expecting me. It wasn't expecting Abigail.

"I didn't think I could do it either," I replied, "but I had to try. I figured it was the only way to save my parents."

"Can I think about it?" she asked.

"Of course you can," I said, "but you're going to have to make up your mind before next Sunday."

"Okay," she said before leaving.

I put the knife and the pendant back in my desk drawer and leaned back in my chair, hating myself for what I was asking Abigail to do.

"How'd it go?" Father Bradley was standing in the doorway of the office.

"About as good as could be expected," I said.

"Do you think she'll go through with it?" he asked.

"I do," I nodded.

Her love for her parents would drive her to do it the same way it drove me to do it. Of that I was certain.

"What about you?" Father Bradley stepped into the office and took the seat opposite mine. "Are you going to be able to go through with it?"

"I will do what needs to be done," I insisted.

As the two of us looked at each other, I thought about the part of my story that I didn't tell Abigail. The part where Father Bradley and a group of men I didn't recognize began executing the parishioners of the church after I'd closed the gateway. No one was spared. Every man, woman, and child who Azbycx had touched was killed, including my parents and the woman who helped me.

I still haven't forgiven Father Bradley for that day, but I now understand why he had to do it.

MORE CHILLS FROM VELOX BOOKS

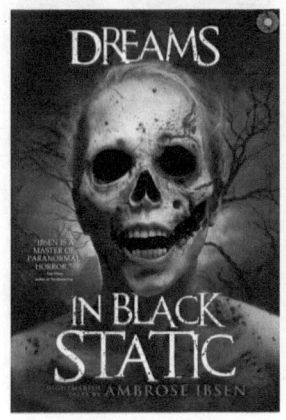

MORE CHILLS FROM VELOX BOOKS

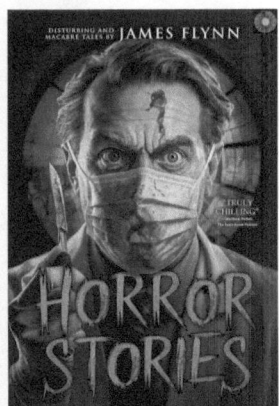

MORE CHILLS FROM VELOX BOOKS

MORE CHILLS FROM VELOX BOOKS

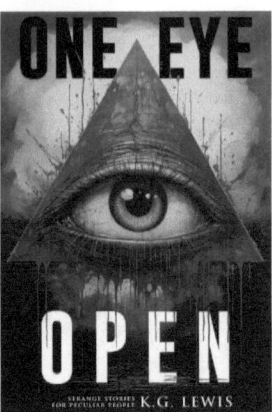
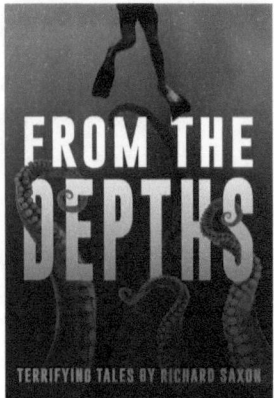

MORE CHILLS FROM VELOX BOOKS

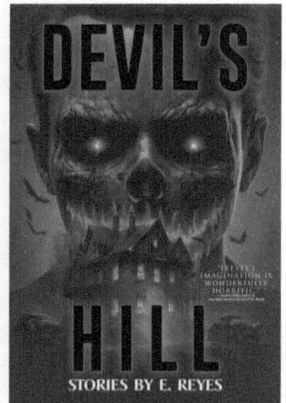

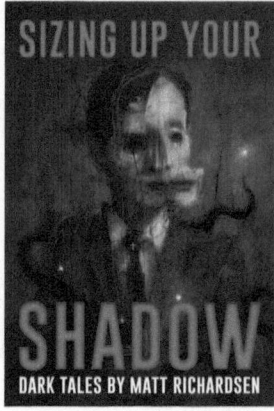

MORE CHILLS FROM VELOX BOOKS

www.ingramcontent.com/pod-product-compliance
Lightning Source LLC
LaVergne TN
LVHW040044080526
838202LV00045B/3477